MAN MADE
MURDER

MAN MADE
MURDER

Z. RIDER

Dark Ride Publishing
PO Box 63
Erwin, TN 37650

Editing: Simon Marshall-Jones
Oops check: Victory Editing
Cover design: DamonZa.com
Interior layout: Heather Lackey

ISBN: 978-1-942234-02-9

For Nick,
who believed in this.

And who owes me a book now.

PART ONE

OCTOBER 12, 1978

1.

THE MORNING of October 12, 1978, Sex Pistols bass player Sid Vicious woke on wet sheets in the New York City hotel room he shared with girlfriend Nancy Spungen. Thinking he'd pissed himself during the night—it wouldn't have been the first time—he stumbled out of bed. Dazed and half confused, he crossed the blood-soaked carpet to the room's bathroom, where he found twenty-year-old Nancy slumped between the toilet and the sink in a black bra and panties, the bra's straps drooping from her shoulders. A hole in her belly gaped black. Her stomach, thighs, and arms looked like they'd been painted red by an artist who didn't care too much about his work. Blood streaked the white porcelain of the toilet, tub, and sink pedestal, as if she had struggled to pull herself up from the cold tiles.

By nightfall, Sid sat in a 17th Precinct holding cell, charged with murder.

Three hundred miles north, rock band Man Made Murder fidgeted in the dim control room at WHAK, the Lakes Region's Only Rock Radio Station. The console lit the underside of late-night deejay Rick Travers's sharp jaw, and a glint sparked his eye as he said, "So, come on, what do you think—did he do it?"

Man Made Murder's lead guitarist, Dean Thibodeaux, dampened the strings on his acoustic guitar as he leaned toward a mic. "Uh…Sid?" It was the band's last night to get some buzz in about the album before they took off on tour, but Dean had no idea how to get buzz in around Nancy Spungen's death.

"It's not beyond the realm of possibility, is it?" Travers's lips brought fish to Dean's mind, even as they thinned to a tight smile. "I mean, we're not talking Donnie and Marie here."

Rhythm guitarist Jessie Moran, one arm hanging over his silent acoustic guitar at the end of the table, drew his brow down. "Wait. Aren't they brother and sister?"

They'd expected to do two, maybe three songs during their spot. The minutes ticked away. Dean had to remind himself this fucked up interview was working in their favor. Almost like fate was in on what they were trying to do. If they embraced this disaster, they could get out of here with just one song. Dean tapped the ash off his cigarette as Travers said, "Paul and Linda McCartney then."

"Nothing's beyond the realm of possibility, I guess," Dean said. "I mean, right?"

Shawn Elija—vocals and bass—nodded beside him, his head bent, knee jiggling.

"He could have killed her, or she could have slipped and fell, or someone else could have been there. I mean, we don't know," Dean said. "It's not up to us to point fingers."

"No one else has an opinion on this?" Travers said.

"It's a shame," Shawn said. "It's tragic. I feel for her family and for Sid, but, man—"

"Did you ever meet them?" Travers said. "The Sex Pistols?"

"No, we never met any of them," Shawn said.

It wasn't like they were going to be doing compilation albums together, Man Made Murder with their grinding bluesy sound and Sid and company shouting about anarchy over their barely tuned instruments. Although, given the chance between working with The Sex Pistols or their own fucking record company, at this point the band would be willing to do a rendition of "God Save the Queen."

"I think I met Paul Cook at a party once," Jessie said. "Maybe."

Travers spun his chair to face their drummer. "Nick?"

"Huh?"

"Nancy Spungen's death—any thoughts?"

"She died?"

Shawn turned away from the mic, lips pressed together, the dimple at his cheek threatening to show. Dean had to drop his head to keep his own cool. It was a shitty thing, Nancy dead, but Travers was milking it for the ratings. He deserved any shit he got for it—and if anyone was going to make sure shit was gotten, it was Nick Costa, in his own inimitable way.

Traver's lip curled as he said, "I guess you could call stabbed to death 'dead.'"

"Oh shi—uh. Man, that's terrible. Who did it?" Nick shirred his tambourine under the table.

"I'm getting the impression," Travers said, "you guys'd rather play a song."

"Well, you know," Dean said. "It's kinda what we came for."

"Hey, far be it for me to stop you." Travers leaned back, clasping his hands behind his head. His button-up shirt had pit stains, and his eyes went flat as he checked out of the discussion.

They fucking hated doing this show.

Jessie leaned toward the mic and said, "This one's for Nancy," as Dean fitted a steel slide over his finger.

"It's not quite the same acoustic," Dean said, "but you'll get the idea. This one's called 'Can't Win for Dyin'.'"

"WELL THAT was thirty minutes of my life that could have been better spent picking my ass," Jessie said as they pushed through the station's side door.

The air had a lifeless quality that didn't quite feel right for mid-October—a sense like the band had already left and been forgotten.

Shawn, hands in pockets, bumped Jessie's shoulder with a smile.

Nick jerked his head to toss his lank dark hair out of his eye, his hand rattling the tambourine against his thigh.

Dean drew a Winston from a half-crushed pack. "Eleven thirty on a Thursday fucking night." The match made a sharp sound as it lit. With his guitar case dangling from two fingers, he brought the flame to his cigarette.

"Well." Jessie dug his keys from his pocket. "At least the three saps stuck on late shift with their radios tuned to WHAK heard the new single." Once again, to no band member's surprise, support from the label was less than stellar. What all those line items that kept adding to their debt to the record company were, they had no fucking idea. None of it seemed to be spent on decent publicity. *Yeah, just stick 'em in whatever shitty timeslot you have available.*

Dean expected to be dead before the band saw a penny in royalties. If he'd known then what he knew now...

Signing a record deal was tantamount to signing your soul to the devil, if all your soul was made of was music.

"For once," Shawn said, "I'm just fine with the job good old High Class is doing for us."

"Feels kind of wrong to be rooting against ourselves, though, doesn't it?" Dean said. "Like there has to be some kind of karmic payback for that." But that was their plan: hope like hell the new album tanked. Make themselves a pain in the ass for the label. Convince them they were half worthless, so maybe they'd get let out of the shitty fucking contract.

It was that or give up music, and Shawn and Dean couldn't contemplate that. Jessie could move on to his second love— working on cars. They'd pulled him off that career path in high school, literally showing up at the back of the shop classroom to say, "We heard you play guitar."

Nick would land on two feet whatever happened; he could drift into things, the way he'd drifted into Man Made Murder after Dean and Shawn had run into him outside a few concerts. Canned Heat, that had been the one they'd met him at first, outside banging on the club's walls with a couple dowels he'd pulled out of the trash—because he'd been thrown out of the club before the show had even started.

Their plan carried its risks—they could make themselves so unattractive no one would pick them up after High Class dumped them. Then it would be starting all over again—shitty bars for crowds who didn't notice there was a band in the corner trying to play over the drunken shouts. They'd toured the shittiest shitholes throughout New England when they were eighteen, sleeping in Shawn's van, panhandling that time they'd run out of gas and cash at the same time in Rhode Island. Signing with a record label had changed all that—exactly the way signing your soul to the devil changed your life.

"It's a necessary evil," Nick said.

Jessie popped the trunk of his Torino—all his advance money went into cars. To make up for it, he lived over his parents' garage, and he seemed fine with that. They left him alone for the most part, and he never had to worry about what to do with himself when Sunday dinnertime rolled around.

Shawn started to say something, but it was drowned out by the guttural rumble of a Triumph pulling up at the bar across the street, joining the thick line of bikes angled out from the sidewalk. If it weren't for the bikes, Dean wouldn't even think the place was open—the windows were shuttered, the place had no neon beer signs flashing. Not even the name of the bar had been posted out front. He could have sworn last time they'd been to WHAK, the place *had* been closed, a tired For Sale sign posted by the door.

"If they do drop us..." Nick said when the engine cut off.

"*When* they drop us." Jessie slammed the trunk shut.

"We fucking hope they drop us," Shawn said.

Dean watched the biker swing off his motorcycle. A knife strapped to his thigh made Dean think he might have been in Vietnam, a fate the band had narrowly avoided when the draft was brought to an end the same year their birthdates entered the lottery. They'd talked about it a lot, though. Even considered enlisting together so they could be in the same platoon, rather than getting picked off by the draft, one by one. (Dean had tried to talk Shawn and Nick into enrolling in college. If any of them were going to make it that way, it'd be those two. No go, though. They'd just finished with high school, and neither was about to start a whole new round of education, even if it kept them safe at home.)

"If or when they drop us," Nick was saying, "the restraints are off. We can say what really goes on. Write a letter about what a losing game it is for musicians, what a sweet deal for record companies. Send it to *Rolling Stone*. See how they like *that* shit."

Jessie reached out and messed up his hair. "Nick never wants to work again, except maybe playing drums at kids' birthday parties."

The biker wasn't alone—four or five men straddled their rides out front, drinking from bottles in brown paper bags. Eyeing the band with aggressive disinterest.

"You looking at something?" called the one who'd just arrived— dark hair, hawk nose, piercing eyes. His glare eased into a smirk just before Dean looked away.

"Anyway." Nick pushed his hair out of his face. "Who's up for some beers?"

Shawn, keys in hand, leaned a hip against his Mustang.

"First round's on me if it helps," Nick said.

"Free beer you say?" Jessie said. "Count me in."

"Fuck it." Shawn pushed off the car. "Why not? It's not like I have to be up early in the morning to get on a van or anything."

Dean clamped his cigarette between his teeth so he could fish for the keys to his pickup.

"Dean? What about it?"

The biker was astride his Triumph again, a brown-bagged bottle in hand. Dean cut his eyes from him, dropped his cigarette under his foot, and ground it out. "Think I'll take a rain check."

He wanted something before he headed out to New York in the morning, but alcohol wasn't it. He needed something that would smooth the rough edges in his brain, and wouldn't leave him with a hangover as a parting gift.

"So where are we going?" Jessie asked as Dean headed to his truck.

"Shorty's?" Nick said. "Hey, how are we handling the shows? Are we diving them too?"

Dean shoved his guitar case across the truck's bench seat. Straightening, he said, "We play the shows like we always do. I'm not shortchanging the audience."

Nick nodded.

"See you in the morning," Shawn said to Dean.

"Yep." He shut the door with him still outside his truck. To Shawn, he said, "You okay?" He hadn't said a whole lot during the interview. The knee jiggling had been more than impatience. In the past ten years, he'd spent more time around Shawn than anyone else in his life. He could tell things.

"Yeah. I'll live."

Dean's eyebrow crooked up.

"Evie called earlier. Don't worry about it. I'm gonna go drown it in some beer and pull out of town in the morning."

"You sure?"

"Yep. See you tomorrow."

As car doors pulled shut behind Dean, three bikers watched him cross the street. Dean was thinking about Evie, annoyed about the timing. *Just let him go already.* She and Shawn were together four years, and the breakup was like a bad landing— every time Shawn finally hit the ground, she bounced the whole thing back up a few feet. Just enough to drag it out.

The biker with the sharp eyes lifted his chin when Dean was halfway across. "Help you with something, man?"

He waited until he was almost at the sidewalk before saying, "You happen to know where I could get something to relax?" In his experience, bikers were a good resource for that. He'd partied with more than a few in the band's tours across the country and back.

The biker settled back on the chopper's seat, brown bag resting against his thigh. "You looking for 'ludes, weed, or pussy?"

Dean was irritated from the radio show, edgy over the impending tour, and the whole let's-tank-the-album thing still wasn't sitting fully right with him. There wasn't a better alternative; it was what it was. But he still didn't like rooting against himself. And then Evie. *Just let him fucking go already.*

He had to be on the road in the morning, though—early. Quaaludes wiped him out, and pussy got most complicated when you least wanted it to. Like Evie.

"Weed," he said.

"I don't have any on me, man, but I know where to get some," the biker said. "You want to follow me?"

"How far?"

"Fifteen minutes. That about right?" He turned toward the others. One gave a shrug, acting like he wasn't paying any attention to what they were saying.

"Fifteen minutes," the biker said, returning his attention to Dean.

Across the street, his bandmates pulled out of the parking lot, one car after the other like a convoy. Shorty's was between here and home—closer to home than here. It was a reliable choice. Just thinking about the place, though, Dean didn't want to be there. It felt too stagnant. He was sick of stagnant.

He really needed to be on the road, playing in front of people. They'd been home for thirteen months. He was crawling the walls. He needed to be someplace where he could forget himself for an hour and a half every night, feel like all of this was worth something. He gave the biker a nod.

They rode out of town, the truck's headlights picking out the details of the cut on the rider's back: Black Sun Riders in gothic script, the "Black Sun" and the "Riders" framing a skeleton on a chopper, its bony fingers gripping ape hangers with a giant full moon picked out in white stitching behind him.

Dean lit another cigarette, cranked down the truck's window, turned up the radio to compete with the wind—John Fogarty singing about going up around the bend.

As the bike picked up speed and Dean pressed the gas to keep up, the wind turned the ends of his hair into whips. He squinted and took another drag.

It wasn't just the interview and the record label and the frustration he needed the pot for. He was actually scared, feeling like they had something in their grip, and they were about to chuck it without being sure they had something better to take its place. Shawn could stomach risk, though you wouldn't know it from his practicality—passing up the opportunity to get the car he really wanted in their early days for that hulk of a van instead. That green piece of shit had hauled their equipment all over the northeast the first few years, and Dean had only caught Shawn craning his neck to look at the sporty cars they passed on the road *every* time they passed one. He'd never said a word about wishing he'd made another choice though. Eventually he'd gotten his car. That was Shawn: put up with discomfort in the near-term to get to what you wanted in the end.

Once they'd done this thing, doing their best to fuck up their contract—however it turned out, he expected Shawn would never say a word about how they could have done it differently.

Ashes swirled in his face as he took one last good pull before flicking it out the window. A trail of sparks skittered in his side mirror.

Another two miles out, the bike slowed, its turn signal beating like a heart. When the bike banked onto a dark narrow road with no sign, Dean followed. His guitar case jostled as the truck's tires bumped over ruts and rocks. The bike crept ahead, dodging the worst parts of the road, the path curving through tall, dead pines with sharp black branches and winding through moonlight. He followed the beacon of the bike's taillight to a crooked one-story house that leaned on its foundation. The truck's headlights picked out weeds growing up through the porch boards, pickets in the railing hanging free, a few disappearing into the undergrowth edging the porch's posts.

The biker cut his engine.

A dog's bark came from out back, like he was happy someone finally stopped by.

The house's windows were dark, the wooden frames sun-faded and paint-peeled so they looked like old bones.

"You got the cash?" the biker asked as Dean let himself down from the pickup, onto the dirt drive.

"How much?"

"Twenty for a lid."

"What is it, skunk?" He followed the biker onto the porch, his calf brushing a spiny weed growing where a chunk of step was missing.

"It might not be what you rock stars are used to, but it'll get the job done." The biker glanced over his shoulder, catching Dean's eyes. "Saw the guitar cases."

"Yeah."

"Anything I would have heard of?" the biker asked as he pushed on the front door, unsticking it from its frame—no lock, just a shaky collection of wood, one of its lower panels cracked. The door scraped the floor as it swung open, and the biker held out an arm.

Dean stepped through to the dark room, thin moonlight playing through the windows to hit against the back wall. No bulky shapes of furniture, no pictures hanging.

The biker pushed the door closed and flipped the switch nearby. It made a firm *click*, but nothing happened. "Sorry. Power's out again."

Dean swept his gaze toward the ceiling. Exposed wires dangled from a fixture. An uneasy sensation prickled, but what was the worst that was going to happen—the biker robs him and steals his guitar? That'd be a sight, the bike racing away with the beat-up Sears special strapped to his back. Teddy'd already come by the house earlier to pick up the good guitars so he could inspect and restring them before they got loaded for the tour.

The place reminded him of a flop he'd visited in San Francisco, except that place had had bodies curled and sprawled and slumped on the floor. Maybe everyone was out.

The dog had shut up for a minute, but it started up again, as though now that they were in the house, it knew they'd surely be coming out the back to see him.

"Don't mind the fucking mutt. Made the mistake of feeding him once, now he's always around."

The floor sloped toward them, a few floorboards rucking against each other. "You live here?" Dean asked.

"I don't live anywhere. Come in. Relax." He clapped Dean's shoulder. "I've got the stuff in the bedroom."

There was a smell, among the earthy must and mildew, underneath the untended aging wood and plaster. Something almost sharp. It made him think of steel, a blade. It made his hand move to his pocket, but he didn't have his buck knife with him. He'd only been going to do the radio show. He didn't generally feel the need to carry a knife in Podunk, New Hampshire.

The biker's boots echoed down the hall.

Dean walked farther into the front room, stepping over the hump in the floor. His toe sent an empty soda can skittering, his shoulders pulling tight at the noise.

The walls were sprayed with graffiti, the kind bored kids left when they got a hold of a can of spray paint. No art in it, just memorials to the fact that they existed: *We were here* they all said, one way or another. *Jimbo '72. Hell no, we won't go. Cara & Michael 4-eva.*

No one here gets out alive.

The dog's pitch grew higher, more urgent.

A door off the room led to the kitchen. From where he stood, Dean could make out cabinets with their doors missing and a gap in the counter like a missing tooth where a stove might once have been. A tree grew against the window, one of its branches reaching through broken glass like an arm.

He stepped back, knocking over a glass bottle with a dull clatter. Looking over his shoulder, the glint of something caught his eye. Crouching, he lifted a thin silver bracelet, dangling it over his finger. He didn't know much about jewelry, but it felt like it was worth something.

Letting it slide back to the floor, he straightened. It was cooler inside the house than out, like the place was an icebox, keeping the cold in. He looked at the ceiling again, cracks crossing the plaster, a dark hole near the corner exposing part of the wooden skeleton above his head.

He was starting to think he didn't want to be here, didn't really need to get high this badly. He hadn't handed over any money. He was free to walk out the door and go get drunk instead. The guys were probably just pulling up to Shorty's right now. He was just going to be sitting on a bus for five hours come morning. With enough aspirin, orange juice, and road vibrations, he'd be over a hangover in time for sound check.

He turned, and the biker came around the corner, almost walking into him. Putting him off-balance.

It felt intentional, the way he'd pushed right in, but as the biker raised a hand, a sandwich bag tumbled in his grip, hanging from his thumb and finger. The thin plastic caught the moonlight like rippled water.

Dean reached for his wallet.

"Need papers?" the biker asked.

"Yeah."

"Consider me your one-stop shop." He put the baggie in Dean's hand while he reached inside his jacket. "These are on the house even."

Dean had a finger in his billfold, the other hand weighing the weed, his thumb rubbing the surface of the baggie—and the biker flipped the packet of rolling papers into the air with his thumbnail. It turned as it rose before arced back down, landing between their feet.

"Whoops," the biker said.

He just stood there.

Dean added the baggie to his wallet hand and bent to scoop the packet of papers off the floor.

The biker's hand dropped to the hilt of the knife strapped to his thigh.

The biker's weight shifted to one foot.

Dean's brain matched the movement with the consequences too slowly—it was only starting to send his muscles the signal to *move* when the toe of the biker's boot caught him under the ribs.

The blow twisted him. The baggie slid off his wallet. He caught the floor with the flat of his hand, hard, the impact jarring his wrist.

The biker's boot swung back again.

Dean got a knee under him and pushed forward, clutching his wallet, his eyes locked on the front door. The closest path to it meant squeezing between the biker and the wall.

The biker's kick grazed his flank as he pushed against the rucked-up boards.

The biker's punch caught him in the side of the head.

His shoulder hit the wall.

Adrenaline spiked, bristling his nerves, but his reactions were half a beat behind. He brought an arm up to shield himself, but the biker's leather-gloved hand caught his face, cranking it aside, grinding his cheekbone against the wall.

Leather and dust and lightly mildewed wallpaper assaulted Dean's nostrils. Gritting his teeth, he clutched the biker's wrist. The grip on his face clamped down harder as the biker pushed in closer, crowding him.

Dean swung the fist holding the wallet around. Connected with the biker's leather. The biker grabbed a fistful of Dean's denim jacket and wrenched it off his shoulder.

Dean brought his knee up, fast and hard, digging his other heel into the floor to keep his balance.

The biker slammed him hard against the wall. Dean's teeth snapped together with a click. But he found his chance to twist and drop, slipping out of the biker's grabbing hands like a wild cat. He launched himself toward the kitchen doorway, finger-tips ghosting the floorboards because he didn't have time to straighten back up.

The biker's blade made a *snick* against its leather sheath.

The back of Dean's jacket jerked, the biker catching hold of the collar. Dean wrenched free. Something plastic crumpled under his foot. His arms flailed. His wallet slid into the kitchen. The trash skittered out from under his foot as he aimed for the back door—just a rickety wooden storm door, its screen torn.

The dog's barking rose, fast and sharp.

The biker growled, his boots scrabbling over torn linoleum as he grabbed Dean's jacket again, yanking Dean back like a yo-yo at the end of its string.

Gasping, Dean let the biker have the jacket, dragging himself right out of it. All he cared about was the fucking door.

He crashed through it in his shirtsleeves. His feet tangled in the drop to the cinder block steps.

The dog was in the middle of the yard, its eyes luminous green in the moonlight.

He hit the ground with one knee, feeling the impact all the way to his teeth. Got halfway up and *oofed* as the wind flew out of him.

The biker's weight buckled his elbow, sending him flat on his chest in the dirt.

The dog bolted toward them.

The biker wrenched Dean's arm backward, twisting it high. He cried out.

Humid breaths hit the side of his face—the dog standing over him, its matted fur smelling like swamp and dead things.

Fingers gripped Dean's hair, dragging his head back.

The edge of cold steel touched his neck.

The weight on him shifted, and the dog barked, three percussive shouts that jarred Dean's skull.

The knife pressed. The fingers gripped harder. "Don't be a pain in the ass," the biker said. "This can go easy, or it can go really fucking slow."

Dean clawed the dirt. The backyard was littered with junk, some of it glinting just out of reach.

The knife slid back into its sheath on the biker's thigh. Dean wondered if there was any chance he could reach it.

"Ain't nothing personal," came the hot growl at his ear. Damp breath curled over his skin, bristling the hairs at his nape. A thumb jabbed below his skull.

The dog's front leg bumped his head, its paw stepping on his hair.

He grasped behind him with his free hand, finding his own shirt, the biker's leather. The biker's body angled off him at the hips, putting the knife out of reach. But he kept trying for it anyway.

Pain like white-hot fire shot down his shoulder and coursed up the back of his skull. It tingled like electricity along his jaw. His mouth jumped open. The yell in his chest was knocked right back there with the surprise of the pain. He dug at the ground with his fingers, knife mission forgotten. Panic and the weight of the biker pushed on his lungs, squeezing the breath out of him. He needed to get out from underneath.

The dog's bark jarred every bone in his skull.

His flesh tore just below his ear with a wet sound that stiffened his toes, made his guts sink cold and heavy.

He needed to focus. He needed to get the fuck *out* of there.

He wrenched his hips, grinding one painfully into the dirt, and threw his elbow back, hard, connecting with the biker.

The biker didn't so much as grunt.

He slammed his elbow back again, ignoring the sick slide of the biker's teeth against tendons in his neck, the pain needle-sharp where nerves had been torn into. A tooth hit one just right and his legs jolted like he'd touched a live wire. He yelled out and flattened his hand on the ground, trying to get leverage to twist free.

The teeth sank deeper. Dean clenched his teeth. His insides bucked. A helpless moan dragged out of him as he stretched to grab hold of a sad clump of weedy grass in the dirt.

The dog stepped over his arm and a weather-beaten can of WD-40. Dean pulled with his strength, the grass ripping from the dirt by its roots. Something glinted just past the half-upended clod.

Ignoring the head rush sluicing through his scalp, he dug his fingers in what was left of the clump of grass and dragged himself half an inch forward. The biker's grip clamped hard on his skull. And he hummed as he feasted—a low, contented sound that vibrated against Dean's neck.

Dean stretched toward the shard of glass. His fingertips brushed its edge.

With a growl through his clenched teeth, he pulled himself—and the biker on top of him—another half inch. The biker's cheekbone ground his jaw.

Wet heat trickled under his collar. Blood. Had to be. His cheeks went cold. His forehead popped clammy sweat. Bile surged to his throat as he hauled himself another half inch closer, pushing the toes of his sneakers hard into the dirt.

For a second, something beyond the glint of broken glass came into focus, and he had to swallow back dinner. His lips—numbly tingling—peeled back. A fresh wash of cold sickness rolled through him.

The biker's teeth clamped down harder, trying to drag him back.

Once he'd seen the chewed-up woman's hand, with its silver ring hanging loose on sun-dried muscle and bone, he couldn't not see it. He dragged his eyes to his fingers, watched them just reach the jagged piece of glass. Gasping, he coaxed it toward him until he could get it in his grip.

With a good hold on it, he leaned his weight to one side and swung his arm back, fast and hard—crying out at the twist of pain in the muscles of his other arm, still bent up his backside.

The glass shard slid against leather, doing nothing except digging into his own palm.

Hissing, he gripped it harder. Leaning his weight, he brought the shard right over his shoulder, hoping to get the biker in the eye—anything that would get his mouth the fuck off his neck.

The shard of glass hit flesh, but it wasn't like the movies. It sank slightly and jolted to a stop when it hit bone. His own hot blood ran down his palm.

The biker growled and grabbed Dean's wrist without lifting his head.

He slammed Dean's arm against the ground. Dean's stomach clenched, his fingertips cold, but he held on to that piece of glass.

The dog yipped and barked.

"Asshole," the biker said, inches from Dean's cheek. He let go of his grip on Dean's other arm and pushed up to sitting, his weight on Dean's thighs.

Blood burbled from the gash in Dean's neck, the air cool against it. He needed to get out while he still could. His scalp was prickling and his lips had gone completely numb—he had no idea if it was too late for "still could," but he wasn't going to lie down and die yet. With the shard clutched in his hand, he dug his elbow and knee into the ground and wrestled himself onto his side.

The biker's eyes gleamed. His lips were black with blood. A thick bead of it shone in his whiskers. His arm came up—

Dean whipped the hand with the glass upward, giving it everything he had.

It struck just below the biker's eye.

With a shout, the biker punched him in the side of the head.

Dean's temple banged the dirt, rattling his head. But he still had the shard of glass. His blood and the biker's ran between his fingers.

The biker's bloody lip drew back, pain turning into a smile, sharp teeth smeared dark.

Dean's breath guttered.

The biker closed his hand around the hilt of his knife.

Dean dug his heels into the dirt, shoving backward, gritting his teeth.

The knife *snicked* softly from its sheath. The blade flashed.

Dean hauled his upper body up. He arced the glass through the air. It lodged in the biker's neck.

A laugh huffed out of the biker. He swung the knife upward.

The dog jumped around them, barking.

"Yeah, this is all yours after," the biker said to it, grinning at Dean. "Don't worry."

Dean scrambled back.

The biker grabbed his knee.

High-voltage adrenaline coursed. Dean kicked out, catching the biker in the chin. Yanking his other leg free, he rolled to his feet, which didn't want to work right. He stumbled a step, like he was dragging his foot—his body on fire with the sense and sounds of the biker getting up behind him. He still had the glass, embedded in his cut-up palm, and he turned on his one cooperating foot, swinging the shard blindly. It sank deep in the biker's face, lodging there.

Dean shoved the biker with his other arm. It was just luck that the dog was in the way. The biker's heel caught it and he went over backward, sprawling in the dirt. The dog panting and barking excitedly jumped on him.

Dean started running, wobbly at first, then getting the hang of it as the biker yelled at the dog. He caught the corner of the building with one hand, using it to push himself around. Skidding on what gravel was left in the dirt drive, he caught hold of the door handle on his truck to pull himself to a stop.

He yanked the door open as the biker broke around the corner.

Dean clambered into the truck. Jammed his key in the ignition—amazed that he got it on the first try. Amazed that he'd even, out of habit, managed to get it into his hand in the first place.

He backed the truck up with the door hanging open, spitting gravel and dirt as he swung around. The truck jolted as it hit the parked motorcycle with its front corner. The bike crashed to the dirt.

He wrenched the truck into drive and floored it, tires spinning until, catching, they jerked him against the seat. His door banged shut. His headlights lit the trees. He swerved to keep from hitting them.

Heart hammering.

Warm trickles sliding down his back, under his shirt.

His rearview mirror went pitch-black. A *whomp-whomp* like huge wings came at the truck from behind.

A thud shook the seat at his back.

He sat forward, his blood-soaked shirt peeling off the seatback.

A hundred yards up, the driveway opened onto the main road.

Sharp things scrabbled above his head. He glanced up—saw nothing but the truck's dark ceiling and put his eyes back on the road. There was nothing he could do about something on the roof except keep fucking driving. He swallowed hard, his breaths fast, his chest aching.

His heart a bomb ticking toward explosion.

He pressed the gas, flicking his eyes toward the rearview. Darkness. Trees.

A foot came down beside him, the toe of a boot resting on the open window.

The truck swerved and corrected as Dean elbowed it out of the way. He scrabbled for the window crank.

A car swept past the mouth of the driveway, as though just over the line, where dirt met hardtop, the normal world existed. Reality. He had a crazy thought that the front end of his truck would crash into an invisible barrier, that he was trapped in this fucked up alternate dimension where nightmares lived.

The biker's boot jammed down hard on the window before he managed to get it up more than a few inches.

Dean pried at it, keeping an eye on the road that was coming up way too fast. He couldn't risk slowing down. He needed to get the fuck out of there. Wind buffeted the open wound in his neck, the pain sharp as he shifted and twisted his arm to force the boot out again.

The leg kicked in at him, its sole shoving, gritty, against his cheek. He slammed on the brake and grabbed it around the ankle. But it just kept pushing in.

The other boot dropped down, getting its footing on the window.

Fuck this. Just *fuck* this.

He jammed his foot on the gas. The tires spun. The truck shot forward, knocking him back. He peeled onto the road, cranking the wheel hard. A horn blared. Headlights swerved. The truck's tires caught the far shoulder, bumping the guitar off the seat. He floored it again. Dirt spit. His tires caught pavement, and the truck shot forward.

The other boot tried to come in.

Dean cranked the wheel.

The truck's back end fishtailed on the pavement.

His lips were numb, his back and neck hot.

He grabbed the biker's foot by the heel and forced it back out—as soon he let go, it swung back in, getting him at the top of his ear, making it smart.

He stepped on the gas again. Caught the wheel with one hand while using the other to knock the boot back out the window.

The biker couldn't be holding on to much on the roof.

He took the truck up to forty, trying to roll the window up again. He made it halfway before the boot stepped down on it again.

He stomped the brakes hard enough to throw himself against the steering wheel.

Put it in reverse and peeled around.

The weight on the roof shifted backward. Boots kicked for purchase against the side of the cab.

Sweat dripped off Dean's hair, trickling down the side of his nose.

His scalp prickled tightly.

Back in drive, he floored the gas until the truck shuddered— sixty, seventy, eighty on the curving back road.

A fist banged the window.

He flinched with every thud.

Gravity pulled on the truck as he rounded a curve going too fast. Two of his tires lifted off the pavement. The body on the roof shifted toward the inside of the curve.

He slammed on the brakes.

The truck juddered as it landed back on four wheels, making Dean's teeth click together.

The body on the roof tumbled down the windshield.

Dean pressed back in his seat, hands braced on the steering wheel.

The biker banged to a stop on the hood. One arm reached back, leather-gloved fingers feeling for something to hold onto.

The biker's face turned toward him, his mouth distorted, black with blood. But still grinning. Eyes feverish and sparkling.

Dean jerked the shifter into reverse and tore backward.

The biker bumped down the hood and spilled over its edge, boots flying into the air, then gone.

Dean forced the gearshift back to drive and gave it all the gas he could.

The truck bumped hard, its front tires riding over the body. A split second later, the back tires bumped over it. All four wheels hit pavement again, the truck speeding away.

Dean fought the urge to ease up and look back. He hunched forward, blinking through sweat, clenching the wheel, focusing on the road.

He needed to get to a hospital.

His shirt clung to his back. The steering wheel was sticky with blood. He didn't hurt—shock had taken him away from that. But he needed to get to a fucking hospital.

He checked the rearview. Nothing but darkness beyond the red glow of his lights.

All the blood in his shirt. His mouth flooded with saliva. A clamminess crawled his scalp, draining the heat from his cheeks.

His lips felt thin, numb. His fingers were thick and clumsy.

He glanced in the rearview.

Trees and empty road.

"Jesus," he whispered. He tried to remember where the hospital was, what roads he needed to take to get there. He could picture the place—ugly sprawling white with a squared-off canopy over the front entrance—but the road leading to it was as black as the night behind him.

"Jesus." He was shaking.

That thing had just killed him.

His blood was pumping out of his neck as fast as his heart could beat, and that thing had just fucking killed him.

Warmth slipped through him, a floating feeling of comfort. He fought his eyes back open, back to the reality of his situation. He tried to watch the road. Something familiar would come along. Something would snap into place.

His hands were like blocks of Styrofoam, useless and light, like they were going to float right off the wheel. He focused on them, on keeping hold of the wheel.

His speed slipped to forty.

He sent a signal down to his foot to put more pressure on the pedal, but lowering that foot was like asking it to climb a mountain with a ninety-pound weight tied to it. The speedometer wavered toward forty-five before starting to sink back.

He wanted to sink too.

Just sink into blackness and not worry about anything…

A crossroad came up. He turned without signaling, afraid to let the wheel go with either hand. He took another turn, wide, the truck ranging into the other lane. He came close to swiping a car parked on the street before correcting. Another turn—no idea where he was going, only that he wanted to be off the road he'd been on, to make it difficult for the biker to track him down.

He wasn't willing to believe running over the guy had killed him.

Jesus.

He saw a dog in the road suddenly—a Newfoundland so black it was only thanks to its eyes that it caught Dean's attention. He swerved, feeling for a second like he wasn't going to be able to get the truck back on the road, and then he had it, the dog disappearing behind him.

Two blocks later, he was drifting toward darkness again. Wanting so badly to just give in to it.

The truck crept to ten miles an hour.

His legs felt like lead. He was losing the fight to stay conscious.

He coasted into a dirt lot beside a disheveled concrete building, its windows boarded. The dirt in the lot was so dead, it didn't even have weeds growing in it.

The truck rolled to a stop in the building's shadow.

His fingers fumbled the keys until he got hold of them and turned the one in the ignition. The engine cut off.

He stared into the dark shapes of trees behind the building. Fuzzy shadows swelled at the edge of his vision.

He made a sharp sound, a *chh* through his teeth. The skin behind his ears prickled as he strained to hear a bike, a dog barking—the *whomp whomp* of wings.

The engine ticked, cooling under the hood.

The urge to throw up tightened his stomach, but he was detached from it. His body couldn't get itself together enough to carry half-digested food up his esophagus.

Air rushed in his ears, like the inside of a seashell—and the blackness came again.

The engine ticked.

Then there was silence.

2.

CARL DELACROIX eased his Cougar alongside the curb, engine idling. So far he'd only seen New Hampshire in the dark, and his impression was there were a lot of trees, most of them ashy black until the Cougar's headlights washed them gray, but he'd seen trees that made him think of bones too, their bark white and peeling.

Colonial homes lined this street, silent and boxy and severe-looking, with either no shutters at all or narrow dark rectangles framing dark windows, hardly any roof overhang, which said to him that sun wasn't the same thing here as it was in New Mexico. Short white fences edged the yards, collecting fallen oak leaves in their pickets.

He flipped the dome light on, unfolded the map he'd picked up at a Sunoco in Keene. It'd been a thirty-four-hour drive across the country, mile after mile of highway. He could have flown—probably should have, but then what? Pay for a rental on top of airfare? That was assuming anyone would even rent to a twenty-year-old.

He'd napped at rest stops, the Cougar wedged between rumbling semis, but sleep, actual sleep? What the fuck was that anymore? The last good night's sleep he remembered getting was in 1976, and he'd been kicking himself in the ass for wasting precious time sleeping ever since.

The map vibrated in his hands—the caffeine, the hours of guiding a steering wheel. The shakiness didn't help his orientation. Where he needed to be was marked with a scribble. Where he *was* on the other hand…He leaned toward the windshield, tilting to see around the school photo and St. Michael medallion hanging from his rearview mirror. Squinting, he made out the street sign, his lips moving to commit its name to his scattered memory long enough to locate it on the map.

When he finally found the street he was looking for, after circling around and going up the wrong street twice—when he found the *bar* with the eight motorcycles parked out front, he laughed, an exhausted, lonely, half-losing-it sound that hung in the car's cabin like cigarette smoke.

A one-story wooden building stained black, the bar was like a smudge of char. Its windows were shuttered. No sign with the bar's name hung outside, but who needed that when you had three Triumphs, an Indian, and four Harley hogs sitting out front?

He sat forward, his back barely grazing the seat. This was it. That was what he'd come for. He swung down the next major street and came around again, stopping alongside a sidewalk three blocks up from the bar.

He cut the engine.

Peered around.

The street was dead, the shops, cafes, and municipal building closed. Across from the bar sat a squat cinderblock building, looking like it had been shunned by the more picturesque downtown area that started closer to where Carl was parked. A fifty-foot radio mast loomed behind it. Call station letters—

MAN MADE MURDER   33

WHAK—rose three feet high on the concrete building's face. Out of curiosity he wanted to dial in the station, but the stereo's light would draw attention to the car, the same way taking his edge off with a few cigarettes would, so he slouched in silence, reached for the last dregs in the cup of caffeine he'd bought in Keene, and put his attention on the bar.

His information could be wrong. Sure, he was looking at bikes, but they could be any club's bikes. Nothing outside the bar or, that he could see, *on* the bikes, marked this as Black Sun Riders territory. He cupped a hand over his wrist and pressed the button to light up his watch face for half a second.

Two a.m.

It wasn't likely they were living in the bar, so they had to be coming out sooner or later. Walker, the last P.I. he'd hired, had tracked them to this point, but either hadn't been able to go any farther, or hadn't wanted to. Carl was never sure, from their conversation on the phone. Something in the man's voice, or something in the spaces between his carefully selected words.

When he lifted his eyes, his gaze reached long, toward the bar again, but the photo hanging from his mirror caught his attention. He brought his focus closer, picking out Sophie's face in the dark shadows of the car. She had that almost squared-off smile she forced on for photos. In real life, she'd had a great smile—contagious, especially when it was paired with a laugh—but every photo she posed for, going all the way back to when she was in diapers, she put the square smile on, like she thought the point of it was to neatly frame her teeth for the camera.

He kissed the tip of his finger and touched her face. The gold Los Campos High School seal in the corner glinted in the light from a streetlamp.

The damn packet of school photos had shown up in the mail the day after her funeral.

Movement caught his eye. He shrank down, knees knocking the underside of the dash. From the dim yellow glow of the bar's interior stepped a biker, about two hundred and fifty pounds, wide shoulders, black leather jacket. Gloves with the fingers sliced off. He swung a leg over the farthest bike in the row, straightened it between his legs, kicked the stand up. With the stomp of a foot, he cranked the bike to life, its rumble crowding the dead street.

Carl's heart beat slow but hard. This wasn't his guy. But he watched, fascinated, anyway. Because this guy probably *knew* his guy.

Were all the Black Sun Riders like his guy? Carl had pored over the stories in biker magazines, the crazy first-person tales of gang rape and strapping dead bitches to the back of their bikes, the smell of burning flesh as the corpse's leg burned on the muffler. He could believe they were all—in these outlaw gangs at least—like his guy.

As the biker pulled out, swinging his bike up the street, the wind swept his blond hair back, and Carl ducked close to the driver's side door, turning his face toward it so only his dark hair showed. The engine rattled his eardrums, vibrated the door against his cheek. It dropped off as the bike kept going. He let out his breath, waiting until the engine was just a fading buzz before lifting his head. The bar was unchanged, just a black bump at the edge of a streetlamp's reach. He shifted around to look out the back window.

The bike was gone.

Seven more to go.

After an hour, the bar's door swung open again, someone leaning in the frame, watching the street as he smoked a cigarette. An engine growled from behind Carl. He slouched, watching over the dash. The blond again, returning.

The P.I. before Walker had sent him a photo, a black and white print of a group of soldiers in Korea. On the phone with that P.I., Carl had said, "This has to be his father. I mean, come on." In the photo, Sergeant David "Grip" Gershon stood smirking beside a Lieutenant, his arm hanging over a gun of some kind he had on his shoulder. And it did look like his biker, but the photo was twenty-five years old.

I'm just telling you what I found, Sanderson had said with a sigh, and Carl had gone looking for yet another P.I.

Watching the blond exchange words with the guy in the doorway, Carl wished he could take a look at that photo now. It was in a folder in the back seat, but it'd just be a smudge in the dark unless he was willing to draw attention to himself by holding it up near the windshield.

It was stupid. He'd had nothing but catnaps for two days. Even if he had the photo in his hand and the fucking dome light on, so what if a guy in an old black and white photo looked similar to another guy a hundred yards away? It wasn't like the world didn't have plenty of large men with blond hair.

The guy at the bar door crushed his cigarette under his foot, and the both of them went inside.

During the drive from New Mexico, Carl had pictured how this was going to go. He was going to walk into the bar, spot his guy, draw the gun out of his waistband, extend his arm. Pull the trigger.

And go to jail, but that was all right. He could do time for this if it meant justice was finally served. Or maybe they'd kill him before they called the cops. That was all right too. He only had one thing he had to do in this life; after that, nothing else mattered.

But he'd pictured himself getting here earlier, imagined the bar being rowdier, neon beer signs in the windows, people coming and going. Women laughing.

Not this shadow of a building.

What if his guy wasn't in there? He'd stand out like a neon light, wandering into an unmarked bar in the early hours of morning, in a town that had otherwise gone to sleep.

By four, his knees were stiff. He turned sideways, putting his back against the driver's door, legs over the console. His feet itched. His scalp itched. The coffee he'd gone through on his way across the state pressed against his bladder. He shifted to get some weight off it, the steering wheel in the way of his elbow. His eye caught his sister's photo again. He touched it with the tip of a finger.

He'd get the guy. He'd put his sister to rest.

The numbers on his watch said it was nearly six. First light wasn't showing yet, the stars still glinting in the sky, but on the ground shapes picked themselves out of the shadows, the grays softening, the details sharpening. If it weren't for the bikes still parked out front, he'd take off, find a hotel to grab a few hours of sleep in. No one was awake this time of the morning except the people who needed to get up to go to work. But he wanted to see who owned the bikes out front.

At the rumble of an engine, Carl drew himself straight.

Up a side street it came, swinging onto the main drag, slowing as it neared the others. In the pool of a streetlamp, one of the side mirrors hung crooked. A tailpipe was crumpled. The bike stopped, and the rider back-walked in alongside the others.

At the sight of the knife jutting from the biker's thigh as he toed the kickstand down, Carl swung his feet back under the dash and gripped the steering wheel. Dark hair, long sideburns. Carl wished he could see better from where he was parked. The biker swung his leg off, his hand releasing the clutch.

Carl strained to make out the patch on the back of the jacket. Binoculars—he needed to find a K-Mart first chance he got. Didn't know why he didn't think to have some already. (Oh right: because he was going to strut into the bar and take care of the whole thing in one swoop.)

The biker stepped onto the sidewalk, yanking one glove off by the fingertips. His step had a hitch, something a little off to it. He threw open the bar door and plunged off-kilter inside. The door fell shut.

Everything returned to dead silence.

Carl squeezed the steering wheel, his breath flooding from him.

It was him—the hawk nose, the thin mouth. He'd seen him pull his gloves off like that once before, from about the same distance, when he'd watched the man stride up the steps of the

Los Campos High School gymnasium, Sophie standing at the top, her fingers fidgeting with the buckle on her purse. She'd seemed to barely notice the biker approaching. Older than her by ten years at least, not worth paying attention to, her eyes had searched past him, looking for someone her age. She'd been waiting for the little snot who'd asked her to the basketball game, then hadn't shown up. Carl, kicking back in the Cougar in the school's parking lot, was ready to wait for as long as it took her to give up. Ready to wait until the game let out, even if the kid did show—just in case.

You couldn't trust a guy who showed up a half hour late for his first date, although maybe he was related to Jonesy Randolph, one of the team's best players and habitually late for everything. Carl had seen Jonesy getting out of his brother's car not long before the game would have started, had watched him jog into the side of the building, his uniform all but spilling from under his arm. Tim Randolph's car, dark burgundy and about fifteen years old, nearly dragging its muffler behind it, had pulled around, getting lost in the traffic from kids showing up to watch the game. And Carl had gone back to watching Soph watch for her date.

Later he'd learned that the kid she was waiting on had diabetes, the kind you got as a kid, and had been rushed to the hospital when his blood sugar tanked. His family hadn't even thought about the ball game or the little girl who'd be waiting on the steps for her date to show. But that was later.

In his car in the high school lot, after everyone else had gone inside, Carl had watched the biker tug his gloves off as he mounted the steps, one finger at a time. He'd had patches on the back of his jacket, a smudge of black and white. Soph might have dismissed him, but Carl didn't. His hand had moved to the door as the guy said something to Soph. In the wash of security lighting, she pointed down the road, like she was giving directions. The biker turned, following her arm. The security light picked out details on the back of his jacket—a skeleton on a motorcycle, it looked like. The outline of an oversized moon. The biker said something else to her. She nodded and said something back, just a tiny thing standing up there in her new dress with its long, tapered sleeves and flared short skirt, her dark hair parted neatly down the middle.

The car's dome light had come on, Carl unintentionally opening the door just enough to trigger it.

The biker glanced toward the lot, said one more thing to Sophie, then turned with a nod and headed back down the steps, slapping his gloves against his thigh.

Carl had let his breath out and settled back to wait some more, pulling the door shut. Thinking he'd take his sister for ice cream when she finally gave up.

He'd stayed in his car that night—had taken his attention back off Soph when the danger had passed.

It had cost him everything.

He reached under the passenger seat now, feeling around the carpet. His fingers bumped the handgun, shifting it. He reached farther, caught a finger in the trigger guard, and dragged it across the scratchy carpet until he could grip it in his hand, solid and cool.

He straightened and stared at the chrome lined up outside the bar. The bar's black door. The building itself, closing the biker inside.

He yanked the door handle and stepped out, his left leg tingling with pins and needles as it unfolded.

He pushed the handgun into the back of his jeans, settling his windbreaker over it.

He looked both ways before he loped across the street.

While the buildings were closely packed on the block he'd parked, they spread out as he headed south—a law office that looked like a home, set back from the street with a neatly tended yard, a frame shop with a sign made to look like a collage of picture frames. A convenience store on a corner, its door set at an angle so it could pick up foot traffic from either direction.

He picked up his pace, feeling exposed in the middle of the road. When he reached the other side, he veered a little, heading for the side of the clapboard bar. He leaned his back against it, catching his breath, collecting his courage. The gun pressed against the wall. Against his back. His heart ramped up to what felt like two hundred beats a minute. He reached back, one hand on the gun, the other scrubbing his forehead. Trying to work out how this was going to go. Was someone inside the door going to throw an arm out, barring the way, arguing him back out of the bar? *Members only. You don't even look like you own a scooter, you little pissant.*

Voices rose on the other side of the wood, but not enough to make out what they were saying.

He put his head against the wall. Swallowed. Clenched and unclenched his hands.

He needed to do this.

A car came down the road, turning onto a street a little ways up. Someone came walking down the sidewalk several blocks down, a Styrofoam cup in hand, a newspaper tucked under an arm. Getting an early start on the day. Carl watched the man shake out a set of keys, put one in the lock of a shop door.

When the street was empty again, he turned toward the front of the building, shoulder against the wall, and started making his way toward it.

At the corner, he put his hand against it, cheek pressed to the wall. A laugh gathered like a storm under his ribs. He was more suspicious creeping along like this than if he'd just manned up and walked up to the door. He pressed his forehead to the wall, heart hammering.

Just as he lifted his foot to do it, to man up to it, the door around the corner opened. Boots thumped out.

"Damn," someone said.

"Pain in the ass," said the other.

"Least it's still drivable."

Silence—Carl guessed they were looking at the bike he'd just watched drive up the street.

He was listening to his guy.

He'd heard his guy's *voice*.

He wanted to flatten his back against the side wall of the bar, but he was afraid to move, afraid the crease of clothing or shift of his foot over dirt would draw their attention.

"You've got a mess on your hands," the one who wasn't his guy said.

"I'll get it cleaned up tonight."

"No fucking shit."

"A little fucking sympathy, huh? I was fucking run over."

"How're you gonna find him?"

"He left his wallet. If he doesn't turn up at the hospitals—" The door swung shut again, cutting them off.

Carl pushed off the wall and stepped past the building's façade, heart thudding. His guy had been *right there*.

Another car swept past, its gust riffling Carl's hair.

He reached behind him as he headed for the door, his other arm outstretched, fingers closing over gun and door handle at the same time.

He pulled.

The door didn't budge.

He took a soft breath, put his teeth together, and pulled again, just to be sure.

It was locked.

He dropped both hands, empty. Stepped back a few paces and looked at the building.

They'd leave eventually, go home. He'd just wait and follow. Once he got to the biker's house, he'd wait some more, let him get good and asleep. Then he'd break in any way he could.

In fact, he liked that plan better—standing over the bed, his gun pressed against the asshole's temple. No way to miss.

OCTOBER 13, 1978

1.

DEAN's eyelid twitched.

He drew his upper lip back, his neck stiff, and he hadn't even moved it yet. His body wasn't in a position he'd expected to wake up in. He forced his eyes open to narrow slits. The steering wheel was directly in front of him, and beyond that the dash, faded in the early morning sunlight.

He squinted until everything was just a sunlit blur before pulling his head forward with a groan. He must have had one hell of a party.

Hugging the steering wheel with one arm, he dragged himself up. His shirt peeled away from the seatback with a sound like old tape pulling free. His head pulsed with hot, cottony murk. Blinking at the sun, he tried to make out the truck's hood, hoping the front end was intact. The last thing he needed to wake up to was the aftermath of a drunk-driving accident.

He fumbled for the door handle, and as he pulled it, he elbowed the door open. It took another grunt to get himself to the ground, one of his knees taking his weight like a rusty hinge. He stumbled forward a step and stopped bent over, hands braced on his thighs.

Sharp lines burned across his right hand, irritated by the rough denim. He was afraid to turn his head or hand to look at it—the movement might upset the very delicate balance of his stomach.

Too late. His sides heaved. Vomit vaulted up his throat, splattered steaming in the dirt.

He wiped his mouth with the back of his wrist, eyes closed—unsteady.

He felt for the door and clutched it, using it to pull himself upright. The lines of pain in his palm throbbed against the sun-warmed metal.

His neck hurt like a son of a bitch. Moving it as little as possible, he took a gander at where he was.

The old, boarded-up body shop looked familiar, but he thought it was a strange place to wind up, on the way to no place he imagined he might have been going to.

He squinted at his watch.

"Shit."

He was catching a ride to the bus in a little over an hour. New York City by two in the afternoon—interviews, sound check, more interviews, and the first show of the tour.

He grasped the back of the driver's seat, then closed his eyes and opened them carefully, taking in but not being able to process the fact that the back of the seat was filthy with rust-brown stains.

The echo of a dog barking scratched the back of his memory, made a shiver dig through him. Suddenly he felt chilly.

He'd worry about the seat later.

He dragged himself inside, his knee complaining again as he pressed the brake pedal down. The engine started right up—he loved this truck, a 1962 Chevy C10 hand-me-down from his grandpa not long before he'd died. Save for the seat, it seemed fine.

As he pulled the Chevy in a circle in the dirt lot, pointing its nose at the road, a fog of déjà vu muddled his head. Shrugging it away, he aimed the truck toward home.

The barking came back to him on the drive home. A shudder rocked through him at a dreamlike memory of a dead hand, its delicate fingers resting on the dirt, one of its painted nails split almost to the cuticle. He wiped his forehead with the heel of his hand and pressed the gas a little harder. He just wanted to get the fuck *home*.

When he got through the door, his bags sat packed on the coffee table, unzipped and waiting for last-minute toiletries. He dropped his keys and headed for the bathroom, mentally running through everything he needed to do before the van showed up.

As he let his bladder go, he braced a hand on the wall and rubbed his forehead against his shirtsleeve.

Bent at that angle, his neck throbbed like a heartbeat. He lifted his head, and stared at the hand on the wall. Smeared with dirt, a scrape on the knuckles. Jesus, what *had* he done last night? There'd been the radio interview...

He closed his eyes, and images jolted him like exposed wires: jagged glass, a dog's barking, struggling on the ground.

Two thumps that made his heart still.

He pressed the flush handle down, his fingers lingering on the cool metal—his mind blank, just the echo of the silence that had followed those thumps.

As he cranked the taps in the shower on, he rewound to the dog in the darkness, its hot breath in his face, its chest lunging over him, his skull rattling with the barks.

He started on the buttons on his shirt, twinges across his palm as he worked his fingers.

He could almost feel the brittle edge of glass, smooth and sharp all at once, cutting into him.

He peeled his shirt off, the fabric adhering to his skin. When he dropped it, it stayed half upright, stained brown down the back, especially at the collar. He stepped on it, flattening it, on his way to the sink. Dreading what he was about to look at, but—

He flinched. Gripping the counter, he pulled himself forward to get a better look.

If he didn't know better, he'd think he'd just climbed out of a dumpster—dirt smeared across half his face, hair sticking up.

He touched his cheek with two fingers and winced at the tender bruise under the dirt.

He dropped his gaze slowly, because he'd already gotten a glimpse of what was there, and he was kind of hoping it wouldn't be as bad as he thought.

His fingertips went cold.

"Jesus Christ," he breathed.

He angled his shoulder toward the mirror.

He closed his fist, the cuts stiff, the pain like holding barbed wire.

He'd needed to get to a hospital. That's the last thing he remembered—giving up on the hospital. Thinking that thing had killed him. That fucking psycho.

He touched his neck, just shy of the wound, and leaned closer to the mirror.

Jesus fucking Christ.

Was that fucking bone? Or just the glare of the mirror's light glistening off his pink insides?

He shut his eyes. He was up and walking around, and aside from the pain, he didn't seem to be any the worse for wear. He'd apparently not lost as much blood as he'd thought, and neither the gouge in his neck nor the cuts on his hand had that intense fire-pain that came with an infection.

And he had twenty minutes before the van pulled up out front. He could spend the better part of the day at the ER, or he could go on fucking tour.

He shoved his jeans off. Steam billowed from the shower. He could use a smoke but didn't have time. He made the mistake of thinking about the wound in his neck again on his way to the tub, and his knees went rubbery, his forehead clammy. He caught hold of the shower's curtain rod. He had bandages somewhere—if he hadn't thrown them out—from the time he'd gone down a hill sideways on a dirt bike. No stitches needed then, no broken bones, just road rash he'd needed to cover to keep blood from oozing through his shirt.

He stepped over the edge of the tub and yanked the plastic curtain shut, trying to think of where he'd put those bandages, forcing his mind to run though his cabinets and closets rather than go back to thinking about what he needed to use them for.

Hot water sluiced his back as he examined the rest of his body. He found a bruise the size of a tangerine on his kneecap, another like a thumbprint on his hip. He had a sore wrist and a hinky elbow—hinky but it worked. It just complained a little when he extended it. Nothing else like his neck, though. Or even as bad as his hand.

He straightened, wincing and turning away as shower spray hit the gash in his neck. He let water run over the cuts in his palm—this was going to be the real problem. It was his picking hand. He fingered a riff in the air. He thought it'd be okay, hoped the cuts didn't open and ooze halfway through the set, but it wouldn't be the first time he'd bled on his guitar.

He found the bandages in one of his dresser drawers, the box still half full of four-by-four gauze pads, just big enough to cover the mess. He grabbed the buck knife out of the nightstand and slipped it in his back pocket. He wasn't going anywhere without that thing after this.

The shower hadn't made his neck look any better. He stood right up against the sink to get another look. The raw edges had dark, coagulated blood around them that flecked off with the scrape of a thumbnail. Between those edges were the bright, moist contours of exposed muscle.

Blood drained from his cheeks. His face washed with heat. Saliva flooded his mouth, like he was going to throw up. He leaned over and spat in the toilet.

You're okay. You're alive. You're gonna be fucking fine. He tore open the packet of sterile gauze.

As he was taping it to his neck, a horn sounded a short note out front.

Smoothing the tape down, he thought he looked better already. Less like he was about to pass out.

He ran his fingers through his wet hair, shaking the ends loose, letting them curl against the bandage.

The horn sounded, longer this time.

He grabbed the box of bandages, the tape, and the moustache scissors he'd used to cut it. Loping out to the living room, ignoring his bruised knee, he stashed the supplies in one of his bags.

The horn again, louder, longer.

He swung the front door open. "I'm coming! Shut up for a minute!" With the door hanging open, he shoved toiletries in his bag. Then went to find his jacket.

He didn't have his fucking jacket. His first thought was the truck, then—no, he didn't *have* his fucking jacket.

He patted the pockets of the jeans he'd been wearing. No wallet either.

Shit.

He hoped he wouldn't need I.D. Maybe he could have Gary work some magic and get something sent to him on the road.

He grabbed a beat-up black denim jacket from his closet, the horn outside blaring again. He caught his two bags by their straps and glanced around the place one more time. Four rooms, modest and easy to manage. He'd put the down payment on it when they'd gotten their first advance, happy to be out of the apartment he'd been sharing with Jessie.

Nothing against Jessie.

He'd expected to be living in a much nicer place by now, maybe a cabin up north, big windows overlooking a lake, floor-to-vaulted-ceiling fieldstone fireplace, a nice crackling fire in the snowy winters. That was before they'd learned that advances were pretty much *all* they got. Those payouts needed to stretch from one album to the next, on top of covering equipment breakdowns, new equipment, whatever they might need that the label wasn't covering. (And when Dean thought in terms of what the label "covered," it was a loose use of the word—the label just put every penny it spent, whether it consulted with the band on the expenditure or not, on the band's account. Try to argue with them, and within twenty minutes you felt like you were being gaslighted. And what could you do about it?)

He could have signed a big mortgage on the strength of the contract they had with High Class, but they were so deep in debt to the label he had a hard time justifying taking on more on top of it.

He *liked* this place too. Liked that it was paid for at this point, just taxes, insurance, and utilities to worry about. Yeah, he'd still like a place in the woods, but that vision had downsized to a one-room hunting cabin with a woodstove and creaky furniture. If there was a lake nearby, fine, but no lake also meant fewer people—just him and the trees.

One day.

Jesus, he felt like he was leaving the place for good. Reluctant to step out the door and never come back.

Someone laid on the horn—and by "someone" he meant Mike, because nobody actually *in* the band was enough of a control hard-on to insist on driving the van themselves, or to keep blaring the horn all over the neighborhood at fuck o'clock in the morning.

He backed out the door, pulling it shut with him, and locked up.

When he climbed in the van's side, their tour manager—behind the wheel just like Dean'd expected—turned his head. "It's not like we're on a schedule or anything."

He started the van moving before Jessie'd even pulled the door shut.

Nick was curled up on the farthest back seat, his jacket covering his head. Dean dropped his bags behind Nick and made his way back up to the front row.

"Anything I need to know about in those bags?" Mike asked.

Since Dean hadn't managed to get away with the nickel bag last night—no. Mike didn't actually care if they had drugs on them; he just wanted to keep tabs on what, where, and how much, in case the bus was about to be searched.

"What happened?" Shawn asked as Dean dropped onto the bench beside him.

The tape on the bandage itched. He touched the edge of it. Felt the ghost of a *thump* underneath him, and his saliva shriveled away. "Dog bite."

"What?"

Dean patted his jacket pocket. Shit. He didn't have cigarettes either.

"Must have been some dog," Shawn said.

"I think it was wild."

Shawn's eyebrows rose.

"I don't want to get into it." He didn't know how to explain a fake dog bite, and he sure as shit didn't know how to explain what he really remembered from the night before.

Jesus—he'd run over some guy.

He reached inside his jacket, hoping, but no—no cigarettes. He'd have settled for stale ones. He leaned forward. "Can we stop at a convenience store?"

"You're fucking kidding me," Mike said.

"Did you get it looked at?" Shawn asked.

"Yeah, I'm fine. Is he asleep back there?" Because Nick smoked, might have some on him.

"Who knows?"

"Aw, fuck, come on," Mike said, the van held up at a red light.

"It's not like we're gonna get there and they've got our shit all loaded and ready to go," Shawn called forward.

"Yeah," Jessie said, leaned back in the passenger seat with his sneaker against the dash. "We'll get there, and they'll just be starting."

"That's because when we get there, they realize they need to move their fucking asses," Mike said. The light turned green, and he gunned it. "We have a schedule. Every day you assholes are on tour, you get a little farther behind on it. I just want to start out even with it instead of already behind the curve, if it's okay with you."

"It's fine with me," Dean said. "As long as we can hit a store on the way."

"You want to stop and get your nails done too?" Mike asked.

Dean stretched his leg out and laid his head back. "Nope. Carton of smokes'll be just fine."

2.

CARL SHIFTED in the midmorning sunlight blazing through the Cougar's windshield, sticky and itchy in his clothes. His hair, when he dragged his fingers through it, stood up and stayed that way.

No one had come out of the building.

He didn't know what to think.

People didn't *sleep* in bars. It wasn't even that big a place. He imagined it had to be just about all barroom in there, a couple closet-sized restrooms, a little office that maybe doubled as inventory storage. The roof was a little high, but not enough for a second floor. Maybe the basement? But there were no windows in the short foundation, at least not that he could see from behind the wheel. Maybe—he hoped—there was a bulkhead on another side of the building. An unlocked one.

His mouth tasted like shit. He'd started smoking once it got light. It hadn't helped. He needed a cold drink—orange juice sounded like heaven right about then—and if he waited another ten minutes to empty his bladder, he was going to lose it right in the seat.

He cranked the engine up. He needed to get a look at the rest of the building anyway. He crawled the Cougar past, craning his neck for a good look. Three shuttered windows, nothing at basement level except weeds and litter. He went around the block and came up behind the building. The rear door was shut, a couple wooden steps leading up to it. The windows on the main level were shuttered just like the others. No sign of a bulkhead

anywhere. He turned up Main Street, the way he'd come, the
St. Michael medal swinging from his rearview. Eggs sounded
almost as good as orange juice—or would once he took care of
his bladder. There was a diner just up the street, close enough to
keep an eye on the bar if he sat in a window booth. He parked
out front, the car easy to get to if the bikers made a move.

He shoved the handgun back under the passenger seat,
reached in back for the manila folder. Leaving it on the table
he wanted, he gave a nod to the waitress and strode through
the scattering of tables toward the restrooms.

When he got back, a menu sat by his folder, a napkin and
silverware. A glass of water. He chugged half of that down,
glanced at the menu, pushed it aside.

The waitress showed up, and he ordered orange juice, coffee,
a couple eggs over hard with toast. When she left, he opened
the folder. Reports and photographs and newspaper clippings
from the series of P.I.s he'd hired over the past two years, his
bank account leaping downward with each new lead. Each had
gotten him closer, but ultimately they'd gotten him nowhere—
until now. Until Walker. Walker who'd got him to the bar and
refused to get him any more information. Walker who'd gone
silent, refusing to take his calls.

The waitress brought a cup of coffee, a little pitcher of cream.

"Thanks." He didn't look up. He'd arrived at the picture he'd
been thinking of in the dark, the one of the soldiers in Korea.
The resemblance between the dark-haired man and the biker
he was tracking was unsettling. Not far from his canary-eating
smirk stood a wide-shouldered man, maybe two hundred and
fifty pounds, taller than the sergeant. While the other guys in
the photo—the canary eater and the other three whose faces
Carl could see—had helmets like metal mixing bowls turned
upside down on their heads, this one was holding his at his
thigh. His hair was short on the sides, thick on the top. Blond.
A lock that might have been carefully combed over to the side
at one point had fallen loose, making him look more like a bar
brawler than a lieutenant.

Of the other guys, one had his tongue out, his eyes rolled to the side. Another had his thumbs tucked under the straps of his backpack. The guy on the far end was angled away from the camera, his face tilted toward it, a scar white at the lower curve of his cheek.

A quarter century ago. The guys in the photo were the same age as the guys at the bar last night.

The waitress came with his eggs and juice. He shoved the photo back in the folder.

He watched the bar through the plate glass as he ate. The row of chrome out front glinted in the sunlight; the building itself was silent, shut up.

When the waitress came by with the coffee carafe, he said, "Hey, let me ask you a question."

She cocked her hip, the carafe jutting out. "It's your nickel." A pocket in her apron bulged with her order book. She acted older, but looked not more than a year or two ahead of where Sophie'd be now, her hair pulled back into a ponytail the way Soph used to wear it. But the waitress had auburn hair, her eyes dirty green and set wide apart. She had a scar under her lip, a pale nick.

"Do you know anything about the bike club? At the bar down the street?"

She shrugged. "I don't really hang out with that kind of crowd."

He smiled. "I didn't think you did. I just thought you might know something about them, you know, in general."

"They have a skeleton on a motorcycle on the back of their jackets," she said.

With the outline of the moon in the background. "They call themselves the Black Sun Riders?"

"I guess. They never come in here."

"Do they ever leave *there*?" He thrust a thumb toward the window.

"I guess. I don't pay them much attention. Can I get you anything else?"

"No, thanks."

"All right." She tore off his check and put it on the table.

"These windows must rattle when they go by," he said. They took up most of the front end of the restaurant.

"Don't hear them much during the day." Her gaze skated over him, and she added, "You don't look like much of a biker," before she walked off.

In another life, he might have liked to have owned a motorcycle. Ride through the desert with hot wind in his hair. Not give a shit about anything except school, bills, falling in love maybe. If it had just been his parents that were gone, he might have been able to do that—knowing Soph was safe, knowing she was graduating high school, maybe heading off to college, his aunt and uncle taking good care of her. Things would have been okay, even then. They'd just started getting over the car wreck that had killed their parents, as "past it" as you got, at least.

When he paid the check, the day was pushing toward noon, the sun high and bright in the sky. Shops were open, doing a steady business. A little ways past the diner, he spotted a pay phone. He stopped at his car to dig out a rattling can, scooped a handful of coins from it into his pocket.

He punched in the apartment's phone number, one eye on the bar.

"Where are you?" Tim asked, his voice sludgy like he'd just woken up.

"Two blocks from the bar."

After the kind of grunt that accompanied a lazy stretch, Tim said, "Was it everything you'd hoped for?"

Carl turned his back to the bar, as if the place could read his lips, and pushed closer to the phone, his fingers bumping over the segmented cord that connected the receiver to the box. "I saw him this morning."

A yawn stretched across the line.

"He went into the bar and hasn't come out. Is that normal, to hang out in a bar right through morning?"

"I'd have thought they'd close at two or something."

Leaving out the part about creeping around the building with a gun, he said, "It's locked."

"Well that's strange, I guess." It came across the line flat.

"They'll come out sometime," Carl said, "or unlock the door for business this afternoon."

"I still don't know what good you think you're going to do." Tim didn't know about the gun. Carl had almost told him, but he wanted to keep Tim out of trouble when this all went down. He wanted Tim to be able to say, *I had no idea.*

Tim said, "He's going to say, 'I don't know what you're talking about. I've never even been to New Mexico. You've got me confused with someone else.'"

"I don't have him confused."

"And then he's going to call the cops and have you dragged off to the loony bin."

"I don't have him confused."

A sigh, and then, "When are you coming back?"

"I don't know yet. I have to figure out how to get him alone."

The silence was more than just a vacancy in the conversation. It was crowded with things said a thousand times, not worth saying again.

Before Soph had gone, Tim had been at the edges of his life: the other side of a social studies class, bagging groceries at the Furr's Carl would buy his cigarettes from, sitting at the counter at the burger joint everyone went to. He'd stepped in from the edges when Soph had happened, just an accident really—he'd been walking by while Carl had sat on the gym steps the afternoon after, Carl too numb for any of it to feel real yet. The only pain getting through at that point was the pain of him fucking up, letting it happen.

Tim had come up to sit beside him, tell him he was sorry.

He'd wanted Tim to go the fuck away, but he'd mumbled "Thanks."

After a few minutes, Tim said he'd seen her that night, when he'd dropped Jonesy off for the game. *I can't believe... she was just... she was just right here.* Tim had gripped the edge of the

steps. His eyes had been wide with the frustration and helplessness Carl himself felt so keenly.

They'd sat at the top of the stairs until the sky had turned
orange.

"Don't do anything stupid," Tim said, finally, all the way in
New Mexico. "Especially if it's not even the right guy."

A recording butted in, asking for money.

Carl looked at the change scattered on the shelf under the
phone. Instead of popping more in, he said, "I've gotta go."

"Don't do anything fucking stupid."

He swept the quarters into his hand, the sun hot on his head.
Back at the car, he smoked three cigarettes, leaning against the
door, looking but not looking at passersby, wondering what
they thought as they passed him. Wondering what they knew
about the bikers.

He tossed the last cigarette on the ground and climbed inside,
cranked the engine, and pulled up in front of the convenience
store, that much closer to the man he was after.

3.

WHILE THE crew loaded equipment into the belly of the bus,
Dean mounted the steps, coffee in one hand, cigarette in the
other, a pair of convenience-store sunglasses perched on his
face. Life seemed a lot more pleasant with those on, and his
last pair was in the jacket he'd lost. He'd had to borrow cash
from Shawn to cover the purchase, but at least he didn't have
to worry about food for the next two months. Per diems would
help with alcohol. He'd be all right.

The bus had that steamed-fabric and burned-vacuum-belt
smell that wouldn't survive more than a day or two of eight
guys leaving their dirty socks in it. One of his bags went under
the bus, the other he dropped on the "junk" bunk in the narrow
sleeping area. In his pocket he had one more thing from the

convenience store, and he pulled it out while he leaned a hip against the bunk.

The bus swayed, people climbing on and off, traversing its aisle. He managed to pluck the cotton out of the mouth of the Tylenol bottle with his cigarette clamped between two fingers. He dumped two pills onto his slashed palm.

His teeth ached, he'd come to realize during the van ride. All the way across the front. He must have hit his mouth on the ground when the biker'd tackled him, though how he hadn't bloodied his nose at the same time, he didn't know.

It was funny how different pains turned on in their own time: the neck and knee when he woke in the truck, the cheek when he'd first touched it—now it smarted whenever he moved his face. And now his teeth.

"Hey, hey." Teddy turned sideways to fit his bulk through the bunkroom door. One of their roadies, Ted hauled equipment and kept fans at bay, usually just by crossing his arms and standing there, but he was also their guitar tech, with fingers more nimble than you'd expect and an almost preternatural talent for coaxing failing equipment back into service.

Dean shifted toward the back lounge to let Teddy drop his stuff in the junk. Heat came off the man like a furnace—ten in the morning and the tips of his hair were already pointed with sweat from loading up.

Dean popped the Tylenols in his mouth and chased them with coffee, grimacing as it went down his throat. Some of the best coffee he'd ever had had come from gas stations, but this made his stomach kick before it even reached it. He doubted he'd finish it.

The first thing Teddy pulled out of his bag was a hand towel to sop up the sweat on his face.

Their first big tour, they'd taken three roadie-slash-security guys, two guitar techs, a drum tech, light and sound guys, someone to handle the merch sales, and their first big-tour tour manager—and why not: the record label was supporting the tour.

Man, they were dumb.

They could still tour with a crew like that if they wanted to—just give in and dig their hole with High Class so deep they'd be able to smell Chinese food when they looked down it. And maybe that was the way they were supposed to do it—shut up, sit back, and enjoy the ride. It wasn't like High Class was going to come after them to pay up years down the road when they were on the downslide side of their careers.

It wasn't like it was *real* money—the argument Nick sometimes made. "It's just numbers on paper. It's make-believe. There's no *money* there."

But there *was* money involved, coming in every time someone walked out of a record store with one of their albums. They were just never going to see *that* money. And *that* was bullshit.

"Man, this is *October*?" Teddy said, running the towel over the wide back of his neck.

"Feels about right for October," Dean said. It was probably sixty outside.

Nowadays they toured with two techs who doubled as roadies, a sound guy who doubled as their merch guy, and Mike—who right then grasped the back of the driver's seat with one hand, his clipboard in the other, and said, "Who's not on the bus?"

Nick's head popped up the stairs behind him. He ducked under Mike's arm, then straightened to swagger up the aisle in a snap-front shirt and dark glasses, his ear, as always, poking through hair he hadn't yet bothered to pull a comb through.

"Is that it?" Mike said. "Everyone else on? 'Cause if you're not on, you've got a long fucking walk to NYC."

"If we're not on," Nick said, "we don't know you just threatened to leave us in Haverhill either." He dropped his jacket on a couch in the front lounge, then dropped himself next to it.

"I gotta piss," Ted said, tossing the towel on his shoulder.

"Watch the sway as we pull out," Dean said. "We're not far enough along the tour yet to have piss all over the floor."

"That's tomorrow, right?" Teddy said with a quick grin before he sucked in his gut and squeezed through the doorway.

Dean heard Shawn saying, "Dean back there?" to Ted, and Ted saying, "Yeah," before the click of the bathroom door came. The "yeah" didn't stop Shawn from showing up in the doorway to check. Behind him, the front lounge was bright—almost cheery. The promise of a new tour about to start.

The bunkroom had no windows, just banks of sleeping berths on either side, coarse burgundy curtains drawn across them. From where Dean stood, looking out toward the front lounge was like looking out from the throat of a cave.

The bus vibrated under his feet. The door at the front squeaked shut. The sound of the engine changed, and Dean put a hand against a bunk as the bus started forward.

The movement made Shawn look back over his shoulder. When he turned his attention back to Dean, he said, almost quietly, "Thirty-nine."

"Thirty-nine what?"

"'Can't Win for Dyin'' charted at thirty-nine."

Okay. Well, that wasn't the end of the world. They'd had singles pop up and sink back just as quickly before. "Probably be seventy-two next week." He dropped what was left of his cigarette into his coffee.

"Yeah."

Even so, there was that pull—that *hope*, turning like something dark and shiny deep inside Dean. "The Fix Is In" had made it to five and held for a couple weeks before sinking like a corpse in concrete boots. "Boiler Room" had popped to number two a couple years back.

Their first and only real hit—ironically titled "Hit Me"—had climbed to number one in December '73. Through the magic of engineering, production, and record label coercion, it had hit the airwaves sounding nothing like what the band had intended. Whether it made it because it was a fluke—the exact right song at the exact right time—or because the label really did know better than the band, they hadn't been able to touch the success of "Hit Me" since.

The last thing they'd wanted was to write "Hit Me" over and fucking over. That had been the start of their struggle against the label.

At this point, even if they did write "Hit Me" again, it wouldn't help: five years was a whole generation in music.

And that was another thing: they still weren't putting out the music they wanted to—*their* music—despite the battles against the producers High Class pushed on them, despite the confrontations—er *business meetings*—with High Class execs, and no thanks to the way their own manager—not Mike, who handled their tours, but Gary, who handled their careers—always came back to them with "just give a little on this one."

We'll get you what you want, but you have to give some too. It's a partnership.

They had one album they hadn't "given" on: *Mercy.* They'd produced it themselves, and it was the best work they'd ever done: rough and raw, honest and broken with a thread of hope running through even the darkest parts. Each song was like a cracked-open chest, a beating heart trying to survive the worst possible conditions—and High Class called it "not ready for the market." "A little amateurish, to be honest."

Which had almost gotten an exec a "little" punched in the teeth.

That album was gone. Property of High Class Records, who'd buried it in a vault. That album was gone, and they had to get the fuck out of High Class before their souls got buried too.

"It'll drop off the list," Dean said about their latest single's charting, because like the others it was a Frankenstein monster of the band fighting to keep their sound, and the record label steamrolling it flat, and that just didn't stick for audiences. "How's Evie?" he said to change the subject.

"Pregnant."

"And since you guys broke up last winter, she was just calling to invite you to the baby shower?"

Shawn crossed his arms, his shoulder pressed against the doorjamb.

"Shit," Dean said. "Really?"

"We fooled around in August. But she was seeing someone else. So."

"Great."

"So it might be, it might not be. Are you coming up front?" Shawn asked.

"Nah. I'm gonna catch a nap." He cupped his hand over the bandage at his neck. "It was a long fucking night."

"I'm still waiting for you to tell me about it."

"I'm too busy tryin' to forget it."

4.

THAT NIGHT at the high school, after the creep who'd come up the steps had disappeared, Carl had watched Sophie stand up there alone, like a ballerina in a music box, turning her head at every car that passed.

Certain it was just a matter of time before Soph gave up on her date, he'd turned on the radio. The pop station she liked blared through the speakers. He turned the knob until he found the middle of Aerosmith's "Sweet Emotion," then stretched his legs and pushed his palms against the ceiling. He had Stephen King's *Carrie* on the passenger seat floor, snagged from Sophie. He wasn't sure how much he was into the plight of a high-school girl getting her first period—or how comfortable he was with the idea Soph had read it—but it was something to do. He scooped it up and creased it open to the page he'd dog-eared.

He didn't mind sitting in the car, really. He'd had the Cougar for all of a month, brand new off the showroom floor. Maybe not the best way to spend part of the money he'd inherited after the wreck that killed their parents—his aunt and uncle had certainly argued against it—but he'd stashed a good bit away for college expenses too.

Besides, it only seemed fair he got something good out of losing his parents. All Soph had gotten—until her eighteenth birthday—was him, and a sewing-room-turned-bedroom at their aunt and uncle's house, a house that was out of district, so he had an extra excuse for the car: he'd needed something reliable to run Soph to school in, so she could keep going to the same one, not have her life turned any more upside down than it already was.

He, on the other hand, had gotten to head off to a dorm at college a month after the accident, a place where he could pretend for stretches at a time that life hadn't changed at all—that he could pick up the phone and call mom and dad and tell them how things were going.

As *Carrie's* Billy Nolan rigged buckets of pig blood in a rafter in the school gym, Carl glanced toward the real-life one.

Soph wasn't on the steps.

He'd folded the book closed around a finger and sat up. The place was deserted.

Maybe she was using the restroom.

Maybe the doofus who was supposed to be taking her to the game had finally showed.

He stared holes into the gym doors, a heavy ball turning in the pit of his stomach, telling him she wasn't in the restroom, and she wasn't standing at the drink table while her date bought her a pop.

He dropped the book on the passenger seat and stepped out of the car. Pushed the sky-blue door shut. The soles of his tennis shoes scuffed over the asphalt as he jogged to the gym, his gaze flicking between the doors and the empty sidewalk. By the time he got to the steps, she hadn't popped out.

The security lights made the concrete landing look like a stage, and the show felt over somehow. He checked over his shoulder as he climbed, making sure he hadn't missed her.

The game bled through the steel doors—a coach's whistle, an opinion from the crowd, the closer murmur of voices in the foyer. He grasped the handle and pulled, and all of it got louder, brighter.

A student behind a folding table just off to the side nudged his glasses up his nose, looking toward the door.

"Hey," Carl said. "Did you see a girl come through a few minutes ago?"

"Nope."

"Sophie Delacroix, do you know her?"

"Yeah, she's in my geometry class."

"Have you seen her?"

He nudged his glasses again. "Nope."

Carl looked around. The foyer was crowded, kids who didn't give a shit about the game but wanted someplace to be. The doors to the gym itself were propped open, giving Carl a view of the backs of people's heads, the ones who hadn't gone up into the bleachers.

"Have you been here the whole time?" he asked the kid at the table.

"Sure. I'd have seen anyone coming in. Gotta get their money." He tapped a metal cashbox on the table. A roll of faded blue tickets sat next to it.

Carl pushed back out the doors, a breeze lifting his hair, skittering a newspaper page across the sidewalk.

No sign of Sophie.

Swearing, he checked his watch. The game was probably half over. A forerunner of the panic that was going to overtake him when everyone started streaming out the doors and Soph wasn't with them started revving inside him. He had to prevent that from happening. He had to find Soph, safe, before that happened.

He yanked the door open and went back in. "Can I walk around and see if she's here?"

"If you pay your fifty cents, I don't care what you do."

He pulled his wallet out and slapped a dollar bill down, heading for the gym floor as the kid called out, "You're supposed to get a ticket."

The bleachers were packed. He scanned them as he skirted the game, looking for familiar faces. Looking for one familiar face in particular, small and framed with dark hair, a great smile lighting up her face when she wasn't having her picture taken.

When he got around to the far side, he pushed through another door, to the hallway with the restrooms. A girl was coming out of the ladies'. He asked if she'd seen Soph.

She shook her head. "One of the stalls was closed, though." With a shrug.

Hope sprouted, tender green shoots of it. He paced the short hall, waiting, worry overtaking hope. A certainty sat in him, a lead weight he was trying to ignore. He wanted to claw his belly open just to get it out of him.

At the door to the gym, he stared through the windows, checking the bleachers. Checking the gaggle of girls standing in front of them. Checking the guys laughing closer to the foyer.

The restroom door opened. He swung around, coming to a short stop at the sight of a tall girl with blunt-cut blond hair. Stuffing a folding brush back into her purse, she looked up, startled at his sudden movement.

"Was anyone else in there?" he said.

"Not that I saw." She snapped the purse closed.

"Could you do me a favor and pop back in and check? I'm looking for my sister."

"Soph?"

"Yeah."

With a shrug she turned back.

He tapped his foot. He looked back through the window again. The girl said Soph's name in the restroom, a question mark at the end of it. He wished he were three people, one to stay here and two to split up and check everywhere else.

The girls' room door opened.

"It's empty."

"Have you seen her at all?"

"She was out front when I got here, waiting for Stephen."

"Have you seen *him*?"

"No, sorry."

He shouldered through the gym doors just as the team made a basket. Half the bleacher crowd jumped to their feet, cheering. He walked the sidelines, his head craned back. No Soph. No Soph. No Soph.

He caught a girl in a pink sweater by the arm. Shelly. She'd been to their house, back when they'd lived in their house. "Hey."

"Hey, what are you doing back here?" Metal flashed when she spoke. Her cheeks dimpled.

"Have you seen Soph?"

"Hunh-uh."

He left her staring after him as he half-jogged back to the front doors.

"That was quick," the guy at the table said.

"Seen her yet?" he asked.

The kid shook his head.

Carl pushed out into the cool air again, the door swinging shut behind him.

No Soph.

No Soph, no Soph, no Soph.

THEY FOUND her the morning after the basketball game, in a dumpster behind the Furr's grocery store, three miles from the school.

Whoever'd done it, they'd said, at least he hadn't "violated" her.

No, he'd just cut her throat open from ear to ear.

Not exactly a consolation.

As THE afternoon deepened, an Olds Cutlass, its blue paint dulled by dirt, turned into the lot behind the bar, the sun orange in its rear window. Carl watched it pull to a stop by the wooden steps. The door swung open, and a man stepped out—early thirties maybe, and so thin his denim jacket and the tee shirt underneath looked like they were walking around on a hanger. His beat-up canvas tennis shoes knocked up dust as he turned to lock the car. His hair was stick straight, a lock of it tucked behind his ear. He mounted the steps slow, fishing a different key from his ring.

Carl glanced around, everyone going on about their business.

The guy fitted the key into the knob lock, turned it, wiggled it back out, went for another key, the deadbolt lock. As he stuffed his key ring into his jeans pockets, he pulled open the back door.

It swung shut behind him.

Carl squeezed the hot steering wheel, working out what to do.

Shit or get off the pot.

Pull the trigger or drag his ass back home and get on with his sorry life.

Except he didn't have a life. He had a roommate who liked slasher movies and an academic suspension from school because he spent more time poring over P.I. reports and newspaper clippings than textbooks.

He popped the Cougar's door open. Got to his feet, to the complaint and then relief of his knees. He glanced up the street one more time, checking the convenience store window to see if anyone was looking out. No one paid him any attention. He crawled back in the car to get the gun and his windbreaker, situating them both before he pulled back out. He shut the Cougar up, stuffed his hands in his pockets, and headed across the street, head down, feet moving fast. Asphalt to concrete to dirt. He tugged a hand out to grasp the wooden handrail at the back of the bar and just about jumped up the bar's back steps.

At the top, with his hand on the knob, he took another look around before pulling on the door, fully expecting it not to give.

It swung open.

He poked his head into a dim hallway with a scuffed wooden floor, its finish worn to bare wood in places. Motes of dust hung in the sunlight coming in around him. At the end of the sun's reach, shadows crowded until the hall opened up to the main room, where yellow lighting made the tables and barstools look like something out of an old photograph.

Someone was moving around up there, a lonesome sound, the scuff of rubber soles on wood, the scrape of cardboard being set down or lifted up.

Carl stepped inside and held the door as it fell quietly closed.

To either side sat unmarked doors. He took a step and put his ear to one. Then, just as quietly, moved across to listen at the other.

Glass clinked up ahead. Water ran.

His hand was on the gun at his back. His muscles itched to draw it out, but not yet. He glanced up the hall before putting his hand on a knob.

Holding his breath, he eased it open, just a crack at first, darkness spilling across his toes. He pushed it wider, blind to what was inside. He risked taking his hand off the gun to feel for a light switch.

It snapped on, the switch loud and the bulbs dim, two 40-watters in a ceiling fixture under a shade glazed with age. Boxes sat stacked against the walls, familiar liquor company names printed along their sides. A trio of metal folding chairs sat in the middle around a table with a scarred top, drink rings worn into its wood.

Rather than risk the loud snap of turning the light out, he just eased the door shut.

Water was still running in the main room.

He reached for the door across the hall. Held his breath as he opened it. Reached for the light switch right away, moving it slowly this time, hoping to muffle the snap.

It clicked, and he jerked his head toward the front, then right back to the room, where a big steel desk sat loaded with papers. A couch that had seen better days had been pushed against the wall, with hardly space between it and the desk to roll the chair out.

What he needed was a basement door, or access to the attic. The ceiling in this room was plaster, stained yellow with tobacco. No trap doors in it.

As he eased the door closed, a "Help you?" jolted him back a step. His hand still gripped the knob. The door clapped against its frame.

"Uh, I was looking for a restroom?"

"We're closed."

"Sorry. It's just that…it's kind of an emergency. Promise I won't take up any of your time, I've just—I've really gotta…"

The wiry guy had a draught glass in his hand. He pushed a bar towel into it as he eyed Carl. "Said we're closed." He lifted the glass toward the street. "There're some places up the way."

Carl's stomach clenched, making him think he really did have an emergency on the way. He opened his mouth, his mind blank. Desperate. "This a biker bar?" rushed out. "I saw a bunch of bikes out front. Some nice ones."

The guy didn't answer.

"It doesn't look like there's anyone in here, though. The bikes wouldn't happen to be for sale, would they?"

"Weren't you about to shit yourself?"

Yes. Right about then, yes he was.

"Sorry. I'll come back later." He started toward the door, stopped. "When do you open?"

"Private bar. No membership, no entrance."

"Right. Sorry." He put his hand against the door. Turned his head again. "There's a Triumph out there…I'd be especially interested in that."

"Get the fuck out." The guy dropped his hands to his sides, one with the towel, the other with the glass.

When Carl pushed open the door, sunlight hit him square in the eyes.

The guy was still standing there as he shut it, starting to give a disbelieving shake of his head.

Carl's feet carried him down the steps and into the dirt. His head swirled with thoughts—no one was in there, but they had to be *somewhere*.

That guy was going to keep an eye on him, no doubt, but the bar's windows were shut up, so he was pretty sure the guy wasn't seeing him crossing the street, pulling out his car keys. At least he hoped not.

His shoulders were tight just the same. The back of his neck crawling.

He started the engine when he dropped inside the Cougar. His heart beat his ribs as he pulled away from the curb.

5.

DEAN'S HAND survived sound check. His head throbbed, though, and when he pushed out the venue's back door to get his Tylenol from the bus, the late afternoon sun flashed off the bus's side mirror, stabbing a headache into the back of his eyes. He hauled himself inside and took the bottle to the back lounge, where the blinds were drawn.

As he shook out a couple pills, footfalls came up from the front.

Nick shambled through the doorway, his hair rumpled like he'd slept on a van seat with a coat over his head—hours ago. "Hiding out? Hey, let me get a couple."

He dropped beside Dean with a sigh while Dean popped the top off the bottle. When Dean held two out on his cut-up palm, Nick pinched them up, saying, "You look half as bad as I feel."

"I thought you went for beers last night."

"*Went* for beers. Stayed for everything else they could pour into a glass. I'm a sucker when other people are buying." He tossed the pills in the back of his mouth and swallowed them dry, his chin tipped, his throat exposed.

Dean pushed the cap back on. The bandage at his neck crackled like insects as he moved, just below his ear. And in his ear, blood chugged—almost a sub-sound. He had the sense that he was hearing Nick's too, just a little off from his own rhythm, a little quicker. Leave it to the drummer to be racing ahead.

As they sat, sensation expanded inside his head, bloating until it swelled to press against his skull. He stood, irritated and unsettled. It was like an itch under his skull.

"We could have some party with those," Nick said.

Dean looked where Nick was looking, toward the ceiling. One of the roof hatches was over his head, a good-sized one, not like the little squares on the last bus. Jessie'd stuck an arm with a bottle of Southern Comfort out one of those hatches a few times as they'd pulled out of venues. But these he could fit his whole body through.

"We need to get one of the flight cases in here to stand on," Nick said. "Pop that baby open."

"Overpasses might hurt a bit."

Nick sat forward with a grunt. "I was supposed to be coming to get you."

"For what now?"

"Another interview."

Dean sighed.

Nick held a hand out.

As Dean grasped his wrist, a restlessness rose in him, traveling up the bones in his arm. A prickling, unsteady sense of some unnamed, unshaped thing.

On his feet, Nick dropped his arm, oblivious.

Dean fisted his empty hand, working the weirdness out of it.

Nick was already moving through the bunk area, tapping the curtains as he passed. "This one's over the phone," he said without looking back.

Dean reached for a cigarette. Lit it with a hand that trembled so slightly it was almost unnoticeable, but the flame danced more than it should in a still room. He let the flame gutter as he filled his lungs with smoke. By the time he got moving, Nick was already hopping off the bus.

"ARE YOU feeling all right?" Shawn asked after the interview. Dean had found a wall to hold him up in the hallway.

"Yeah, the Tylenol's working. Headache's gone at least." It had slunk away when the sun went down, or maybe as a result of things picking up at the venue. The longest parts of day-to-day touring were the late afternoons—post-soundcheck, preshow. Time dripped like syrup.

Shawn tilted his head and touched two fingers to Dean's neck, just below the edge of the bandage. "Are you going to be okay for a show?"

Dean pulled back, raking a hand under his hair, dragging his thumb along the skin Shawn had touched. That fucked up feeling again, that restlessness he didn't know what to do with. "Yeah. Fine."

A sign taped by his elbow read "Bus Rolls At 2 A.M. Whether You're On It Or Not." Mike's handwriting.

"I'll be fine," he said. "Better once I get out there."

They'd opened the doors at the front of the house; the murmur of a gathering audience ran underneath the backstage bustle.

Dean wanted to jump forward a few hours, be out there on stage, guitar in hand, eyes half closed, fingers on strings—quickly losing his sense of where his fingers ended and the strings began.

He wanted to be anywhere but standing around backstage with people jostling him and strangers clapping him on the back like they knew him.

Their support act—Thieves—scurried from their seats, chairs scraping, nervous looks casting back and forth. One of the guys grabbed a last slug from a plastic cup, swiping his mouth with the side of his hand as he followed his band through a black door that eased shut behind them, the word *Stage* stenciled in white on its back.

Half a minute later, feedback sounded, an eruption of applause. The first high, fast notes of Thieves's opener vibrated through the thick walls.

Another night, Dean would be out by the stage entrance, checking out their support act. Checking out the crowd—were they the kind that gave their attention to the opening band, or did they go back to their conversations after their initial applause? It made a difference to the whole vibe of the night.

Tonight, though, he just wanted to—

What?

Get the fuck out of here was what the heart tripping inside his chest was telling him.

"I'm gonna hit the head." He turned away, swerving to avoid people.

Locking himself in a stall, he sat down. Dug his elbows into his thighs and pushed his thumbs against his eyelids.

Maybe he should have gone to a doctor after all. Last night had fucked him up, and he didn't know if it was the attack itself or the psychological aftershock of running a man over.

Had he run a man over? He wasn't even sure at this point. The fucking toilet under his ass didn't feel quite real—how much could he depend on the shattered recollections from the night before?

He kept feeling that ghostly *thump-thump*, the bounce of the truck going up and over. He could feel it right in his bones, feel it in the palms of his hands, as if they were still clutching that steering wheel.

He eased a cigarette out of his pocket. The tip jittered as he tried to light it. When he had it going, he covered his eyes, curled his upper lip up to keep it from pressing against the dull ache in his gums, and hoped Thieves got their set over with quickly.

Hoped, too, that he wasn't wrong about going out on stage. That'd be just what he needed: a nervous fucking breakdown in front of twelve hundred people.

The restroom door swung open, startling his cigarette out of his fingers. He picked it up from the floor, eyed it to make sure it wasn't wet, and took a drag over the sound of someone's zipper coming down.

Piss hit water, and Dean licked his lips, the sharp tang of tobacco blooming over the tip of his tongue.

"Are you hiding or shitting?" Nick called over piss hitting water.

"Meditating."

The urinal gave a sucking gush as it flushed. An arm came over the stall door. Brown eyes appeared, peering over it. The sneakers below rose up on their toes a little.

"Good thing I wasn't shitting," Dean said.

"So how'd you manage to get bit by a dog?"

"By going someplace I shouldn't have been." The cuts on his palm crinkled as he flicked ashes on the tiles with his thumbnail.

"Are you gonna stay in there all night?"

"That was the latest plan."

"Fuck that. Let's get out of here. We've got a good forty minutes."

Dean took another drag before hauling himself up. *Out* sounded good. He dropped the butt in the toilet, and Nick stepped back from the door to let him out. Nick, smiling, opened his jacket. The screw cap of a pint bottle poked from the inner pocket.

"Hair of the dog?" Dean asked.

"Hair on my balls. Come on. I bet there's almost no one out back now."

They headed up the hallway, chins up, eyes forward, like they were on a mission—*Can't talk now.*

Mike caught him by the arm, tried to tell him something. The heel of Mike's hand pressing on him scrambled the words, and Dean nodded quickly, pulling away, following Nick, who'd stopped and turned to see what was holding him up but swung toward the door again when he saw Dean coming.

Nick shoved it open, and as Dean stepped out, cool night air swept his face. He could almost drink it.

And Nick was right—almost no one was out there.

"Bus?" Nick said.

Dean slid his gaze toward the straggle of fans in the building's shadow—three guys, hoping to get a look at the band. One shoved another in their direction, and the shoved guy stumbled half a step, looked back at his friend, and gave him a return push.

"Yeah," Dean said quietly.

Nick pointed his sneakers toward the bus, not giving the group of admirers a second look. He slipped the Jack Daniels from his pocket, unscrewed the cap. Tipped it up while Dean rapped on the bus door.

The bus shifted slightly. The door opened.

Wayne, their drum tech, backed up the steps, hopping into the driver's area to give them room to get by.

"Holding the fort down?" Nick asked.

"Just about to head back in."

"Have fun."

Nick handed the bottle off to Dean and collapsed into a seat in the front lounge, knees splayed, Adam's apple bobbing as he tipped his head back, eyes closed.

The bourbon splashed in the bottle after Dean's pull on it, and Nick lifted his hand out, not bothering to raise his head.

Dean handed it over before taking a seat across the aisle.

"I hate the first show of the tour," Nick said, the bottle on his knee.

"Why?" Blood thudded in his ears again, but the bourbon was warm and distracting in his gullet. He leaned across the aisle and plucked the bottle back, took another slug as Nick said, "Pressure. So much pressure. New songs, old songs, all in a different order than last time."

"I swear you were there at rehearsals."

"Not the same." He stretched his arm out.

Dean threw back another swallow before handing it off. "You do this every time." Handing over the bottle made the blood noises rush back in.

After a pull off the JD, Nick said, "How *did* you get bit by a dog?"

Dean dropped his head. Every breath in turned the volume up on the rushing blood; exhaling pushed it back down, but not completely out. It was ready to come back the next time he opened his lungs.

He said, "I was dumb enough to pet it."

"That'll teach ya."

Dean drew air through his nose. Cigarette smoke and bourbon fumes, deodorant and dried sweat. Underneath, something warm and spicy, like the feel of liquor in his chest.

His teeth throbbed, under his gums. He canted forward, arm out for the bottle. Eyes going straight for the pulse at Nick's throat, the quick little beat against his skin. He dragged his gaze down as his fingers closed on the bottle.

He took three long swallows, shutting up the pounding in his eardrums.

"Maybe I should've brought two," Nick said.

"Sorry." Once it was out of his hands again, he fumbled another cigarette out of his pack, back on his feet. Pacing. He stopped to cup his hand around the lighter's flame, suck-started the cancer stick, and closed his eyes as he breathed in a thick lungful of smoke.

Last night had him all fucked up. He'd give anything to be able to go backward in time, tell the guys, "Yeah, I'm game. I'll go for a beer." That's all he'd had to have done. One measly meaningless fucking decision made differently and he'd be standing in the shadows off to the side of the stage right now, enjoying Thieves.

At the squeak of the bus door, Nick sat up and Dean lifted his head.

Teddy stepped up, looking over the railing. "Jesus. Mike's been yelling all over the place for you, D. He said he told you not to go anywhere. WKRB's on the line, threatening to hang up if you don't get your ass on the phone yesterday."

"Shit." He needed another interview right now like he needed a second asshole.

Nick waved an arm without getting up: *Go, go.*

"Come on," Teddy said, "before Mike blows his top."

People pressed in as soon as he was through the back door—roadies and staff and hangers-on and who the fuck knew else. Teddy parted the crowd with his sheer size, leading him to an office where Mike said, "Here he is," into a clunky receiver before shoving it at Dean.

"Hello," Dean said.

"Heeeey," came a voice through the line. "Dean Thibodeaux from Man Made Murder. How are ya?" So they were live, no quick chat with the producer before being switched over.

"Folks want to know why you're all beat up," the voice said.

Dean pressed his fingers to his eyes. His bruised cheek throbbed. Word fucking traveled fast. "You heard about that, huh?"

"That's the word we're getting from people who've seen you walking around over there. What happened?"

Dean dragged out the dog story again, the "stupid enough to pet it" excuse, adding, "Dogs normally like me, though. I don't have anything against dogs. This one, though, he must've had something against me. Maybe he doesn't like our music." Automatically switching into interview mode.

"Maybe he just confused you for a giant steak," the deejay said.

"Must have."

"Hey, we have the new album here."

"All right. You gonna play it?"

"I'm queuing the single as we speak."

"Just the single? Man, I hope callers light up your lines demanding the whole thing."

The deejay laughed. "You guys have a good show. And watch out for those dogs."

When Dean hung up, Mike said, "You guys are the biggest pains in my ass."

"As well as your main source of income," Dean said. "Have you thought about blood pressure pills?" If they'd wanted a laid-back tour manager, though, they'd have hired one. Mike's state of agitation got them places on time, got them paid on time, got shit done. He was a thorn in their feet ninety percent of the time, but they'd tried using people they got along with easier, and it wound up being more of an aggravation in the end than getting groused at by Mike.

"Try not to disappear before the fucking show starts," Mike said as Dean headed out of the office.

6.

CARL CIRCLED the blocks near but not in sight of the bar, not getting more than a glimpse of the bikes out front with each pass. He'd gone to a gas station for a soft drink, a fresh pack of cigarettes, and the bathroom. He had the radio playing, a commercial segueing into Man Made Murder's new single, the deejay announcing their tour over the intro—New York City tonight, but catch them right here in December when they end their tour back home.

He remembered when he'd been into them, a few albums ago. Or, *probably* a few albums ago. He hadn't kept up. Hadn't kept up with much of anything the past couple years.

He turned the volume up—"Can't Win for Dyin'."

Yeah, that's how he felt too.

Maybe he should stop driving past the road that would take him back to the interstate. He needed a hot shower, a good week's worth of sleep. The thought of catching some of that sleep in his own bed, in the cool dark of the apartment he and Tim shared, it pulled at him, making him feel the weight of all this chasing that much more keenly. *I was out of my mind there for a while*, he'd say, and Tim would pop the top on a cheap can of beer and say, *It's about fucking time you realized it.*

Instead, he pulled up along Main Street—different spot, different direction, different vantage point. The streetlights were coming on, weak in the lingering daylight. He shut off the engine, and the radio blipped off in the middle of the outro.

Shops were closing. The diner had shut its lights out an hour ago. The convenience store's windows glowed with warmth, and across from it, the bar was fading into shadow.

Carl scooted down, bracing his knee against the dash. It was light enough out that smoke wouldn't draw attention, and he lit up while he could, using a match from the book the gas jockey had passed him with the fresh pack. He shook it out and dropped it in the ashtray.

With nothing but time on his hands, he thought about buying the new Man Made Murder album. You know—why not? Tim would be surprised, seeing him show interest in something. Maybe he'd go out to a movie with Tim, even one of those shitty slasher films. He'd done that once, thinking *It's just a movie. It's not real. I can handle* it. But no—as the young girls screamed and the guy in the jumpsuit came relentlessly after them, he'd had to get up and leave, and throw up in the men's room. He hadn't told Tim about the throwing up, just met him in the lobby when the show let out.

But once this was done, maybe he could stomach it. He could watch it as someone who'd vanquished that kind of evil.

It'd be a new start, when he got home.

If he got home.

He wondered if they allowed music in prison. Maybe inmates could have radios, or maybe they'd have one in the rec area or something. If that was the case, he could handle it.

If his problem was taken care of, he could put up with just about anything.

His worst fear was that he'd fuck up what he was trying to do, and go to jail anyway. Stuck behind bars for three, five, ten years while that asshole walked free. That had to not happen.

That had to definitely *not* happen.

The bar's front door opened.

Carl dropped his knee, pulled himself up by the steering wheel.

The wiry guy from earlier came out with a broom, the door falling shut behind him. He swept it over the sidewalk, walking the length of the building, a cigarette jammed in the corner of his mouth. He'd stripped down to his tee shirt. Some kind of tattoo showed on his bony arm.

Carl slipped down in the seat until he was watching through the open spaces in the steering wheel. The wiry guy leaned on the broom, taking the cigarette from his mouth, blowing a stream of smoke. He looked up the road, down it, eyes not falling on anything in particular. Carl brought himself down another half inch, his knees jamming under the dash.

The wiry guy squinted in the smoke as he dragged on his cigarette. Carl's hand twitched, holding the last of his own smoke between two fingers resting on the gearshift.

The guy ground the butt on the sidewalk, let himself back into the bar. The door swung shut behind him.

Carl pulled himself up. With his eyes still on the bar, he stubbed his own cigarette out.

Evening had started to settle in, a few stars glittering in the darkest part of the night sky.

Maybe the guy had locked the door behind him, maybe he hadn't. There was only one way to find out. He leaned over the passenger seat, planting one hand on the manila folder, and reached beneath it, fingers feeling along carpet. It was easier to get to this time—either it hadn't shifted as much in his slow driving or the last turn onto Main Street had brought it toward the front.

He straightened with the gun in his hand. Leaned against the wheel to shove it in his waistband. Was just reaching for the door handle when the bar opened again.

His hand stilled.

His guy strode out, looking neither left nor right, moving straight for his Triumph. He grabbed the clutch, swinging his leg over, the key in his other hand heading for the ignition. He straightened his ride, nudging the stand back. His foot kicked down. The bike swung away from the sidewalk, the biker picking his feet up, gaining speed quickly.

Carl turned his own key. Got himself backed up, did a wide U-turn across the main drag, and followed, the red taillight far ahead of him, zigging and then disappearing around a curve.

He caught sight of it in a few seconds, pushing the Cougar harder, his focus bouncing between the red light ahead and the trees rushing past on either side of the road.

"Where the fuck were you?" he said to the distant taillight. His foot moved off the gas instinctively as another curve rushed toward him. He forced it back down, afraid to get farther behind. He gripped the wheel through the bend, grinding his teeth together, his shoulders tense. They eased down a little as the road straightened again.

He ached for a cigarette right now.

The scenery sped by, as dark as when he'd arrived. He had no idea where he was, figured he could deal with that later. Or the cops would sort it out. He just hoped he didn't rocket past any cop cars right now.

Long stretches of woods were broken by the occasional yard , the occasional church here and there. What looked like a volunteer fire post flashed by. He adjusted himself, getting a little more comfortable—taking off had caught him off guard. He flicked a look toward his mirrors, making sure there weren't any flashing blue and reds behind him. There wasn't anything behind him.

The bike banked, hardly slowing as it rounded a turn onto another road. Carl tossed a prayer toward the St. Michael medal and did the same, tires fighting to stick to the road. Back on the gas, he registered, barely, the houses flying by. Another turn, sharper this time. He took it slower, praying no one was flying down the road as he entered the intersection. His wheels straightened. He picked up speed.

They drove for an achingly long time, Carl's fingers stiffening, his knee jumpy. The radio was singing about running with the devil through the Cougar's speakers. Carl didn't know the band, but he could appreciate the sentiment.

After miles of emptiness, houses showed up in groups, followed by long stretches of them. Suddenly they got bigger—bulky boxes with strips of yard on one side, a driveway between them, the occasional chain-link fence enclosing a property.

On the radio, The Who were asking "Who Are You?" and one side of Carl's mouth curved upward. The WHAK deejay was soundtracking his chase just fine.

Four-way stops slowed the biker. Carl kept two blocks back at each one. A car turned between them, slowing his race from one sign to the next.

Up ahead, the bike banked onto a side street.

He rode right up on the bumper of the car in his way, swerving around it as soon as the other lane was clear. He jumped onto the cross street.

He leaned toward the windshield to the gallop of Heart's "Barracuda," all his focus on the taillight ahead, swooping right at another intersection.

Small houses now, single-story boxes, more yard between them but not a lot. Fences skirting some, toys scattered on grass. Someone had a boat on a trailer in their driveway, someone else a Jeep.

The bike slowed. Carl eased off, keeping back. Spent an extra half second at a four-way to leave some space.

The bike pulled over at a sidewalk.

Carl passed, going twenty, eyes flicking from the biker dismounting to the gray-sided house, noting the dark windows, the old powder-blue pickup parked under the carport. At the end of the block, he turned, turned again, came all the way back around until he was at the intersection, looking down toward the house.

The biker was on the front porch, bending sideways at the waist to peer into a window, his hand a salute against the glass.

Another circle around, and the biker was walking away from the window on the other side of the door, one fist twisting in the other. His knife jutted from the scabbard on his thigh.

Another circle, and the biker was nowhere in sight, but the bike still sat parked on the street. The house was as dark as it had been on the last pass.

Carl put on his turn signal and went down the street. Slowed one house before the bike and nudged the tires up near the curb, beneath the reaching branches of an oak.

He shut off the engine and listened. Couldn't hear anything through his windows.

Across the street, light flickered in a window. A TV. The target house, though, remained dark.

Carl got out and pushed his door quietly shut. He approached the edge of the house's yard. A hedge separating the yard from its neighbor scratched his jeans as he stayed close to the perimeter, watching the windows. He kept his back hunched, ready to duck. He reached behind him and made sure the gun was still there, even though he could feel its weight in his waistband. He just needed reassurance.

Beyond the reach of streetlights, the yard was black. He stepped in a gopher hole. His ankle started to buckle. He caught himself with his arms out and whipped his head toward the house, in case anyone had seen.

Still. Silent.

He checked the neighbor, a light on, bleeding through thin curtains. No one watching.

He left the hedge, crouching low, making his way toward the corner of the house. When he got there, he leaned a shoulder against it and peeked around the edge. The shape of a porch in the back. At the top, a door hung open.

One more glance toward the road, then he moved to the bottom of the steps, staying at the far edge of them so he wouldn't be visible through the open door. He came up carefully, the skin behind his ears tight, his eyes darting.

The porch creaked. He held his breath, took the final step, and peered inside, his arm against the outside wall, his other hand gripping the doorframe. Just inside was the edge of a counter. Soft sounds came from within, things moving, being shifted.

He slipped his hand behind him, under his jacket.

When he pulled it free, his arm was heavy with the weight of the gun. A good, solid feeling. He stepped inside.

A wall faced the back door. He thought he could make out a table pushed up against it. He glanced over his shoulder before moving slowly across the kitchen, to the doorway pointing toward the rest of the house. Other doors came off from it—pantry, he guessed. Basement. Around the corner, probably a bathroom. Something banged a wall near the front of the house.

Carl ducked his head, standing against a wall again. His lips moved in a short, silent prayer. Then he swung through the doorway, arm outstretched.

The front door was wide open, light from the street ghosting in.

Shit.

His arm dropped as he jogged across the room. The throat of the bike's engine sounded before he reached the door. He got there in time to watch the bike speed through the cross street.

Shit!

His legs wanted to run down the steps and get to his car—but what was the fucking point? In just the time it took for him to think that thought out, the bike had probably gone a quarter mile.

By *now* it was probably a half mile out.

Just keep standing here thinking about how you lost him. That's helpful.

The biker would go back to the bar eventually. Carl would start up the watch all over again. And next time—*next fucking time*—he wouldn't be so cautious. Caution was getting him fucking nowhere.

He started to step onto the front porch.

Stopped.

What the fuck had the biker been doing here anyway?

Carl pulled the front door closed, shutting himself in darkness. The street was quiet with the motorcycle gone. He'd have to figure out where he was, then how to get back to where he wanted to be, but it could wait a second. He brushed his hand along the wall, his thigh bumping a table. His fingers found the switch. A ceiling light came on.

All the odd shapes whose contours had been ghosts when the front door was open snapped into clear focus. The expected stuff—the couch, the coffee table, the chair and the TV on a brown metal stand—barely blipped as his gaze crawled over practice amps, a couple guitars, odd electronic boxes here and there, some of them with their guts open. Stereo components were racked against a wall between crates full of record albums. Two hip-high speakers angled out from the corners of the room. Ashtrays, emptied but not washed, except for one that held a single butted-out stub. Tour flyers, rock magazines, receipts and papers of all kinds bulged from boxes.

The table he'd walked into in the dark, papers were spilled across it, some of them scattered on the floor. He hadn't heard paper falling when he'd knocked it. In fact, it looked like a hand had swept them across the table to get a look at them. With the gun in his hand, he pulled them together, scanning the top page as he dropped to a crouch, feeling with the tips of his gun-holding fingers for the others.

Revelations popped into place in his head: the guy who lived here was in a band.

The band was Man Made Murder.

And the invoice he was picking up from the floor said this guy was Dean Thibodeaux.

His heart raced in a mix of awe and excitement and confusion. Why Man Made Murder? What was the connection there? (And, farther back in his head: *Holy shit. I'm in Dean Thibodeaux's house.* He wouldn't have guessed it from the look or location of the place. Didn't stars have mansions? Garages full of cars?)

The deejay on WHAK, he'd said they'd just headed out on tour.

He looked up, his eyes crawling the equipment again but not really seeing this time. What was Man Made Murder to his biker? What had the biker come here for? What had he left with, and where was he going?

Did he know the band was gone, is that why he broke in tonight?

The papers in his hand, one of them was the second page of a tour itinerary, put together by a typist who'd had to backspace and change a letter every couple dates. That was to say, a not very good typist.

All he had was the second half of the tour here, the half that ended with them back in New Hampshire in six weeks.

He shuffled through the pages again. Equipment list, radio stations in the markets they'd be playing, a couple press releases, confirmed interviews, interviews yet to be confirmed, special appearances—apparently there was a meet and greet in Pittsburgh. No first page of dates. He looked under the table. He walked around the room, dipping and crouching, moving stuff, poking into boxes, his heart ticking away the seconds.

List of radio stations. Phone numbers included.

Stuffing the gun behind him, he went to the kitchen and dialed WHAK on a phone mounted to the wall. Waited forever for someone to pick up. Asked them where Man Made Murder was playing tonight. Stood on hold while the info was dug up.

The kitchen was clean. He stretched the cord over to the fridge, looked inside. No perishables. He twisted a can of Coca-Cola free of its plastic, clamping the phone against his shoulder.

"New York City tonight," the phone said.

"Where in New York City?"

He got a venue name and hung up.

North or south? Check the bar first, or go with the hunch?

Why the fuck was the biker interested in Man Made Murder?

Because he was cleaning up his mess, the one he'd mentioned outside the bar early this morning. There was a mess that was all his to clean up.

Like Carl, and the mess *he* was cleaning up.

New York was a long shot. A long fucking shot.

You know where the bar is. You know he's coming back to it.

Right. Even if the biker went to New York, he'd be coming back to the bar eventually.

But Carl couldn't sit and wait; he'd done two years of that.

And the Man Made Murder thing made trying to catch the biker in New York all the more irresistible.

7.

THE CROWD had seen the shapes of them emerging from the shadows at the back of the stage, Jessie first, grinning as Nick slipped behind his kit. They yelled as Shawn walked out with that self-satisfied smile he got when he could tell a show would be good. Dean took a step half out of the shadows, and the sheer presence of the audience hit him like an anvil to the chest. He staggered, and Teddy caught him under the arm, Dean's guitar ready to go in his other hand.

With his eyes pinned on the dark crowd beyond the stage lights, Dean got his guitar strap over his shoulder.

The shouts and whistles were distant, like they were coming from a can at the end of a string, but the *thud-thud-thud* of twelve hundred hearts pumping...

He glanced toward Shawn, panicked, and Shawn shot a smile back, oblivious.

His fingers vibrated as he stepped up to his pedals. He ducked his head. The crowd had a smell—sweat and alcohol and cigarettes. Hairspray and aftershave. And under that, something rich and enticing. Something that made him dizzy.

A girl reached over the edge of the stage, her fingers straining toward him, her arm white and delicate and breakable as bisque.

For a split second, he could hear *her* blood, over all the others thudding in his ears.

Nick counted them in with his sticks.

Dean tore a look toward the set list, his mind a cliff, his thoughts falling off it. "Boiler Room" was scrawled at the top of the sheet. He gripped his pick and tamped down on the fret board. The roar of the audience's pulse drowned under the sound blasting from the monitors at his feet, the stacks at his back. He slipped his eyes closed and hit the opening chords, curling his lip back, his body holding to the guitar like it was the only thing keeping him in the real world.

An hour later, he stumbled backward, his eyes somewhere above the audience, Shawn waving like it was good night, Nick already halfway out the stage door.

He felt stunned, like he'd been hit in the back of the skull and was only now just waking up. He dragged his head over to see Jessie give a wink to two girls in the front row. Dragged his head over more to see Shawn throwing a look back from the doorway, raising an eyebrow at him. Him just standing there with his fingers wrapped around the neck of his guitar.

The audience stomped. Teddy eased the Les Paul from his grip, and Dean fought dueling urges to grab his arm, hard, or duck and run.

Free of his instrument, he spun on his heel, nearly tripping over the drum riser before making his way around it and off the stage. Where he bounced off Shawn's chest, Shawn still waiting for him.

He threw a hand out to the wall to steady himself.

"Are you all right?" Shawn asked.

"Yeah." He dug his fingers against the cool cement. "Yeah, I'll make it." His throat was so dry it hurt to swallow.

Shawn crooked a finger into the collar of his jacket—"Come on"—and dragged him along. "Sit," he said when they got to a metal chair in the back room. He pushed Dean a little to get the message across.

Dean dropped. Leaned forward and scrubbed his face while Shawn fetched water.

Dry as his throat was, he didn't touch the water, reaching instead for cigarettes, finding the pack empty. Crushing it, he looked around. All these people. All these fucking people. He shot to his feet.

Shawn caught him by the arm.

"Bathroom," Dean said.

Shawn let go.

He wasn't all right, not by a long shot. Someone pushed past him on their way out the mens' room. Another Bus Rolls At 2 sign was pasted to the goddamned door.

What he wouldn't give, though, to be on that bus right now, rolling away.

The door fell closed, and he didn't have to look under the stall doors to know he was alone. The layers and rhythms of all the pulses in the building were muffled through the bathroom's walls.

He gripped the sink, the porcelain solid and cool. He rocked on his feet. Clenched his teeth together.

Under his gums, the roots of his teeth throbbed, top and bottom, beating in time with his heart.

Three more songs.

He swiped his forehead against the sleeve of his shirt. Clutched the sink harder. Just three more.

He needed a good night's sleep, that's what he needed. And maybe antibiotics. He should have gone to the ER, gotten antibiotics at least.

The face in the mirror was pale. Purple smudges darkened the skin under his eyes. The bandage at his neck wasn't pristine anymore; sweat and skin oils had turned it gray. Letting go of the sink, he straightened, swallowing, fingers trembling as they reached for the tape. He peeled some of it up, lifting the bandage back.

The door flipped open behind him.

Nick appeared in the mirror, an apple in his hand, his jaws working a bite. He looked over Dean's shoulder, into the mirror, meeting Dean's eyes before dropping his gaze to what Dean was looking at.

"Holy shit," he said, a chunk of apple lodged in his cheek.

What had been raw and red in the morning was gray now, like old meat. The edges of the skin around it were jagged and blueish.

"What the fuck happened?"

He didn't know. He had no *fucking* idea. His lips tingled, numb and cold. His knees started to buckle. The mirror fell away.

Nick caught him, the apple thunking to the grime-streaked tiles. Helped him, half dragging, half stumbling, to the floor where he could lean Dean against the wall, the bandage flapping from his neck like one of the perforated all-in-one envelopes their checks came in.

Nick set a foot between Dean's shins, his hands under Dean's armpits, his hair falling in front of his face. His dark eyes peered through it, searching Dean's. "You are so not okay." His voice sounded like it was coming through a conch—far away, lost in the rush of Dean's pulse. Or Nick's. Nick's pulse.

God, his teeth hurt. It was the one brightly shining spot in the fog. He clutched Nick's shirt as Nick smoothed the tape back in place.

The door popped open, Jessie swinging in, saying, "Hey," before looking—his gaze sweeping before dropping.

His brow furrowed. Words came out of his mouth—the ones he'd no doubt had in mind when he pushed the door open: "Time to finish it. Is he okay?"

"I don't know." Nick untangled Dean's fingers from his shirt.

Jessie stepped closer. "He's kind of glassy-eyed." He waved his hand in front of Dean's face.

Dean turned his head away, blinking.

"What happened?" Jessie asked.

"I don't think he's okay," Nick said.

"Should I get Mike?"

"No," Dean managed, putting a hand up, leaning his weight on his other hand to push himself up. *Don't fucking get Mike.* "Give me a minute. No—don't" *touch me.* "I've got it." He waved them back. "I just can't handle the sight of my own insides is all." He meant looking under the bandage, which had been bad, but it was only the cherry on top of the pile of shit he was worried about at the moment.

Right now this second he was worried about how enticing the sound of Jessie's pulse was.

"Well, it was pretty fucking gross," Nick said.

"It's the stuff they put on it," Dean lied, bumping his shoulder against the wall, trying to navigate to the door without coming too close to his bandmates. "At the hospital." He would have liked to have just leaned against the wall for a while. Any minute, though—any minute and Mike would be poking his head in. *Do not get Mike.* "Let's do this."

"Are you sure?" Nick asked.

"Yeah. Let's fucking do it." He pushed off the wall, his feet sludgy, his ankles wobbly. He got them working, got himself headed to the door, waving Nick's arm off again.

As he stepped into the hallway, he forced himself to walk normal. People were watching. People—as the WKRB deejay'd reminded him—talked.

OCTOBER 14, 1978

1.

TRAFFIC CONGESTED around Worcester and again around Hartford. Carl jiggled the gas, impatient to break free of the logjam and get moving again. His eyes stung with exhaustion. He had the A/C cranked, cold air blowing on his feet, the radio dialed up, the window open, one elbow leaning on it. He stopped for his third coffee in Bridgeport and dumped quarters into a pay phone in New Rochelle to call the venue and get directions for someone coming down I-95.

"They're almost done with their set," the woman who'd answered said. "You wouldn't make it."

No shit, but he was most of the way there, had no choice but to keep pressing on.

The coffee didn't give him the jolt he'd hoped for. It just coated his mouth and made him have to piss again.

New York City was overwhelming—he'd never been in anything like it. This time of the early morning there was more traffic than he saw at midday where he came from. Buildings stretched up to the dark sky, one after the other. Shops crowded at street level, dirty and scrawled with graffiti. He jammed on his brakes as a young guy in a purple leisure suit stumbled into the road. The guy gave him the finger. Carl pushed his heart back down his throat and crept forward, until he had to pull

over, parking lights flashing, to study the notes he'd taken at
the pay phone.

When he glanced up to double-check where he was, Sophie's
face caught him, hanging from the rearview. A neon sign turned
her skin green, made her look dead. He straightened, checking
for traffic, and pulled out again, flicking the lights off.

After another four blocks, he had to admit he was fucking lost.

His chest tightened. To come all this way…

Soph looked at him as if to say it was okay, he'd done the
best he could. But he hadn't, had he? He'd wasted time sneaking around the edges instead of charging right in. He'd spent
two years going to classes, trying in vain to keep up with his
schoolwork, writing checks that meant he could sit back while
someone else did the digging.

He was on a fool's errand anyway. What good was this going
to do?

New York choked him. He had no idea what fucking borough
he was in—uptown, downtown, it was too goddamned much.
Failure broke in his chest, tight and aching. The street blurred,
traffic lights and taillights widening to starry blots.

What was he going to say when he went home?

I failed? I quit? I gave up?

You came to your senses, Tim would say.

Horns blared—he didn't even know if it was him they were
honking at, him they were annoyed with, him who was breaking
some kind of rule everyone else around here knew about.

A yellow taxi swept past, picking up speed as it went by, as
if to make a statement.

He swiped his eye with his sleeve and looked around.

Where the *fuck* was he?

Waitwaitwait.

That street he recognized, right? That was on the directions.
He scrabbled for the scrap of paper, pressing it against the
steering wheel as he crossed lanes—to the complaint of drivers
behind him—and turned up the cross street.

Okay, he could be anywhere on this street. This street could be ten miles long for all he knew; he could be halfway down the wrong end of it going the wrong way, but if he stayed on it until the end, and if he then turned and came back up it, even-tually—*eventually*—he'd find the next street on this list, and that street—*that street*—was the fucking one he wanted.

That street right there.

He slammed on the brakes and made a right, horns rising in his wake.

This street.

This street with the fucking Triumph *parked on the fucking sidewalk.* The venue's marquee jutted out over it, the ticket box dark. The doors dark.

The fucking Triumph was fucking here.

He circled the block, clutching the steering wheel, looking for a place to park. The area was so crowded, not only were all the places taken, but a few cars were parked right alongside them.

Coming back around toward the venue, he said *Fuck it*, and pulled in close beside a Volkswagen bus, just beyond the mouth of an alley where he'd seen a crowd milling around a real bus about halfway up.

The photo of Soph wouldn't come off the mirror, the ribbon he'd tied to it getting caught on its edge. He yanked it, and the ribbon tore through the hole he'd punched in the paper.

He leaned forward to put the gun under his jacket again. Grabbed the keys out of the ignition. Opened his door and stepped onto the street in New York City, the whole thing unreal. Like a movie—that was the only place he'd ever seen New York City. *Mean Streets, The Anderson Tapes, Midnight Cowboy*. All brought to life. He pushed the door shut as someone leaned on a horn, dodging him. He headed around the VW bus with his fists shoved in his jacket pockets, Soph's picture tucked behind his wallet in his jeans.

The crowd outside, hoping to talk to the band, was probably forty people thick, crammed between the bus and the alley wall, blocking his view of whatever might be going on at the venue's side exit. Exhaust puffed from the bus's tailpipe, rising gray in the night. A good half of the crowd were girls, their heads low enough to see over even as they rose on tiptoe and turned to grin at their companions. He rose on his own toes, looking over the taller heads—long hair, short almost military cuts, moustaches. An arm pumped up every now and then, a smart retort rising in response to something someone from the band—the band *must* be up there somewhere—said.

So where was his biker? Inside? Farther up? Maybe in front of the bus, with Dean pulled aside?

Carl was still a good twenty feet from the rear end, ready to break to the empty side and come out around front, when his gaze, lifting, caught movement above. His eyes followed a figure jumping down from the back corner.

He took a step back without thinking.

His hand went back, under his jacket. Fingers closing over the gun's grip.

The skeleton on the back of the leather jacket picked up light from the security lamps along the venue's side wall, and Carl was still registering what he was seeing as the biker half turned, digging something from a jacket pocket.

Seeing Carl, the corner of his mouth rose. He brought a black-gloved finger to his lips. *Shh.* His eyes caught the light, glowing like an animal's for the flash of a second. He spread the dark shape he'd tugged out of his pocket and drew it down over his head, first over those eyes—dark now that the light wasn't hitting them—then his nose. Then the smirk, and then that was gone too, and Carl, taking another step back, picked up on another odd thing: the ski mask had no eyeholes. No mouth, no nose—he'd seen that before. But no eyes?

The biker ducked, grasping the bus's back bumper, and snaked into the narrow space under the bus. His feet turned over as he went, coming up off the ground. They disappeared too. All of him disappeared.

With the knurled gun grip under his palm, the back of his jacket brushing his knuckles, Carl crouched, moving quickly, dropping even lower as he neared the bus. He put his free hand on the asphalt and ducked to look beneath it.

The undercarriage bulged and bumped with grime-black shapes—pipes and housing, axles and hoses. A softer, stranger line of shapes didn't fit with the rest—the biker was nestled up against and clinging to the underside of the bus, one foot hooked in who-knew-what, the other braced against something else. Carl couldn't see the other end of him, had no idea how his arms were holding on, what he was doing to support his head.

The edges of the black shape shifted, the biker fixing himself more firmly into the bus's belly.

The bus moved too, jostling from above. Voices to his right became clearer, and he caught sight of a couple passing. The guy gave him a curious look—*The hell are you doing, man?*—as they walked by, the girl clutching something precious in her hands, something with signatures on it, probably.

More of the crowd broke off, heading back up the alley.

The tone of the bus's idle changed.

A light squeal brought him back to elementary school days— the bus door closing.

Shit.

He straightened as he backed away, his feet nearly tangling. He smoothed the back of his jacket over the gun. Turned on his heel and speed-walked to the street, around the VW bus, through the blare of more horns as he yanked his door open and dumped himself in his car, dragging the door closed as he pulled his foot inside.

This was good, though. This was good. Wherever that bus was going, the biker would be stuck on foot, his Triumph left sitting out here on the sidewalk. Carl's ability to keep up just got a whole shitload better. How fast did a bus go, right? It wasn't like it was going to lose a tail. And the biker wouldn't have any idea he was back there. This was perfect.

He popped the Cougar into reverse, threw his arm across the seat, and cranked his body half around to watch the faces of oncoming drivers contort as he backed up, confident they'd be smart enough to get out of the way—not particularly caring if they didn't. He was going after that bus even if he had to drag his rear bumper behind him.

He turned into the alley. The bands' hardcore fans, lit by his headlights, jumped out of his way, hitting the hood of his car as he pushed between them. They yelled at him, and he did not give one shit.

The bus had a hundred yards on him, but it wasn't gaining speed quickly.

This is such a joke, Tim-in-his-head said. *You're like a fucking cartoon character. It's like you don't even* want *to catch him. You had him you asshole.*

How long do you think he can cling to a chassis? Carl asked back. *Once they get out of the city, onto an interstate, how long do you think someone can hold onto a chassis with pavement racing under their back?*

If the biker were to lose his grip—oh fuck, man, how awesome would that be? To see the biker suddenly appear right in front of his tires? Bump, bump, motherfucker.

Getting out of the city was a shitload easier than getting in: he just had to keep his eye on the back of the bus and let their driver do the hard work. In the meantime, he entertained himself with visions of pulling his car over on the interstate and walking back toward the bloody pulp of a man lying on the road, cars swerving around the mess.

He'd make sure the biker was looking at him, make sure he *knew* he was there. Then he'd point the barrel of his gun at the guy's skull and blow it away.

He was fucking *exhausted.* He felt like he should be thinking about this more—not about what he was doing, but about the fact that a man had crawled under a bus to ride it to who knew where. And those eyes—like a coyote's in the moonlight.

He was so tired he was losing his marbles. But the biker had been real, and that was all that mattered.

God, he hoped he'd been real.

Why wouldn't the biker have just followed on his bike, the way he himself was following in his car? Why force yourself into such an uncomfortable position, take such a big risk of fucking up life and limb if you fell off and hit asphalt going fifty-five miles an hour on a busy highway?

He wondered if there was a trap door on the bus, if the biker might have crawled up through the floor while the bus was ambling out of the city. Had he slashed all their throats already? Hell, he could have even done the driver in and taken his seat.

But that wasn't likely. Otherwise, why was the bus in New Jersey now, headed south, getting farther from the Triumph with each turn of its wheels?

And how many people were on that bus? The band, yeah—he thought there were four of them, unless they'd added or lost someone since he'd stopped paying attention. The driver. There had to be roadies, whatever other guys a band needed on the road. So say somewhere between seven and ten people on that bus—and one biker, on it or under it.

The dark swept past him, gray smokestacks to his left, picked out against the sky by the light of a waxing moon.

Exhaustion was catching up, creeping through his muscles like fog.

He stretched his non-driving leg, shook his head, and pulled up straight, blinking himself awake. The burst of adrenaline he'd had when he jumped in the car slipped away, leaving traces of irritation and impatience in its wake.

Ten minutes later, the car was drifting right, and he jolted himself, gripping the wheel, guiding it back.

Follow the fucking bus. He wished for something cold to drink, and lit a cigarette instead.

2.

JESSIE HAD a girl's phone number on each hand. Nick had the rest of his bottle of J.D. in his. The bus was barely out of the city when Dean said he was going to lie down.

Nick was enthusiastic in his support. Jessie nodded, like, yeah, that's a good fucking idea, man. Neither had told the others about the bathroom, as far as Dean could tell, though Shawn watched him thoughtfully. Dean dragged in a steadying breath and focused on getting from here to there without looking like he needed help.

The front lounge buzzed in ways he was sure no one else noticed, electric fields sparking around everyone. He focused on the doorway.

Just get through the fucking doorway.

He'd felt better once he'd gotten back on stage. After the show, by keeping his distance yet not going off on his own, he'd been able to maintain some kind of equilibrium. Telling himself he just needed sleep.

But the minute—the fucking minute—he'd climbed on the bus, a black dread had washed through, clenching his insides, leaning in his chest like a boulder.

He pulled the bunkroom door shut.

And the dread only grew, as though the heart of it was right here, beating beneath his feet. Waiting for him.

In his bunk, black and cramped as a cave with the curtain and the doors to the two lounges shut, he curled into a ball with his back to the aisle.

Panic picked over his nerves with sharp fingers.

Danger and dread consumed him, and he didn't know what it was. Couldn't even *think* with all the noise from the lounge—the talking and laughing, yeah, but the *other* noise, the one he had beating against his eardrums. Secret, private noises amplified to a steady *whoosh whoosh.*

Whoomp whoomp unfolded in his head, like big, slow wings, and then he was back in his truck, trying to get away—the scrabble of fingers on metal, only it was beneath him. Scraping and shifting and waiting. His moan stirred him, and he turned, restless on top of the sheets. Still fully dressed, his boots scuffing the far wall of the bunk.

He clutched the curtain, his eyes shut tight. His mind trapped in the memory, black fingers reaching into his truck—that hadn't even happened, but it was scaring the shit out of him right now.

He fucking killed me.

The biker coming after him.

The crew closest to the bunkroom door burst in when he shouted himself awake, the others pushing in behind them. He blinked in the light, someone having yelled for the driver to turn it on. He was still clutching the curtain.

Faces crouched at eye level. Someone put a hand on his shoulder.

"Bad dream," he whispered, shifting away. "Just a bad fucking dream."

Shawn and Jessie lingered, watching until Dean dragged the curtain shut, mumbling one more time that it had just been a bad dream.

He buried his head under the pillow.

After the door to the lounge closed, while everyone was gathered up front, talking in hushed tones about him, he dragged himself from the bunk to feel in the darkness for his bag among the others in the junk. Dug through it till he found his knife.

He unfolded it and put it under his pillow, his hand tight around the handle as he stared at the inside of the bus wall.

3.

THE MILES spooled out, and Carl had every trick going to keep himself awake, including a stinging palm print on the side of his face from slapping himself. His thoughts bounced from that night in the high school parking lot to the fact that he'd been in

Dean Thibodeaux's house—*Dean Thibodeaux*, he couldn't wait to tell Tim that—to the way the biker had looked at him behind the bus, raising a gloved finger to his smirking lips. The two of them sharing a secret.

Whenever he got to that point in his thoughts, they split off in one of two ways: you should have fucking shot him while you had the chance, and *Did you* see *his fucking eyes?*

And teeth. The biker's lips had pulled back in a grin, and his mouth had been like a wolf's.

I'm losing my mind.

He laughed, sharp and edgy. In a singsongy voice, he said, "I'm losing my *mi-ind.*" At least that'd help keep him awake, talking to himself. "Did you see that, Soph? He had some *fucked up* teeth. What do you think, Sophie, am I—" His eyes searched the space under the mirror. Soph was gone.

His heart slammed to a stop for a second.

Right, his back pocket. He'd put her picture in his pocket. He turned his grip on the wheel. This was the first time since the week after she'd died that she wasn't hanging from the mirror.

It's pathetic, isn't it? he'd said to Tim.

Why? How else are you going to remember her if you don't see her face?

The road funneled under him. His eyes itched. He snapped his attention to the lights ahead of him.

How long had it been since he'd slept? How fucking long?

He checked the gas gauge again, his new nemesis. Fully in the red now. They passed another exit, him and the bus, another chance to stop and refuel. He'd lose them if he slipped off the interstate on his own. The question, though, was whether it was better to lose them for the ten minutes it would take to fill up, or the hour it would take to hike from wherever he ran out of gas back to the nearest station and then back to his car. Then he'd *still* have to stop and refuel because he could only lug so much gas in a can.

Next chance, he had to stop. *Had* to. He just hoped he hadn't held off too long already.

The bus was going fifty-five. If he could get back on the interstate doing eighty, and assuming the bus didn't pull off in the meantime—how long would it take to catch up?

Jesus, as little sleep as he'd had, he didn't even know how to *start* to figure out the answer to that.

Fangs. That was the answer to that. -was half hysterical. He was definitely losing it.

The sun, though. That was welcome. It nudged against the bottom of the sky, lightening the black night to dark purple. That gave him a hope. With daylight coming, he'd get a burst of energy. Maybe manage to get this thing done before he ended himself in a fiery crash against the guardrail, the bus lumbering on down the road without him.

They were nearing a city. He had no idea what city. He'd spaced out on the signs.

Another exit finally, just a road name.

A glance in the rearview gave him a welcome sight: the cars behind him were more than just twin beams of light. They had outlines to their roofs. The night was coming to an end.

When his eyes dropped back to the bus, his heart beat a quick tap dance: a red signal flashed. The bus slowed.

He followed it right off the exit ramp. And right past a gas station. He gripped the wheel and sat forward, staying with the bus, unwilling to lose it now. It made a straight line for a mile or so, stopping for red lights. Finally putting on its signal. The turn took them down a tree-lined residential street for a while. Past a school, its crossing guards not out yet but a scattering of cars already in the parking lot. Eventually the houses moved closer together, and Carl could make out glimpses of downtown buildings up ahead. Then they were there. They waited at a light at the intersection to the main drag, the bus's left signal blinking. The light turned green and the bus rolled forward.

Carl pressed the gas.

The Cougar died.

Shit.

He turned the key off, back on, giving it gas—what gas was left. It sputtered, coughed, and died. A car swung around him. *Great. Just fucking great.* He looked left, right. Leaned forward to check the drag. *Fuck.* More cars swept around him; he was the rock in the middle of their stream. He turned, squinting against the orange rise of sun.

There. Three blocks back. He turned his hazards on, locked up. Headed for the sidewalk and hiked up the road. He'd made it to the next city at least, wherever the fuck that was. Once he got his car moving again, he could find them. How many buses with Massachusetts plates were sitting around downtown, right?

The only catch was, where would his guy be then?

Worry about it later. He needed to piss now—so urgently he sped up his steps, trying to walk as quickly yet gingerly as possible. As he crossed the street to the gas station, the need got so strong he started to worry it was just going to spill down his leg. Wouldn't that be just great? Not enough to be unwashed, unshaven, and unkempt, but he could smell like piss too!

At the urinal, he almost didn't get his dick out in time, but once he had it emptying into the bowl of cool water—pissing had never felt so good in his life.

He left the men's room with a lighter step and a rumbling stomach.

He tore chunks off a Snickers bar while a gas jockey filled a metal gas can at the pumps for him.

Maybe he'd lost his guy. Maybe the biker had dropped out from under the bus while he was busy leaking his lizard, and he was on his way to take care of whatever he'd ridden a few hundred miles under a bus to take care of. Maybe the biker would be on his way out of town before Carl even got to his car with this can of gas.

Maybe his quest was over. No point in hanging around here, right? Get in the car, circle the block to get it to this gas station, fill the tank to the brim, and head west. West and west and west, all the way home. A load off his shoulders. He'd tried, and he'd lost him—it was time to move on with life. He stuffed the last of the chocolate in his mouth as he fished a dollar bill from his pocket. With the gas can heavy in hand, he headed back to his car, where people kept pulling up, pausing, then going around.

The sun was up. A new day had broken. He'd make a quick check downtown—if he didn't see the bus, he'd go home. That was the coin he'd flip. He was already rehearsing the phone call to Tim:

Where are you?

Missouri.

What are you doing in Missouri?

It's kind of hard going from the northeast to the southwest without going through something like Missouri.

Are you coming home?

Yes, and don't use up the hot water. I'm going to need it when I get there. And pizza. After I catch up on a week's worth of sleep.

He was smiling a little as he screwed the gas cap back on. Someone honked. He waved a hand—*sorry.*

After stowing the can in his trunk, he got in and turned onto the main drag. No bus on that. Fine by him. He peered up side streets—no bus, no bus, no bus.

But he spotted a venue, right up around one corner, facing a one-way street. *Man Made Murder* on the marquee. Well shit. He eased over and turned onto the narrower road.

The building was concrete blocks painted brick red, three stories high with windows only at the very bottom and very top, the ones at the bottom plastered over with tour posters.

The place looked dead, litter swept against its dark front doors, the ticket booth shuttered. As he passed an alley running along the far side of the venue, he saw the bus, sitting quietly within it. He pulled up along the curb past the alley and shut his engine off.

Here we go again.

He just had to look under the bus. No biker, no job to do, no reason to hang around. The gas station was just a few blocks away—he didn't even need to go back down to the main drag to get to it. Ten minutes, he'd be out of here.

As he was locking up, a white taxi pulled up to the mouth of the alley, its engine running. Waiting. Carl didn't know if he was waiting for the space Carl had taken. The driver was sitting not ten feet from him, smoking, tapping his wheel.

He couldn't very well go peer under a bus with this guy sitting there.

He went around his own car, to the sidewalk, where he shoved his hands in his pockets and looked around. Across the street, a jewelers hadn't opened yet. Next to that, a pizza place, also not open yet.

Footsteps brought his gaze back. A middle-aged guy in a windbreaker and well-worn tan trousers came out of the alley, opened the back door of the cab, tossed a small bag in ahead of him before dropping into the backseat, pulling the door closed. The driver straightened, hit his meter, and put his signal on. Carl watched the cab drive on past him.

With his hands still pushed in his pockets, he turned on a toe and strode into the alley. It was cooler there—bright from the sun-lightened sky but shadowy near the bottom. He stuck close to a wall, throwing looks over his shoulder.

Either the biker was there or—more likely—he wasn't.

Christ, he might never have been there at all. He could have hallucinated the whole thing. He wasn't discounting that possibility, not completely, though as he played it back, it still *felt* real. Crazy as it was.

His shoulder brushed the wall as he slipped between it and the bus. This side of the venue hadn't been painted red—like they'd run out of that and had had to settle for grime blue. Graffiti scrawled on the walls said Killroy had been there, and "Peace Nation '77," whatever that meant.

One more look toward the street as he hunkered down, duck walking toward the side of the bus—listening for noises, from inside and outside…and noises from beneath. He ducked low. The underside of the bus was pitch-black at first, his eyes accustomed to the sunlight. He closed them, counting silently, then opened and stared, concentrating, looking for the softer bumps he'd seen the night before.

His mouth opened. His breath caught in his throat. He looked up the alley, like he was looking for someone to share this with.

There was a fucking guy clinging to the bus chassis. *Still.* Well shit.

Cars passed the alley at a steady rate. People on foot.

The band, for all he knew, was still on the bus.

He probably couldn't shoot the guy here. Who knew what he'd hit. He didn't mind blowing himself up, but the band didn't deserve to go out in a ball of flames.

But if he could lure the guy out…well, different story.

"*Psst.*"

The black lump didn't move.

Fuck.

What it must take to cling to brackets and pipes for hours on end.

"Hey," he whispered. If the band *was* on the bus, he didn't need them coming out to see what was going on.

A little louder: "Hey."

Maybe he was wrong. Maybe this was something else under there—who knew what, but what'd he know about buses anyway?

He glanced up the alley before ducking low enough to stretch an arm into the shadows. The air coming from the ground was cool, but heat radiated from the undercarriage. He shifted his other palm on the asphalt and reached farther in, his fingertips just brushing fabric. His arm and shoulder blocked his view. The side of his thumb brushed something more rigid. Could be the collar of the leather jacket, and his fingers could be touching the ski mask. It wasn't warm, the way you'd expect a hat someone had been wearing to be warm.

Holy fuck. What if this guy'd crawled under here and died?

That would be kind of cool actually. No less than he deserved.

He turned his toes a little, reaching farther, pebbles grinding under his sneaker.

Hard fingers clamped his wrist.

Air sucked out his lungs like a high-power vacuum had switched on.

He tried to rock back away from the bus.

The hand gripping him yanked him farther in.

His knee hit the pavement. The back of his head slammed the undercarriage.

The hand gripping him twisted, dragging him another few inches closer.

Carl dug his knees against the pavement. His other hand scrabbled forward.

Another yank on his arm from the black, faceless thing clinging to the bus.

In the dim undercarriage, without the sun to interfere, Carl's vision was adjusting quickly. Even as he bent his elbow to try to gain some leverage, his eyes were on the outline of the knife jutting from the sheath on the biker's thigh. He pushed forward with his toes, lunging for it.

The snap holding it popped as he jerked its handle.

The blade *sssed* softly as it slid free from the leather.

The biker released his wrist to reach for the knife.

Carl clenched its hilt in his fist and plunged it into the biker's leg.

A hiss of pain came from the mask.

The biker grabbed hold of Carl's hair.

Carl rocked the knife out and pushed it through leather, into the biker's side. The biker *oofed*, then slammed Carl's head against the underside of the bus, but the angle was awkward, and though it made his ear bleat, it also made it possible for Carl to wrench his head free. The hand came at him again. He banged his head on the pipes as he lunged to meet it with the bloody blade.

The biker's hand didn't have enough weight behind it. The knife pierced the leather but didn't sink far into flesh.

He pulled it back and plunged it into the biker's side again.

As the biker reached for him again, he caught his arm and shoved it downward. And buried the knife up to its hilt in the biker's neck.

"Fuck you," Carl whispered hard, spittle wetting his lips. "*Fuck you.*" As he pulled back, dragging himself backward toward the light, the knife still stuck in the biker's throat, he heard a gurgle of a laugh.

The words that crawled out from under the bus were wet and burbly, but there was a smirk in them. "I smell you, asshole. After this, I'm coming after you, you little *shit.*"

Carl's sneakers scuffed over pavement as he hauled himself into the sunshine.

"I'm coming after *you*. And I ain't gonna leave nothin' but bones."

He slammed his back into the alley wall. Above, the blinds were drawn on the bus's windows—no one peeking out as far as he could tell.

His heart pounded, big booms in his chest. His nerves jittered. He felt high—like crazy high. Like nearly-fucking-got-killed high. It thrummed through him.

The biker chuckled, a gurgling, sucking sound. It stopped, and in its place Carl heard the sick, wet sound of the knife being drawn slowly out.

"Asshole," the biker muttered.

Jesus Christ. Jesus fucking holy fucking Christ.

Carl pushed to his feet, the wall against his back, his palms flat on the bricks. He looked down at one of his hands, blood smeared in the crook of his thumb, wet and glistening along a finger. Seeping into the crevice of a fingernail. A streak of the stuff had followed his palm up the wall.

His cheeks were cold. Numb. Tingling a little. His mouth was dry—he was gasping in gulps of air.

Holy fucking shit.

He pushed off the wall and walked away, trembling.

He just fucking—he just walked away. No idea where he was going, he just needed to move. His feet needed to move so he could think, so he could *process* this shit.

Once his hand was clean—wiped on a shirt he pulled out of the duffle bag on the back seat—and he had two cigarettes smoked down to the filter, he headed toward the main drag, looking for a pay phone.

It took forever for Tim to answer, and when his groggy voice—it was probably six in the morning there—said, "'Lo?" Carl ran right over it: "I'm losing my fucking mind."

"Wha? Where are you?" No snappy comeback on the mind losing—no, *Hey, admitting you have a problem is the first step*, or *Tell me something I didn't know.* Tim must have been dead to the world when the phone rang.

"I have no fucking idea," Carl said. "You're gonna love this, though, as much you love horror movies. Wait'll you hear this. Holy fucking—I'm losing my mind. Are you ready for this?"

"Can you just—"

"I've been tracking a fucking vampire."

Silence. Then: "Are you out of your mind?"

"*That's what I've been saying!*" Only he wasn't out of his mind. He'd just stabbed a guy in the neck, and the guy was still alive back there—not just still alive, but threatening to leave him nothing but bones when he got a hold of him. And why hadn't he gotten a hold of Carl yet? Because he couldn't come out in the sun! "He can't come out in the sun!" he said into the phone.

"What the fuck are you talking about?"

"He can't come out in the sun. He's hanging onto the underside of a bus. That's why he couldn't just take his bike."

"What the *fuck* are you talking about?"

He couldn't even try to make sense. Thoughts collided, smashing into each other. Banging against his skull. "I need to find a stake."

"What? Hold on. Hold up. Now you *are* talking crazy. What the fuck?"

But he did: he needed to find a stake. Assuming stakes actually worked—and why not? Apparently vampires actually had to avoid sunlight.

Holy shit.

He was losing his fucking mind.

He could drag that thing out into the sunlight and *then* stake it. He needed a stake.

Downtown turned out to be no help. He got directions to a hardware store from a woman behind the counter at a pharmacy and swung by the gas station to fill up on his way. When he got there, the hardware store was just opening, and he went straight to the back, looking for lumber. He didn't have anything to shape the stake with himself, so he was hoping for some kind of picket, preferably a small, easy-to-wield one.

The proprietor asked if needed help, and he couldn't imagine describing needing a stake, so he said he was fine.

Finally he found what he needed farther up in the store, sitting in a bin near the plastic For Rent and No Trespassing signs: thin wooden sign posts, about three feet long each, pointed at the end to help you shove them in the ground. He brought a handful to the counter.

Back on the venue's block, his spot was gone. The best alternative was two blocks up. He circled for twenty minutes, waiting for something with a view to the alley to open up. He had time—the biker wasn't going anywhere.

There were people in the alley now—roadies it looked like, smoking cigarettes and drinking coffee in the sunshine. One of them stood not four feet from the thing under the bus.

Parked in front of the pizza joint, Carl slouched in the driver's seat, his fingers resting on the bottom rung of the steering wheel, his head turned to watch the alley in the breaks between passing cars.

Crazy stuff, Soph. Crazy stuff.

She hadn't liked vampire movies. Found them too ghoulish. He remembered when she was four, she had this thing where she pulled her sheets all the way up to her chin, because maybe if a vampire came and he didn't see that she had a throat, he wouldn't bite her on it. He'd been more of a Westerns fan himself, always wanting to go to the pictures to see the cowboys. Indians—that's what had scared him, their whooping and tomahawks. *Scalping.* The thought always made him shudder.

Vampires.

As he thought of those old movies, his forehead slid slowly toward the glass of the side window.

His fingers slipped from the wheel.

Seventy-some-odd hours with nothing more than catnaps to keep him going caught up with him in the morning sunshine, and he wasn't even aware of the blackness rushing in on him until it was too late.

4.

FOOTSTEPS APPROACHED the bunkroom. In the dark, Dean inhaled, tasting the scent of whoever was heading his way. He found light sweat from someone who'd only had a sink bath after the last show. The subtle pulsing of blood under skin.

The curtain rustled before lifting at the corner. Shawn crouched, resting his chin on his hand, hanging on to the edge of the berth. Aftershave. Coffee in his exhale. "Hey."

When Dean said *hey* back, his voice rasped like he hadn't used it in years.

"We're sound checking in fifteen. Meet and greet later this afternoon."

"Okay."

"You feeling all right?"

"Think I'm coming down with a bug."

"Are you good for this?"

"Yeah, just let me piss and wash my mouth out."

"There's a sandwich on the table for you."

"Thanks."

Shawn didn't move. Neither did Dean. He'd rather the curtain be pulled shut again—let him lie there in the darkness.

"If you can't do it," Shawn said, "let us know. We'll have Teddy handle sound check. Anything else—"

"I'm there." He rubbed his face. "I'll be fine. How are you doing?"

"Fine," Shawn said, but he seemed tired. After another moment, he said, "See you inside."

The curtain dropped back into place.

Shawn didn't close the bunkroom door. Faint light filtered through the edges of the curtain.

Dean dug his hand from under his pillow, leaving the knife for the moment. He rolled onto his side and opened his palm. The skin looked sickly, but the cuts—the cuts were the same dull, dead gray he'd seen in his neck. He was rotting from the inside out—whatever had gotten into him was making its way downward.

He put his nose to the cuts, inhaling a faint, sweet, fermented meat odor.

Rotting from the inside fucking out.

He clenched his hand shut. He was dying inside, and he was damned if he was going to do it lying on a thin mattress while some other guy played his guitar. *His* songs.

They'd talked about pulling out one of the *Mercy* songs for this tour. A jab at the record label.

They should do that tonight, while he still could. Who knew where this fucking thing was going.

He rolled out of his bunk, the boots he'd never bothered taking off hitting the floor with a thump. He needed smokes, and he needed to get his hand covered up before anyone saw it. Wouldn't be a bad idea to change the bandage on his neck too. Aside from being filthy, the tape wasn't holding so well anymore.

He popped a cigarette between his teeth and wrapped his hand around the bandaged part of his neck, one eye sneaking toward the sunlit front lounge. It irritated him, just from here.

He slipped his gas station sunglasses on before heading out of his cave.

HE'D BEEN engulfed in the dread for so many hours it had become part of him, so he was surprised when he jumped off the bus and the dread eased up a little. Just a little.

Enough to make him rub his chest, like he could feel congestion breaking up in it.

He banged the venue's back door, the sun hot on the back of his neck, and slipped inside as soon as the opening was wide enough.

The congestion broke even more when the door closed behind him, and by the time he'd found his way to the stage door, he could almost breathe again.

Shawn's voice was saying, "Check, check," through the mic. He swung the stage door open.

Yeah—tonight was definitely the night to do that song from *Mercy.*

"It lives," Jessie said. He had his guitar strapped on, a plastic beer cup in his hand.

Dean picked up his guitar, slung the strap over his head. "What are we doing?"

"Boiler," Shawn said—and to Janx behind the soundboard on the other side of the room, he said, "Can I have a little more in my monitor?"

"How about 'Sidelined'?"

Shawn looked at him. "Yeah?"

Dean shrugged. "Fuck it, why not?"

"I'm game," Jessie said.

"Game with what?" Nick was recapping a water bottle. He set it on the floor.

"We're pulling out *Mercy* apparently," Shawn said.

"All right. 'Bout fucking time." He bounced the hi-hat pedal. Shawn tweaked a peg. When he was ready, he gave Dean a nod.

With a nod back, they started into it.

They'd run through it in rehearsals the week before, so it was still fresh in their fingers. It came off easy. Smooth. Real.

When they finished, Janx called out, "Heavy," from his board, and Dean could hear the smile in it. It *was* nice. *Fuck* High Class Records.

5.

CARL JOLTED awake to the sound of idling engines. He sucked back drool pooling at the corner of his mouth. Dried spit tugged at the skin on his cheek. He sat up, cotton-headed and sweltering, wiping his mouth with the back of his hand.

The afternoon sun beat through the windshield. The back of his shirt was soaked through. His brain had been replaced with steel wool, prickly and irritable. He was confused for a few seconds over where the fuck he was or what was going on.

A bicycle whizzed by, one of those gazelle-like ten-speeds.

His bladder set off an alarm as he shifted. He straightened a knee that felt like a rusted-shut hinge. Shoving his hand through his greasy hair, he squinted toward the alley. Bus still there, so there was that.

He needed to piss. Needed to get a fucking drink before he died of dehydration, and maybe eat something.

He stepped out of the car and into the street. He looked like a fucking bum. No doubt he stank like one too. He straightened his back with a grimace. The pizza place was in full swing, the aroma of baked dough and melted cheese making his insides twist with hunger. He ducked back into the Cougar to grab a change of clothes.

After a sink bath in the tiny stall of a restroom at the back of the building, after deciding the clothes he'd been wearing could just go in the trash—especially the undershorts—he sucked down two colas and a couple of cheese slices, sitting at a table right in the window, where he couldn't see far enough into the alley to keep an eye on the bus but could see fans stopping at the mouth, lingering to talk amongst themselves before moving around front—to get in line, he guessed, or get their tickets before finding their own dinners before the show.

It struck him that he was going to be around for a Man Made Murder show, and three years ago—man, he would have loved to go to a Man Made Murder show. Bands didn't come where he lived; you had to drive up to Albuquerque for that, and he hadn't had the Cougar then. He *did* have two parents and a sister, though. Wished he'd appreciated *that* a little bit harder at seventeen.

Yeah, he was going to be around for a Man Made Murder show, but it wasn't likely he'd see it.

So he wondered instead what it looked like when you staked a vampire—was it going to burst into flame and disintegrate to a pile of ashes, like in the movies? Was it even going to be as easy to stake him as they made it look?

The leather jacket was going to be a problem—another reason why he couldn't just stake the fucker where he was. It was zipped up, and the zipper was pressed against the belly of the bus. As he wiped pizza grease off his fingers, Carl decided you *could* technically stake a vampire from behind, but the leather jacket was still a problem.

Three guys huddled at the mouth of the alley, nodding toward the bus, bumping each other with their shoulders.

In all likelihood, Carl thought, when you staked a vampire, he bled and he died, and everyone would think you'd just killed a man. And then you'd go to prison, and everyone there would think you were off your rocker when you told them your story of revenge against the vampire who'd killed your little sister. They'd probably fuck him up the ass while they made fun of him, and that would be his life, for the rest of his days, however long that lasted.

But *he'd* know. He'd know what he'd really done.

He dropped a tip on the table.

6.

SOUND CHECK ran long. They were having too much of a good time—they pulled out a few more *Mercy* tunes, ones they hadn't rehearsed, laughing as they lost their way, fumbled back. The longer they played, even without the heat of stage lights, the more they perspired. The stronger they smelled. By the third time through "Josephine," Dean had an edge in him—restless and pacing, like a caged lion. He wiped his brow, grabbed the cold beer Teddy brought him. Tried to drown the restlessness with a big gulp of it.

It hit his throat and he started coughing, his stomach lurching. He spat what hadn't gone down his throat onto the floor.

"All right?" Shawn asked.

"Fuck. I should've started with the harder stuff."

Nick grinned from behind the kit.

His stomach rebelled. He hoped to fuck the harder stuff didn't do the same because right now he needed a fucking drink. He coughed and wiped his mouth with his sleeve. "I think that's a good sign to let the other band have a few minutes of their sound check."

The others were grinning as they set their equipment down.

Teddy was there to take the guitar. His fingers brushed Dean's shoulder as he lifted the strap.

The edge inside Dean reared up, and Dean pulled away, slipping free of the strap and guitar, walking away fast without a word. Clenching his damaged hand just to feel something besides the demon rocking in him.

"Food's on the way," Jessie said as Dean passed through the dressing room.

"Save me some," he said, his stomach wrenching at the thought.

He found Nick around the corner, chatting up a chick with Farrah hair and a beauty mark on her cheek, her lips like pink raspberries. Sidling up to him without getting close enough to touch, he said, "You got any of that JD left?"

"Hi!" the girl said with a smile, the gum she was chewing even pinker than her lips.

"Nada," Nick said. "Mike's got drink chits, though."

Dean wondered if Mike had enough chits to get him a whole bottle.

"Oh, hey, I like that," the girl said, reaching toward Dean's wristwatch.

He slipped away before her fingers could touch it. "Thanks," he said to Nick, getting away from the bubblegum and the sweet berry scent of her lip gloss, the dark earthy notes pulsing underneath.

Thieves's sound check bled through the walls.

He found Mike, asked for chits.

"You look like shit, you know."

"Yeah. It's just a bug."

"So you're going to use these for orange juice?" he said about the two tokens he dropped in Dean's hand.

His stomach clenched as the cloying sweetness of that thought splashed through his brain.

"Sound check was good. You've got a meet and greet in a few," Mike said, and before Dean realized what Mike was doing, Mike had a hand to his forehead.

Dean reared back, stumbling over his own foot. "Don't think I'm gonna make it."

"You don't feel warm."

"I'm just wicked run down. Vitamins and some rest, and I'll be good for the show."

"All right. Get on the bus. I'll send someone with juice. Go on."

He went on, straight through the door to the main hall, music blaring as he crossed into it. Ignoring the band on stage, he made a beeline for the bartender, who was pulling bottles out of a cardboard box.

"Whiskey, double. Put it in something portable."

While he waited, he watched Thieves start then stop a song, their electric piano cutting out on them.

MAN MADE MURDER   115

He slid the chits across the bar and took his drink. Headed back out the door while the other band crouched around the Wurly, trying to get it running again.

The sun was an orange tint low in the sky when he shoved open the venue's back door. He ducked his head, keeping his eyes on the ground. He made it to the bus with only traces of an irritated headache, fumbled his bus key out of his pocket, got himself inside, half stumbling up the steps. Dread tightened his chest again. Fuck it. *Fuck* it—he was alone. He could sense no living thing on the entire bus, and he was closed in on all sides. He could live with the dread if it got him a respite from the restlessness.

The bunks, once he shut the doors on both ends, were blessedly dark, and the low throb of the nascent headache at the back of his eyes went away as quickly as it had come. He raked the curtain open and sat on the edge of his bunk. Tossed the whiskey back and closed his eyes at the trail it warmed down his gullet. No queasy stomach from that. Thank God for some favors.

When the whiskey stopped burning his nostrils, he picked up a smell again. One he'd gotten used to overnight. He lifted his palm to his nose, sniffing the bandages. It was that—but it wasn't *from* that. It was all around him.

Actually, it wasn't a smell at all; it felt like one because it was high up in his nostrils. Not like the tickle of a sneeze. Just…a sense.

He pulled to his feet and walked toward the back lounge. The sense in his nostrils faded a little—even more so once he yanked the flimsy door between the lounge and the bunks shut. He sat on the couch, feeling for his cigarettes, still holding the empty plastic cup in one hand. He was going to need more of what had been in that cup. A lot more. When the orange juice showed up, he'd send the runner back to the bar.

Why did it all have to get fucked up now? Those fucking *Mercy* songs—they were going to blow people away. And here he was falling apart, just when they were ready to start bringing them out.

He had to hold it together for this one show, just one fucking show. Then maybe check into a hospital. Find out what was wrong with him, before it really did kill him. He was fucking *losing* it.

7.

EVENING BLED across the late afternoon. Traffic congealed. Activity around the bus, if not *at* the bus, picked up. One of the guys from the band had staggered out of the venue, not looking too well, and climbed on board about ten minutes ago. And in the time since, Carl had paced. And watched. And gritted his teeth in frustration—a roadie came out the back door and opened one of the bays under the bus to dig for something. Fans stopped, some of them brave enough to walk right up to and around the bus, their sneakers passing where the biker was nestled.

Carl wondered if maybe he was wrong and the biker had maybe in fact bled to death there under the bus. He'd hunkered down to the ground—a good thirty feet back from the bus—to take a look, and he couldn't tell anything from that distance.

No, he wasn't going to know until he reached under there again and tried to grab him out.

Three more goddamned fans wandered into the alley, talking about the bus, wondering if the band were inside. Daring each other to knock.

Given what had happened last time, he was thinking it'd be best to go for the biker's feet. If he could get the ankle that was hooked around the under-workings of the bus and pull that out from under the edge of the bus, he'd have the leverage of the bus itself to brace against as he struggled to drag the rest of him out.

The plan of exposing him to sunlight, however, was rapidly getting away from him.

The three stakes leaned against the wall of the building opposite the venue in the alley, a women's clothing store with white mannequins in its windows—dresses, hats, and gloves in the browns, yellows, and oranges of autumn, with a scattering of construction-paper leaves around the toes of their smart shoes.

New plan, if he didn't lose the fucking vampire as soon as it got full dark: wait until the show was starting. Fans would be inside, along with the band and, hopefully, the crew.

After another twenty minutes, the street took on that cozy evening feel—the pizza place was lit up, headlights were on, the sky a deep magenta heading toward black. The first few stars twinkled in the heavens.

Carl shifted his weight to his other foot, arms crossed, neck stiff from sitting and sleeping in his car.

One last huddle of fans hung on, reluctant to leave the proximity of the bus to join the crowd shuffling into the building.

Carl pulled in a deep lungful of air. He had to do something. Letting it out, he said, "Hey, do you know who's opening for them?"

A guy with his back to him half turned. "Thieves."

"Shit. Really?"

"You heard of them?"

"My brother saw them open for Aerosmith. He'd fucking kill to see them again. I wish he'd known."

"They're that good, huh?"

"That's what he says. He'd know better than me. He deejays, out in—" He caught himself on the brink of naming his own town, leaving something for the cops to go on, assuming he managed to get away after taking care of the biker. "Out in Los Angeles." There, that should have enough prestige. "They'll probably be hitting the stage soon. You should check them out."

"What about you?"

"I'm just waiting for my sister. Supposed to take her to dinner for her birthday. If I'd known Man Made Murder was playing… Hey, you guys have a good time in there."

The guys talked for another minute or two amongst them-selves before shrugging and heading up the alley, around the corner, digging in their pockets for tickets.

Carl let out a pent-up breath. Grasping the stakes in one hand, he turned his attention to the bus.

It jostled. He chalked it up to the guy inside walking around.

Moving quickly, he crossed the alley and stayed close to the venue's wall, praying the door didn't swing open and spit more people out.

He made it to the rear tires and slowed, calculating distances, stopping shy of where he wanted to be, giving himself a chance to duck for a look.

With the sun behind the building, the underside of the bus was black as night.

He didn't see what he'd expected to see—but it was dark. He slid over a few feet, to where he wanted to be, and checked again.

Shit. His eyes must be fucking with him. He'd been right *here* the whole time it'd been getting dark. He'd have seen the fucking biker walking around.

Swearing in a whispered breath, he flattened himself to get underneath the bus, just to make sure.

There was fucking nothing there.

8.

As HIS third cigarette burned down to the filter, Dean heard a scrape from farther up the bus. His orange juice, hopefully—which meant he'd be able to put in an order for whiskey. He stubbed the cigarette out, his lip curling at the thought of the juice.

Another scrape, and the skin behind his ears tightened, his chin lifting toward the bus's roof. He got slowly to his feet, an arm out to steady himself, a hand reaching back to his pocket, where he'd stowed his knife. He turned his eyes to the ceiling.

The voice of a rational Dean—the old Dean, before all of this—was telling him it was just a pigeon or something.

At night?

An alley cat then.

A quick shuffle overhead, farther up the bus, was followed by a *thump* he felt through the bus floor.

Your orange juice, old Dean said, but today's Dean unfolded the knife, gripping the handle tight. He switched out the light in the back lounge before darting a glance through the darkness, trying to think of where he could go.

It's Nick, fucking around. He'd been eying those hatches on the roof.

He flattened himself beside the door. Trying not to breathe.

His bones felt like they were starting to crack under the weight of dread. He felt like he was back in his truck, out on that black road—like he'd never left it. Like there was no escape, really. His throat held back the edge of a noise. He touched his fingers to the back of the door—cheap plastic with a lock a four-year-old could break.

He didn't need to hear footsteps: he could map the approach with that weird sense high in his nostrils. He turned his cheek to the wall, teeth gritted. Breathing out his nostrils so he wouldn't breathe in the fermented meat smell.

The knife handle was hard in his fist.

From the bunkroom came the light scrape of curtain tracks, the soft rustle of fabric.

Then silence like a precipice.

He wanted to be anywhere but here. Anyfuckingwhere.

The door made a quiet click before it juttered on its tracks.

He felt like he was free-falling off the precipice.

The full smell of the biker rolled in—leather and exhaust, road grit and oil, and that hint of fermented meat.

Two eyes reflected what light the lounge had in it, and Dean raised his arm.

The biker grabbed his throat with a gloved hand, slamming him to the wall. His weight leaned against Dean's shoulder. The arm with the knife wasn't pinned; Dean swung it around the biker's back like he was giving him a hug and buried its blade in leather and flesh.

Cold breath puffed over Dean's lips.

In the darkness, a grin.

Gritting his teeth, Dean pulled on the knife.

"You're a pain in my fucking ass." The hand gripping his throat tightened. Dean's air cut off. He scratched the biker's jacket with the fingers on his pinned arm. The knife wiggled in the biker's side, but wouldn't come free.

"Bet you're feeling pretty shitty these days, huh?" The biker's thumb jammed harder into his neck.

He wrenched the knife from the biker's side. The rich scent of blood burst into the room. His mouth opened wide at the smell. His head pushed against the cheap wall at his back. It was so rich, it made the edges of his brain fuzz.

"Gimme that fucking thing." Without releasing Dean's throat, the biker grabbed Dean's arm.

Dean sank the blade again, higher, steel sliding along the underside of bone, making his teeth tingle at the sensation.

"*Enough* of this shit."

With a grating, almost burning pain, Dean found himself on his knees, bent over the couch, his now-empty knife hand pinned to his back.

His chest heaved against the couch cushion.

He should just let the asshole kill him.

Just get it the fuck over with.

His nostrils flared at the smell of blood all around him. His throat opened, wanting it.

The biker yanked the knife from his side. It thumped on a couch cushion. Another blade snicked softly against its leather sheath.

The tip dug into Dean's cheek.

His stomach contracted, drawing in against itself. He hadn't eaten in days. His head was going light. He was so hungry all of the sudden; he felt like he was going to puke. Pass out. His eyes rolled, his lids fluttering. He moaned and at first didn't even realize it was him.

"Yeah, that smell'll do it to you," the biker said, close. "Sadly for you you'll never get the joy of it." He twisted Dean's arm higher. Sharp pain, something on the edge of breaking, forced a choked noise from his throat.

And he didn't care. He let out a broken breath—desperation for what was so close—even as the tip of the knife pierced the flesh of his cheek with sparks of cold pain.

"I don't know you from fucking Adam," the biker was saying. "You're not one of us. You don't get to *be* one of us." He forced the knife deeper.

Its tip pushed through Dean's flesh. Metal scraped tooth with an electric pain that flew through his nerves like ice.

The biker twisted the blade.

Dean cried out.

It tugged flesh as the biker worked it back out. He wiped it clean against Dean's cheek.

Dean had time to push his tongue against the hole, taste the tang of his own blood, and then his mouth and eyes stretched open in surprise at the cold pierce of pain at the side of his neck. His throat constricted, his body trying to swallow by reflex around the steel blade lodged across its opening. He dragged air in to yell, but all he got was a wheezy gurgle.

"Shhh," the biker whispered, jerking the knife out.

The gurgling became louder.

His flesh made a sucking sound as the last of the blade pulled free.

His eyes were still open in surprise, his fingers weakly grasping for purchase on the couch cushion. The knife plunged into his back.

Air stopped almost completely. He tried to suck, but the bag wasn't filling.

He scratched at the cushion. The knife's hilt leaned on the hand the biker had trapped behind him, but there was no getting a grip on it.

Up close to his ear, the biker said, "Don't worry. You're not gonna die from this. Not *this*. We'll get to that a bit. First: payback."

The knife wrenched free, leaving him fighting to breathe.

A hand clutched in his hair yanked him backward. The biker tripped him to the floor, planted a knee on his chest to hold him there. Dean wasn't sure he could have gotten up anyway. He reached out, fingers grasping air weakly as he tried to suck air in.

"Hurts like a bitch, doesn't it?" the biker said. "Getting run over's no fucking fun, either, just so you know."

The knife plunged into his gasping mouth. Its tip lodged in the back of his throat. He choked around it, his shoulders banging against the floor. Blood surged into his throat. He tried to claw the biker's face, but he couldn't even *see* the biker's face for the panic and pain.

He could hear him, though, every word as though it was whispered in his ear just for him: "I could suck what's left of you out right here, leave you for your friends to think you're dead. If you're lucky, they'll cremate you."

He braced a hand on Dean's forehead to draw the knife back out.

"If you're not so lucky…I gotta say, forever's a long fucking time to spend staring at the walls of a coffin."

A weak cry came out of Dean's throat along with the blade. He grasped the biker's arm. Watched the biker's thumb flick the metal pommel off the knife's wooden handle.

The biker flipped the knife around, handle down, and Dean could see the wood had been carved like a fat pencil.

"I'm not gonna leave you like that, though. You've been too much of an unpredictable pain in my ass already." He raised the sharpened handle over his shoulder, his fingers tented on Dean's chest. "My fucking luck, someone'd lean over your body with a bloody nose, and you'd be my fucking problem all over again."

Dean's back was soaked in blood. One of his lungs had to have collapsed. Blood gurgled in his throat. He held the biker's wrist, but his strength was washing out of him. The pointed end of that handle was going to swing down and end him with the cracking of chest bone and the sick squish of organs underneath.

And he hadn't even gotten to play that *Mercy* song for an audience.

He coughed, and blood spattered his lips.

His vision blurred.

At least let it be quick.

The door made a soft pop. Somewhere far back in his brain, he realized the latch had been lifted.

No! broke in his chest.

He was one thing, but not his guys—*not his fucking people.*

9.

THINK. THINK. *Think.*

The biker had come after the band—after Dean Thibodeaux specifically, or at least that's how it looked. If he wanted to get to the band, where would he go? *On* the bus. He had no idea which of the guys it was who'd boarded earlier. If it was Dean, the biker had who he wanted. If it wasn't, he had a hostage to get who he wanted.

If *he* were the biker, he'd have gotten on the goddamned bus somehow.

He backed up and looked at its blank windows, the rounded slope of its roof. The door—he should probably try that first. And if that didn't work, he could always bang on the venue's back door and say he saw someone get on the bus with a gun. It'd cause confusion and might make it tough to do what he'd come for, but he had to do something.

Bus door first.

And the door—was unlocked.

He boarded and dragged it closed behind him.

At the top of the steps, he listened. Voices. He followed them up the hall, no lights on in the place at all, but the fact that there was just one straight aisle made the going easy: just put one foot in front of the other. His fingertips brushed a tabletop, a doorframe, the stiff, scratchy fabric of drapes. He reached behind, into his waistband, and pulled out the gun. Pushed the pile of stakes onto a bunk, taking just one with him, clutched in his fist.

Bodies thudded. Someone grunted. The sound of something hitting flesh, followed by wheezing, gasping. His hand found a wall. A crash against the floor shook it. He patted for a light switch. Nothing. Grasped the doorframe.

"I could suck what's left of you out right here," someone growled, "leave you for your friends to think you're dead. If you're lucky, they'll fucking cremate you. If you're not…I gotta say, forever's a long fucking time to spend staring at the walls of a coffin."

That was him. That was his fucking guy. His fingers found the latch on the door, worked it open despite the clumsiness of the stake clutched in his hand. Pulled the door open to near darkness, and got knocked so hard by what felt like someone's shoulder into his thigh that his jaw slammed into the doorframe. The gun flew from his grip, landing in the bunk area.

Half stunned, he got his footing and tried to shake it off.

A boot heel stomped his toe. He put his hand against a hard back and felt no body heat, just denim shifting over a frame as muscles twisted, trying to wrestle free of the other's hold.

The denim jacket backpedaled, driven by the other guy, and slammed into Carl, making him *oof*, making the stake drop from his grip in a clatter. The weight of the guys against him sent him back a step, wood thunking softly under someone's heel. Carl, with his hand against someone's hip, crouched to retrieve the stake.

"Pain in my *fucking* ass," a voice growled, and the body Carl was bracing against pulled away from him.

Carl closed his hand around a stake and turned, rising.

"*Fuck* you," said a different voice, the words sounding like they'd been bit between clenched teeth.

Carl pushed through the doorway, his free hand feeling in front of him.

Someone cried out as Carl's fingers brushed leather. He reached higher, found the fold at the top of the collar. Closed his grip on the jacket and yanked, hard, dragging back and downward.

The biker's arm shot out and around, elbowing him just above the jaw so hard his knee started to buckle with the pain.

The fist gripping the stake caught him against the floor, his fingers pinched under the wood. The biker tripped backward over him, driven by the guy in the denim jacket, who was yelling—a long wordless shout as the both of them tumbled over Carl's shoulders, knocking him forward, their weight falling hard across his back in the bunk area. Carl's hand slid out from under him. The two guys kicked, and Carl twisted sideways, crawling from underneath, shrugging his way free.

His eyes were used to the dark now. He saw the punch come up, heard the musician's head snap back. He grabbed that guy by a fistful of hair and yanked with everything he had, pulling him enough out of the way to get in there himself, between them, straddling the biker.

"Oh, you fucking too?" the biker snarled. He grabbed for Carl's face.

Carl plunged the stake downward with everything he had. In that split second he had time for a thousand doubts—bone, wood, how fucked he was going to be if this didn't work—and when the sharpened point hit chest, jarring his arms and the wood in his hands, he thought for another endless split second that it *had* failed.

The wood cracked.

The tip did nothing but dent the leather.

The musician's arm knocked it out of the way, shouldering him aside. A knife swung down, the edge of its blade catching a gleam in the room's thin light.

Steel cracked bone, and a laugh huffed out of the biker, but the other guy, with a hand shoved against the biker's chin brought it down again, pulling it like a gear shift when it stuck deep in the biker's chest. Grinding out a hole there.

The biker bucked against the floor, his fingers circling the musician's wrist. Carl grabbed the biker's arm, digging a thumb in to try and break the hold. And the musician kept working on his hole, widening it with sick wet sucking sounds.

"Stake," the musician breathed, adjusting his knee to hold the biker down, working the knife around in his chest.

Carl had only the broken one. He held it out, and the musician took it, sliding the knife out and slamming the stake in its place. He leaned back as the musician rose to a crouch and brought his foot high to stomp the stake farther in.

The biker coughed. His fingers moved weakly, trying to get a hold of the wood.

Something in there squished, then burst with a gush, like an overripe tomato being stepped on.

The coughing turned wet.

Carl's hands turned wet.

The biker's shirt—he was pressing down on his sternum, his ribs—became soggy with cool blood.

"Get out," whispered a voice near his ear.

Carl looked over.

"Get the fuck out now." His lips were drawn back in a snarl, his eyes narrow and wild.

Carl's sneakers slipped. He struggled with the doorway, trying to get over the body lodged in it. He fought free, and then he was running down the bus aisle, his heart slamming, his hand wet to the wrist with blood.

Those eyes clear in his head, even in the darkness.

10.

As sneakers pounded down the bus steps, Dean buried his face in the hole in the biker's chest, butting his mouth against the stake, making it shift in the wet insides. He wrapped his hand around the wood and drew it out, wet and squishing. He licked it, then clutched it against the biker's shoulder as he pushed his mouth back into the wound, biting and swallowing—sucking air through his nostrils. At the back of his mind realizing he *could* suck in air. He could fucking breathe again.

He shoved his thumb into the edge of the wound and pulled, trying to get at more.

It wasn't enough.

He turned his knife around and plunged it into the biker's chest cavity, hacking at the ribs. Sharp cracks. The stab of bone shard in his hand as he broke one and wrenched it out of the way. What he wanted was underneath the sternum, but that was too much bone to force his way through. He cracked another rib, wincing as its jagged end bit his palm. It gave a sharp, crisp sound as he broke the rest of it free.

Tossing the knife on the biker's hip, he scooped his hand under the inside edge of the biker's lung, working his fingers between the organs, getting underneath the heart. With a grip on the sternum, he rocked and twisted the heart out of its cavity, its veins and arteries like cords trying to drag it back in.

He bit through them until he could lift the heart clean away, heavy and cool in his fist.

He sank his teeth in it. Rolled his eyes as he sat back, chewing. Breathing. Swallowing. Opening his jaws for more.

What had been a dark room, lit only by moonlight ghosting in the windows at the front of the bus, was becoming easier to make out by the moment—a little grainy, mostly black and white, but if he leaned down a little, he could read the "Levi Strauss & Co" imprinted on the button at the biker's fly. Read it clear as day.

Blood trickled along the inside of his wrist, under his jacket cuff.

He took a deep breath and tore off another piece of heart, eyes rolling back again, taking more until he had just a couple bites left. As he swallowed, he peeled back the biker's upper lip.

Yeah, that's what he thought he'd seen.

He let the lip sag back into place. Brought the chunk of heart to his teeth again, wrestling another chunk free.

A squeak came from the front of the bus, the door opening.

On his feet in a flash, without a thought to the injuries he'd sustained during the fight, he hopped over the biker and threw himself at the bunkroom door, dragging it shut.

Footsteps rounded the railing at the front and came up the aisle.

Leaning his head against the bunk nearest the door, Dean said, "Is that my orange juice?" Wonderment that his voice sounded so normal.

"Yeah."

"Just leave it on the table."

"'Kay." The footsteps came a little closer before pausing at the table.

Dean wiped his mouth with two fingers—wet, sticky. He looked down—his hand smeared with cool blood.

The footsteps started away.

"Hey," Dean said.

"Yeah?"

"How much time do I have?"

"Thieves is getting ready to go on. You've got a little while." It sounded like Janx. And Janx was waiting out there to see if he was going to say anything else.

"Okay. I'll be out in a bit."

"'Kay."

After a moment, he was alone on the bus again, a hand against his chest. There was a hollowness there—something had wrenched free when he'd stomped the stake into the biker's chest.

Free was the right word. There was something free in him now.

He wiped his bloodied hands on his shirt.

The biker blocked the door to the back lounge, his face smeared dark—his chest worse.

Dean balled up the blanket on his bed and shoved it onto the bunk above his. He stuffed the pillow in with it before tearing the sheets off his mattress.

He liberated his cigarettes, matches, and sunglasses from his jacket before he dropped it on the biker's chest. Another good jacket gone. He dropped his shirt on top of it.

Leaning through the door to the back lounge, he assessed the amount of work he had in front of him. He could just call the cops—he'd been attacked after all. *Good luck explaining the missing heart.* And once they checked out the guy's teeth—there were probably other things they could look at too, things that said he wasn't human…maybe the next place they'd look would be him.

He couldn't have that.

He pulled his head out of the lounge, ready to raid the bus's inadequate stash of cleaning supplies. But first he rubbed his cheek, feeling an itch there—and found his skin knitting back together already.

He walked back to the biker and took a good look.

Nothing was fucking knitting together in that mess. So there was that at least.

11.

CARL BEELINED for his car, stiff-legged, brittle, his heart thudding like a sledgehammer. He held his bloody hand out from his side, like it had been contaminated. He didn't know what else to do with it. Headlights caught him, making him raise his other hand and blink as the oncoming car slammed to a stop. It honked as he stood there, then went around, and Carl, snapping out of it, made it to his car door. Got it unlocked. Got inside and, holding his hand up like a doctor who'd just scrubbed in, he dragged his duffle bag open and yanked out the first piece of cloth his fingers fell on.

He wrapped it—a tee shirt, it turned out, one from the bowling alley Tim worked at—around his hand. He gripped it. He wasn't hurt—he knew he wasn't hurt. Or at least was pretty sure he wasn't hurt. He just couldn't shake himself loose enough to manage cleaning up yet.

He leaned back in the driver's seat, tipping his head back, and let out a long, long breath.

He'd done it.

He'd done it.

Or…the other guy had done it, but he'd been there. And he'd brought the stakes. If he hadn't shown up, the other guy might very well be dead by now.

It had to have been Dean Thibodeaux.

And Dean was…

Yeah.

Yeah, he probably was.

He felt dull inside, hollow. He couldn't even feel his heart thudding anymore. He turned his head to look at the medal dangling from the rearview mirror. St. Michael, leader of the army of God in the battle against Satan. How appropriate.

No Soph, though. He'd never got around to putting her back.

Feeling rushed back in again, his chest heaving with breath, his jaw throbbing. Bruises complained as he shifted.

He clutched the shirt around his hand. He'd have to get that cleaned off. He pulled the door handle, kicked the door wide enough to get out. Staggered against the car before getting the door shut and heading into the pizza place. It had a different feel than in the afternoon—more life in it—and even after all the blood, the fresh-baked dough and sauce made his stomach growl, his mouth water.

The hallway to the bathroom was narrow and white and well lit. His shoulder bumped the wall. In the little cubby of a toilet, he dragged the shirt from his hand, blinked at the blood, and ran it under cold water while he checked out his damage in the mirror. His jaw was a puffy. He had a tender knot in his skull, mostly hidden by hair.

Maybe by morning there'd be bruising, but for now he looked halfway presentable.

He trashed the tee shirt—same can he'd thrown his dirty clothes in—and tore paper towels free to dry his hands.

When he went back outside, nothing had changed with the rest of the world. Cars idled while they waited for the light to change. People walked by. The opening band's set seeped through the venue's walls.

The bus was dark and still.

Carl leaned against the Cougar's door, forcing cars to move around him. He stuffed his fingers in the front pockets of his jeans and watched the alley. Not ready to leave yet. Too much adrenaline jangling through his system. Too much shock that it was *over*.

He realized he wasn't hearing the band anymore.

No light came on in the bus, no one came off it.

He shifted, curving his back a little, stretching it.

It was over.

After a while, the venue's back door opened. A heavyset guy in a tee shirt and jeans went up to the bus, stopped to unlock it, realized it was already unlocked—let himself inside.

Carl held his breath.

Two long minutes later, the door opened again and the heavyset guy came out with the musician who'd been in that back lounge following behind.

He'd changed clothes. He was walking straight, almost a bounce to his step.

His eyes cut over, found Carl's.

And then he was passing into the venue, the heavyset guy holding the door for him.

Tires rolled over pavement. The female half of a couple passing behind him on the sidewalk laughed. The wind had developed cool fingers, and Carl shivered under its touch. He pushed his hands deeper into his pockets, waiting for a break in traffic, and finally crossed to the alley.

The bus was a hulking silence, its metal skin cool against his fingertips as he tried the door.

Locked.

Behind him, another door yawned open, someone stepping out.

"The fuck are you doing?" a gruff voice said. "Get away from there. Go on. Get out before I throw you out."

Carl got barely a look before stiff-legging it back out of the alley, his back prickling.

It was done.

It was done it was done it was done.

There was no reason to hang around.

He could go home.

PART II

OCTOBER 15, 1978

1.

DEAN came off the stage with the roar of the audience at his back. Shawn grinned, sweat dripping from the tips of his hair.

Dean grinned back. A slight resistance pulled at his cheek where the knife had gone through—but if anyone could tell something had happened, they weren't mentioning it.

The house lights were up, but the audience was still back there stomping, chanting for a second encore.

They'd saved "Sidelined" for second to last, tying the whole show up with "Can't Win for Dyin'," which, if rumor was true, was poised to hit higher on the charts Thursday. Gary'd told Shawn on the phone earlier it could make it to number two, maybe even pull it out and hit number one.

Dean didn't know how he felt about that—the one time they hoped an album would just sink into obscurity, and they got this.

Didn't it just figure?

But at the moment—at the moment.

Never mind the dead body wrapped in blankets in his bunk— the show had fucking *killed*.

And it wasn't just because they'd nailed "Sidelined." He was amped up. The music had jangled through his blood, swelling in him until he felt he'd burst like a firecracker. The applause and the cheering and the thousand hearts pumping—he'd never been this high in his life.

He had shit to do, but it was okay. He could handle this.

He could handle anything right now.

"Where're you going?" Jessie asked as he split off from them.

"Get some air." His nerves thrummed. The lights on stage, all those beating hearts. The vibration under his feet from their amps, from the crowd. Everything in Technicolor. Technitaste. Techni*life*.

He'd played right off the audience, the smell of their sweat, the pulsing of their blood.

At least once in each song, his thoughts had slipped to the biker. He'd close his eyes and strum his hand down, and feel himself reaching into that dark cavity. Taking what he wanted.

Try to kill me once, shame on you. Try to kill me twice? *Fuck* you.

On his way to the back of the building, he nudged open the door to a storage room he'd scoped out on his way in.

"Hey," Mike said from halfway up the hall, heading his way. "Dean, got a minute?"

He leaned his shoulder against the doorframe, his thoughts picking through the boxes inside. "What's up?"

Roadies scuttled equipment down the hall, dodging around them.

Mike braced a hand against the wall. "You know, I'm a little concerned ab—"

Dean nodded toward the front of the house. "Did we put on a good show?"

"It was a great show, but—"

"Everyone have a good time? Leave happy?"

"They probably didn't want to leave at all," Mike admitted.

"I don't know what we need to talk about then." He put a cigarette between his teeth. The boxes just beyond the door tugged on him. He had shit to do, and only so much time to do it in.

"Listen…"

"Later, all right?" With the unlit cigarette dangling, he shoved the door the rest of the way open.

"Dog bite's better already, I see," Mike said.

Dean pushed the door shut behind him. Didn't bother listening to see if Mike went away. He had work to do.

When he came back out with four large black garbage bags stuffed down the front of his jeans, the hall was mostly empty.

Back on the bus, with the scrape and thump of equipment being loaded beneath his feet, he closed the bunk door and swept open the curtain.

The body-sized mound lay where he'd left it, with two thin wooden stakes he'd found poking out of another bunk piled on top. Which made him wonder about the guy who'd brought them—where'd he come from? What was his involvement?

And where had he gone to?

He wished now he hadn't been quite so quick to send him off—but at the time…He put a hand on the blanket, the lump underneath. Whatever had been enticing in that body was all used up now. It was just a cold shell.

He had no idea when, or how, he'd be able to get rid of it. Now was definitely not the time, not with Wayne and Teddy streaming back and forth with gear.

For now, he needed to minimize any potential smell.

He yanked the blanket away, tumbling the stakes to the floor. The biker was wrapped tightly in sheets, blood blossoming darkly through the cotton. The damp wads of paper towels he'd used for cleanup tumbled onto the mattress. He pushed them back onto the biker's stomach before shaking open the first of the garbage bags.

He started at the biker's feet, lifting them onto his knee so he could get the bag over the biker's heels. When he pulled the bag as far as it would go, it came halfway up the biker's thighs.

As he shook out another bag, he turned an ear to the door. Everyone was still outside. He climbed back in the bunk and pulled the bag over the biker's head, wrestling with the biker's shoulders, pushing wads of blood-streaked paper towels back onto his stomach.

He wound gaffer tape where the bags overlapped.

The remaining two went on a little more quickly, sliding over the first two. He sealed them with tape, then wound bands at the neck, stomach, thighs and ankles. When he was done, he had a black torpedo in his bunk. He shoved it close to the wall before laying his blanket over it, tugging it to cover feet and head.

Leaning close, he sniffed: plastic, tape adhesive, the faint scent of fermented meat. Wasn't a lot he could do about that, and he suspected he was the only one able to smell fermented meat, at least at this point. It tickled the new sense, high in his nostrils. He tossed the tape into the junk bunk and let himself off the bus, needing air, needing to step away from where it had all gone down. Now that he'd taken care of what he had left on his list for the night, a secondary sort of adrenaline hit, making him antsy.

The alley glistened under the security light. A soft rain had come through during the show. Oil rainbows rippled as he skirted a puddle on his way to the back wall of the venue. He dropped against it and lit a cigarette.

Wayne swung the cargo doors down. Teddy stretched with a grunt.

Dean was seeing everything with new eyes, literally. Nothing looked the same. Bright light made things harder to make out. Darkness soothed the strain, brought out the definition. In the shadows of the alley, the colors were vibrant, if a little off. A little more magenta and yellow, like the color on his TV was adjusted wrong. As he looked nearer to the security light, the colors lost their hue, fading away.

Teddy, as he lumbered toward the venue's door, looked like a big piece of meat.

Smelled like hot blood and sharp sweat.

Dean took another pull off the smoke, images of taking Teddy down and ripping his throat out playing at the back of his mind.

When the draft had been going on, when there'd been a good chance he'd wind up in southeast Asia with a helmet and an M60, he'd imagined what it might be like over there—the humidity, the bugs, the mud and C-rations, an enemy hiding in the rice paddies. What it would be like to have to kill someone? How would he know it was the right thing? What if he hesitated?

What if he shot too soon?

A little pressure on a trigger, and there went a whole life. A whole future. *Bam.*

Gone.

He massaged the palm of his hand—a palm that looked like it had never been through all he'd just been through, except for two faint lines. The hole in his cheek was all but gone, skin knitted back together. The hole in his neck— He'd had to pull the bandage off when he was cleaning up; it had been covered in blood, his own and the biker's, and half shredded by the biker's knife. When he'd peeled it away, there'd been a small puckering scar underneath. It looked like it was swallowing itself.

He wondered if underneath all this new skin he was still gray and rotting inside.

He sucked a long drag, watching Wayne move around inside the bus, in the warmth of the front lounge's lights.

The driver trudged by, back from his day's sleep at a motel. Dean gave him a nod.

Did it *matter* if he was rotted inside? The biker'd had no trouble getting around with the same condition, right until the stake through his heart. Maybe it wasn't even rot—just the new normal.

Jesus, it had really taken a stake through his heart.

He stubbed out the cigarette, wanting to get the fuck out of Dodge now. Not that he'd be leaving his troubles behind, but he had a sudden yen for the roll of wheels over road.

When he climbed aboard, Wayne, slouched on a couch with a can of Dr. Pepper propped on his knee, said, "What's up?"

"What'd you think of the show?" Dean asked.

"Balls fucking out. Whatever you guys were on up there, you need to sell it by the dime bag."

Dean smirked. His teeth felt big in his mouth, strange against his lips. Like he was a wolf. He ducked his head, turning sideways to get by Wayne's jutting leg.

The bus shook as Nick pounced up the stairs, Shawn right behind him, smiling. Dean leaned over to look out a window, his mouth closed, hiding the mouthful. Their scents wafted toward his nostrils—not helping.

Outside, Jessie had his arm around a girl's waist, saying something in her ear that made her laugh. Janx squeezed by them to get on the bus. Mike strode from the building, clipboard in hand. He caught Jessie by the shoulder, and Jessie grasped the girl's hand, making her a promise he wouldn't keep as he backed up the steps.

As the bus rolled out, the guys talked about the show—for an hour they talked about it, going over the highlights, then going over them again. Arguing over which other *Mercy* song to slide into the set tomorrow, with Mike arguing against adding a *second* song from an album nobody could get hold of.

"So, they'll make bootlegs," Shawn said. "That's not a bad thing." He reached between his feet for his drink. "Not a bad thing at all. If 'Can't Win' does what they're saying it's gonna do, we're gonna be stuck with High Class. Maybe some bootlegs will prompt their asses into releasing *Mercy*."

"Fucking album we *paid* to make rotting on a fucking shelf," Nick mumbled, shoving his leg into the aisle. Slouching down with his thumbs hooked in his belt loops.

"Have you considered maybe it's time you made your peace with them?" Mike said. "You guys have been fighting the label as long as I've been working with you."

"Longer," Jessie said. He sucked a swallow off a plastic cup of whiskey

"So maybe if you stop *fighting* them and start working with them—"

"Don't even start," Shawn said.

"Is there any chance of tanking 'Can't Win'?" Jessie said. "I mean, it almost feels like they knew we were trying to leave and paid off whoever they had to pay off to move us up the charts—you know, just to keep us hanging on their line."

"I can't even believe we're annoyed our single's charting," Shawn said.

Dean, leaning in the bunkroom doorway, faked a yawn behind his hand. The last thing he felt like he needed was sleep, but this was all just talking in circles, and talk wasn't going to do anything for them one way or another.

"What are we supposed to do," Shawn said, "tell people to stop buying our single? 'Don't buy our fucking album?'"

"I'm hittin' it," Dean said.

As the others broke long enough to say goodnight, he held up a hand, turning away, dragging the door shut behind him.

The hallway had the light scent of fermented meat, stronger when he slipped into his bunk. He put his back to the curtain, his front nudging the blanketed torpedo. He propped his chin on his hand.

What now? he thought to the biker. The biker didn't answer.

He reached under his pillow until he found the smooth wooden handle of the biker's knife. He dragged it out, its end cap dangling from a thin chain. Dried blood streaked the wood.

He closed his hand around the handle, opened his palm to test its balance.

The others kept talking outside the door. Someone turned the radio on while Mike was in the middle of making a point, cranking it up until Van Halen was a garbled mess coming through the wall.

He moved the pommel back over the handle and clicked it into place, making it look like just a knife again instead of a miniature stake.

He settled his head on the pillow. It was tight in the bunk with the biker sharing his space. The garbage bags crinkled softly under the blanket as he shifted his hip.

He wanted to tell the body it was its own fault. The asshole should've just left him alone to begin with. Should have just told him didn't have any weed. Or at least let him run off when he'd gotten away.

He held the knife above his face.

It was his now, he supposed.

What next? He thought to the biker again.

What the fuck am I supposed to next?

He needed to get rid of the body, before he was forced to explain it. And since he couldn't do it right then, he just studied the knife, the feel of it in his hand. Its real purpose hidden under that engraved end cap.

One thing it told him was that while vampires may or may not be afraid of people—he didn't feel too afraid of people himself—other vampires, that was a different story.

2.

THE BLACK road rushed beneath Carl's tires, hypnotizing. Leaving him with nothing but space between his ears to replay the thuds and grunts from that dark back lounge, the wet squish of wood forcing its way through organs.

He pulled off the exit and up to a McDonald's drive-through, tapping the steering wheel while he waited for his food to be bagged. He looked from the shadows of the parking lot to the gaping drive-through window, empty while the guy working it walked off to get his fries.

His imagination brought a vampire to the window, grinning around a mouth full of fangs. He pictured it launching itself over the ledge, reaching into Carl's car to grab him by the throat.

Trees crowded the edge of the parking lot, their dark leaves drooping like sleeping bats.

The pimply kid handed the paper bag through, and Carl got back on the interstate without touching his food, needing to put miles between himself and his imagination. Needing to get road moving under him again.

The realization was sinking in hard: *vampires existed.* And they were mean motherfuckers.

He clamped his soda cup between his thighs, a chill seeping through his jeans.

His car filled with the smell of French fries and Quarter Pounder.

By the time he'd settled enough to eat them, they were cold, and eating was just a masticating of jaws, a contraction and release of throat muscles. He washed the food down with watered-down Coke.

The road fed under his tires, endless and black.

After an hour and a half, the Coke wanted back out.

He hit his turn signal and banked down an exit toward a truck stop, turning on his wipers as fat drops of rain splattered his windshield. He'd take a piss and refill his soda cup, then jump right back on the road. He pulled around the pumps—all of them self-service, and there was no way was he standing outside long enough to put gas in his car, not until he had to.

A rig with a cab and trailer as black as night chugged around the side of his building. He hit the brakes, heart thudding all over again.

If you were a vampire, wouldn't trucking be a good occupation? Drive all night, go from shithole gas station to shithole diner to shithole rest stop—plenty of victims, plenty of anonymity. With a sleeper cab in the back, you could hide all day. Made a whole lot more fucking sense than riding a motorcycle.

The longer he watched the lumbering truck, the easier it was to imagine the driver, with his grizzled, sunken-in cheeks, hunting down food at lonely rest areas and three-a.m. truck stops. Feeding on throats. Grinning as he wiped blood from his chin.

As soon as the way was clear, Carl zipped around the pumps and right back onto the interstate. His bladder could wait.

A stretch farther down the road, the asphalt—slick with a light rain—wavered. He leaned his elbow on the door. Opened the vents to let cool air in.

Drove and drove, until he came awake with a jerk behind the wheel. He tightened his grip, guiding the Cougar's front end away from the shoulder.

Another five miles, and he couldn't fucking make it. He'd kill himself trying.

A motel sign loomed. He drifted toward the exit, his exhaustion drawing him down it, the tires on wet pavement trying to whisper him to sleep.

The act of parking made him a little more alert—the fact that he was going to have to step out of the car. The motel, one of those thin L-shapes, was mostly dark, but the office gave off a warm, if dim, yellow glow, and one or two of the rooms had a little light peeking around their drapes. Across the street sat a closed café and a couple of dark stores. To his left, the interstate; to his right, the main road heading into town. No cars on the go. Nothing but quiet.

He stepped out and eased the Cougar's door into place, soft rain hitting the back of his neck. The dome light stayed on, the latch not quite caught. He leaned on the door with his hip, every nerve ending aware of the darkness and shadows just beyond the motel's lot, until it clicked into place.

Seven strides to the office. A bell on the door tinkled as he let himself in. The front desk was unmanned, and he shifted his weight from foot to foot, looking for a bell, looking for signs of life—imagining the worst, that the vampires had already arrived, killed the clerk, and were just waiting for him to show up.

Crazy. How would they know?

Shuffling came from the hall. Carl crossed his arms, hugging himself. An older man made his way through the doorway, his gray hair like a neat Brillo.

"Help you?" He had creases around his mouth, eyes that drooped like a basset hound's. He at least didn't look like a vampire.

"Could I get a room?"

"Just yourself?" His teeth were square and a little yellowed.

Carl nodded, chewing the edge of a thumbnail, watching the parking area beyond the doors.

"Be twelve dollars. Checkout's at eleven."

Carl nodded again, dragging out his wallet. Fingering through the bills he had left. The clerk licked his thumb before he counted them, tapped them into a neat pile before opening the cash drawer.

"Do you have anything close?" Carl asked.

The desk clerk laughed. "*Close?* Close to what? We don't got anything closer than this place right here."

"Close to the road, I mean." Away from the edge of trees in the back, nearer to the lit-up office. "My car's right out front. Is that first room open?"

"One over from that is." He turned the registration book around for Carl to sign before searching the wall of keys for a fob with a number two on it.

Thirteen quick steps, staying close to the building. He missed the keyhole the first try, the back of his neck crawling with a feeling like he was being watched. He got it in, got the door open, slammed it shut once he was inside. A loose chain swayed against the wood, and he hooked it in place. Flipped on the lights. Every light. Checked the little closet, peered under the bed, swept back the shower curtain.

Let out a breath of relief.

As he pissed into the toilet, something tapped the edge of the bathtub.

His hip banged the sink as he swung around.

A Japanese lady beetle struggled on its back on the edge of the tub, its legs dancing in the air.

He pressed a hand to his chest and decided he'd just take off his shoes and crawl in bed, fully dressed. Getting naked and showering could wait until the sun came up.

3.

AFTER THE bunks filled with slow, shallow breaths, sleepy
mumbles, and Teddy's snores—after the front lounge had gone
silent—Dean slipped from his bunk. The smell was getting to
him—plastic, adhesive, and dead vampire.

The sheath for the biker's knife was taped in with the biker.
Dean carried the weapon in his hand to the back lounge, a pack
of cigarettes in the other.

Rain pattered the bus's roof.

Sitting on the back couch, he ran his thumb along the edge
of the blade. His skin opened with a thin sting. He turned his
hand over and watched the edges of the cut meld back together
before more than a slight line of red could well.

He looked toward the door, sure no one was up but self-con-
scious anyway. Then back at his hand. Holding his breath, he laid
the edge of the blade against his palm and drew it across. His
lips tightened. His teeth felt odd but not huge, not like before.

He watched his skin open up, the insides gray like wet ash.
A thin strip of blood oozed, and the skin started knitting back
together, starting before he even lifted the knife away.

He licked the blood, leaving nothing but saliva and a fine,
pale line where the cut had been.

He dropped back on the couch, an arm behind his head, the
biker's blade tapping his thigh.

A low moan came from one of the bunks, the sound thick
with sleep.

No one stirred. In a moment, there was only the sound of
the road again, wet under the bus's tires.

He lit another cigarette.

He needed his brain to stop jittering so he could figure out
how to handle his problem, but he was still high. Every thought
was slick and fast moving—any he tried to grab hold of popped
like a soap bubble as soon as he touched it. The biker, the guy
with the stakes, the teeth, the album, the single, the fucking
record company.

The smell of blood, hot and rich and enticing, making his nostrils flare as he tried to just sit there and breathe.

4.

LIGHT FILTERED through a gauzy curtain hung between the drapes Carl had forgotten to close. He pulled his pillow closer, sliding his knee up the mattress. He had morning wood and a full bladder again, and his tee shirt was twisted around his middle, but he didn't want to get moving yet. The bed was the most comfortable place he'd been in days.

Kids ran by his room, their footsteps quick and light, one of them calling to the other about the pool.

There was a pool?

The mother—he assumed it was the mother—said swimming season was over, and one of the kids yelled, "But the pool's still open!"

"And you don't have a swimsuit! Don't go out in the parking lot." And then she was talking to a man, and it was going to be endless, the noise. The world was fucking awake.

He rolled onto his back.

Normal. That was the word he was looking for to describe the feeling he had right at that moment. Not a fleeting sort of normal either, but a *this was how life was going to be now* kind of normal. The obsession, the thing that had driven him, was gone. Behind him.

Soph was avenged, and he hadn't even had to kill anyone.

In the soft morning sunlight and bland beigeness of the hotel room, it was hard to grasp that he'd battled with a vampire the night before. He was losing it if he thought that's what the biker had been.

And in any case, *it was over.*

His life was his again. His future his own.

He stretched to turn the alarm clock toward him.

Shit.

Well, he deserved a late morning. You know what else he deserved? A fucking shower.

While the spray beat the back of his neck, he decided he'd call Tim and tell him he was on the way home. *'Bout fucking time*, Tim would say. Tim, he'd imagined, had spent the week staying up till three, the glow of old horror movies ghosting his face as he ate chips and tacos on the living room couch, wrappers piling up around him. Or he'd slipped out to the "nowhere" he sometimes went, pulling his windbreaker on, lacing up his tennis shoes. *Where you going? Nowhere—just need to get out of this box for a while.* He never said, *Want to come?* and Carl had been fine with that. He hadn't wanted to go much of anywhere.

That was going to change. He had new ideas, rising up and folding around him like the steam in the shower. New ideas for his new life.

He hiked across the street with a pocket full of change to the little café—now open—and fed quarters into the pay phone on the outside wall. He punched in their number. It took a second for the first ring. The first became a second. He watched the motel parking lot, his Cougar dull with road dust, its long nose pointing at the building. Four rings, five. At nine he hung up.

He'd lost track of what day it was. Tim could be in class. He consoled himself with a plate of pancakes at the café, smoked his last two cigarettes, and as the waitress dropped off the ticket for his meal, he found himself torn between the itch to talk to Tim—talk to *anyone*—and the desire to just *be home*. It wasn't so much that he wanted to tell Tim everything that had gone down—the story of the night before felt like a weight he didn't want to disturb. He'd already sounded crazy enough the last time he'd called.

But he wanted to tell him his new plan—investigative journalism. He had an ambition now, to travel, to poke into things. Maybe eventually he'd be the one to reveal that vampires actually existed—or prove to himself that they didn't. A momentary break with sanity might have been all he'd had. At any rate, going back to school would give him access to news reports from all over the country, if not the world, as far back as he wanted to look. He'd start with research. Move on to interviewing people who'd been affected by anything that looked like vampire activity. Starting, maybe, with bodies that had been dumped like Soph's. And if he didn't find proof that vampires were at work, maybe he'd find proof that solved some of those cases.

He'd learn how to take photos—not like Tim's Polaroid, but with a 35 mm. Eventually he'd go back to that bar in New Hampshire. In the daytime. Taking precautions, the most important of which, he was sure, was finding someplace secure to be at night. He'd do an exposé on the biker gang, whether they were vampires or not, because they were definitely up to shit. Definitely causing trouble.

He needed to save up money. When he'd withdrawn the cash for this trip, he'd left three hundred and sixteen dollars in his bank account. All he had to his name. Two years ago, he'd had a little over eighteen grand. When his sister had been killed and the money Soph had gotten from their parents had been transferred to him, that stash had more than doubled.

He'd blown through nearly forty thousand dollars between school and living and hunting down the biker. *Forty fucking thousand dollars.*

He needed to be more careful—needed to do as much of the work himself as he could, as cheaply as possible. He needed to get a job. He wondered if he could get one at the local paper. Didn't even matter if it was emptying wastebaskets. He'd learn stuff while he was there.

One day, he was going to have an article about what he found, someplace big. Maybe the *New York Times* or *Rolling Stone.*

Habit had him reaching for the empty cigarette pack. He crushed it in his hand. He could start cutting corners right here. Give up the smokes. Give up the sodas.

He paid the bill, left a tip a little short of ten percent, and fed coins back into the phone.

Eleven unanswered rings later, he shoved his quarters back in his pocket, got in his car, gassed it up at the place next door, and got back on the highway.

5.

"Hey," Shawn said.

As the word worked its way through layers of sleep, Dean shifted. His foot dropped off the couch. He cracked his eyes open. Light that stabbed his retinas haloed around a dark blob. He snapped his eyes shut, pulling his hand over his face.

His hips pressed on something hard. He worked his fingers between himself and the couch back, trying to find what it was.

"Bit too much to drink last night?" Shawn said.

"Must have." His fingertip slid along something sharp, opening it up. He jerked his hand away, lifting his hip. Got his fingers around the knife's grip as his fingertip tingled, knitting itself back together.

"Shut the door." He pushed the biker's knife between the couch cushions, out of sight. His tongue hit the back of his teeth as he spoke, and it didn't feel like the right architecture in there. But mostly—ugh, the light.

As Shawn rose and turned, he tried opening his eyes again.

A faint strip of sun cut across the lounge's floor and burned right through his pupils. He buried his head.

Shawn pulled the door shut, turned on the light, and Dean peeked. Bright—weirdly bright for a shitty bus light—but not intolerable. He pushed himself up, groggy and sluggish. "Are we there yet?" The bus didn't feel like it was moving.

"Yeah. We've got some interviews in a bit."

Dean pushed his hands up his face, trying to wake up.

"If you're not up for it…"

He breathed in, deep, the room full of smells: sweat, the light oil of an electric shaver's motor, orange juice. Old sweat under fresher sweat. It was pulsing off Shawn, signaling, stirring an edginess in his nerves.

"What's this?" Shawn stooped to pick something up.

Dean's heart kicked into gear. Had he dropped the knife?

And at first, he had no idea what Shawn held pinched between his fingers. It looked too smoothed out to be a broken-off piece of something. Hard and a little yellowed, like aged ivory badly carved into a tadpole shape.

Shawn laughed. "Is this a fucking tooth?"

Dean pushed his tongue against the backside of one of his teeth. Its unfamiliar contour.

Shawn rolled the tooth between thumb and finger, making it twirl. Smiling, he said, "You didn't lose a tooth, did you?"

Covering his face with his hands like he was still trying to scrub himself awake, he said, "Not that I know of."

"Weird."

"Do me a favor?" Dean said.

"What?"

"Shut the bunk door on your way out?"

"It's that bad, huh?"

"Cheap fucking whiskey," he said as he lay across the couch, burying his face in his arms.

"Want some aspirin?"

"Nah, just shut the doors. Let me finish waking up. I'll be out."

Shawn's footsteps grew distant.

The far door slid shut.

He launched himself from the couch. He needed to get to the bathroom mirror to see how bad it was, and he needed sunglasses to get from the back of the bus to the bathroom. He dug them out of his bunk, sending a silent *You're a fucking asshole* to the body he had to reach across to find them.

He dragged the curtain shut to hide it. Pulled his sneakers on. Went back to the lounge for the knife. When he pulled the couch cushion up, another tooth shook loose from it.

He ducked to feel around on the floor, and pocketed one more. That was three. As far as he could tell, he was only looking for four—two uppers, two lowers.

He found the fourth deep under the back cushion. As he looked at them in his cupped hand, his shoulders shuddered. He'd never really thought about what adult teeth looked like, how they embedded themselves so deep in your jaw.

He had the biker's knife in his other fist. Tried shoving it in his back pocket, then in his waistband. Under the leg of his jeans, tucked into his sock. He could point it blade up, but the round handle didn't sit well with his ankle.

He hated to leave it, but he had no way to carry it. Wishing he still had his jacket—*either* of his fucking jackets—he pushed the knife down between the biker and the wall. Slipped his own folding knife into his back pocket. He'd have felt better with the one that doubled as a stake—having possession of the thing that could kill him seemed like a sound idea—but any knife was better than none. Not that it had been much use last night.

More use than the fucking stake the other guy had brought on. That thing had snapped like a toothpick.

He needed to get a new jacket, something with an inside pocket.

When he slid the door to the front lounge open, the sunlight through the front lounge's windows reached around the sides of his glasses. He drew back into the shadows of the bunk area. His pulse beat—slow and sluggish but hard.

No one was out there. He just had to make it three steps. Taking a deep breath, he walked, head down, to the bathroom, and yanked the door shut behind him.

Yeah, there they were. Not much longer than the teeth he was used to, but they curved forward and ended in points sharper than his normal teeth. Holding his upper lip with his thumb, he touched the tip of his tongue to one. Not sharp enough to cut on contact, just sharper than they used to be.

Blood pounded in his eardrums.

He was, at some point, probably going to use these new teeth again. How long would the biker hold him for?

The thought horrified him—and stirred him. As he strode back to the bunks, he could feel his teeth grow, pushing against his lips.

After shutting the door, he walked to where the biker'd bought it and dropped to one knee, sliding his hand across the floor. Looking for blood stains. Anything that would give last night's struggle away.

His tongue worried at a tooth again.

He was something else now. It wasn't just funky tricks of the light, or hallucinating that his skin was healing. Shawn had held his old fucking tooth between his fingers.

A shiver went through him, ending in the cold pit of his belly.

He was something else now.

As he stepped to the ground, the sun, no longer restrained by the bus windows, hit him square in the face. He narrowed his eyes behind the shaded lenses, squinching them down to slits, tears welling. He brought his hand up like a visor as he searched the side of the concrete building for anything that might be a door.

A rectangle moved, distorting into a trapezoid. A hulking shape appeared alongside it. The shape gave a quick whistle.

He walked toward it, his hand pressed to his forehead like a salute. He hoped he didn't step in a hole on the fucking way. He was walking almost blind.

Jesus—was he going to be able to do this?

"There's breakfast upstairs," Teddy said as he slipped through the door.

Teddy pulled it shut.

Dean blinked, floats of light ghosting his vision. "I'm good." He wasn't sure he was, but he was still walking upright. He'd take what he could get.

He grabbed the bannister and hauled himself up, following his nose, his insides clenching at the sweet scent of doughnuts.

Raspberry, powdered sugar. Ripe bananas. Coffee. The higher he climbed, the less he wanted to keep going, his guts churning.

Voices spilled down the stairwell, the melody of chatter. When he came around the corner, Shawn stood at a table pouring coffee into a mug. When he saw Dean, he reached for a fresh mug, upside down on a tray.

"I'm good," Dean said.

Jesus, the coffee smell was strong.

"All right—everyone's here." Mike checked his watch. "You've got fifteen minutes each," talking not to the band but to the people who'd come to meet the band—music journalists and local reporters gathered in a clump with mugs and pastries, notebooks stuffed under their arms. Cameras hanging from their necks.

The band mustn't have been the only ones who'd heard "Can't Win" was making a run for the top.

Mike herded the guys into what amounted to a glorified closet with a swaybacked couch shoved against shelves of audio equipment, binders, and cardboard boxes. A metal folding chair faced the couch. A dinky box of a coffee table had been placed between the two, most of its space hogged by a green, pirogue-shaped ashtray.

Dean walked to the far end and put his shoulder against a wall while the others squashed together on the couch.

The first interviewer smiled as she took the folding chair, setting her bag down, flipping open a notepad, smiling at them again. A dangling silver earring flashed light at Dean like a message. With each beat of her pulse, a flowery perfume rippled toward him. He tilted his head up a little. Lifted his cigarette to his mouth. Breathed in the smoke to cover the coffee smell crowding the room.

He put his eyes on the pirogue ashtray, like he could get in it and float away...

...on a river of blood. He closed his eyes for a moment while the others answered questions. They were still thrilled from the show last night, thrilled with the attention they were getting this morning. It was like going back to '73, when they'd thought it would always be like this. Or that it'd get even better than this.

Dean braced his elbow on the wall, his fingers sinking into his hair. Cigarette burning away. His thoughts were having trouble staying put. Under the coffee smell was the other—dark and secret and enticing.

Their interviewer turned her smile toward him, and having no idea what she'd asked, he mumbled, "Nice earrings, darlin'," his mouth hardly moving to keep his teeth from showing. Her pulse sounded like it was beating just for him, and he shifted a bit—excitement rising up in his jeans.

After a laugh, she started to repeat the question, something about how he'd gotten started playing—and the door swung open, banging Nick in the knee. Mike's head poked in. "Time's up." Then they were on to the next, a twentysomething guy who was already having to resort to a comb-over to cover his scalp.

And his blood smelled just as good as the other's.

By the end of it, Dean was on the floor, his back against the wall, chin tipped up. Watching the ceiling. Thrumming with the buzz of life trapped in the room with him. His fingertips tingled as the baritones of his friends' voices bounced off each other in the room. Nick's pulse was still the quicker one, running ahead, and Dean broke off listening to it to light another cigarette.

This last interviewer, another chick, looked his way, and he caught and held her eyes, green flecked with brown. He wanted her, but it wasn't in the way he used to want. He wanted to crush her against him and sink his new teeth in her neck, tasting the smell of her. Feeling her struggle against him.

A detached part of him tried to be shocked, or at least disgusted. He could barely feel it.

His teeth shifted forward as he pictured her screams, imagined the thud of pulse pounding under skin. He tipped his head down, pressing his lips together.

Whatever she was saying wasn't getting through his ears. They were too full of the rush of blood.

The room was a balloon, pressure filling it and filling it, until it felt like it was going to burst.

The door swung open. Mike again, bringing the sharp smell of sweat with him. The rapid beat of his own pulse. "Time's up. You guys've got sound check."

The others protested but started pulling themselves up.

Dean pushed to his feet.

The interviewer fumbled her pencil as she was trying to put her things back in her bag. It clattered lightly to the floor.

As he handed it back to her, he said, "Want to watch sound check?" Keeping his head ducked, his lips moving against teeth that felt huge.

She looked up, startled. Smiled. "Is that all right?"

He shrugged, like *Why not?* The *thub-thub* of her pulse was a jungle drum, vibrations he could almost feel in his fingertips.

"Can I get photos?" She had a padded camera bag with her.

"Snap away," he mumbled as he turned away. His head felt like it could lift his feet right off the floor. "Get everything you needed?" He stayed a little ahead of her, a good bit behind the others. His head full of helium, the rush of what was within reach.

"Oh yeah, it was great. Thanks. Thanks for taking the time." Her breath tumbled against the side of his jaw as she hurried to keep up. He fought the urge to turn and kiss her, right by her mouth, then down a little, making his way to the throb in her neck. The meat of the meal.

Sensations crowded in—crowding him out. Threatening to take him over. He put a hand out to stop a door from swinging shut behind the others, waited until she was a few steps down before following, keeping a cushion of distance between them. Staring over her head.

Sliding his tongue down the back of one long tooth. It almost seemed to tingle in his gums.

Down a hall, another door, and finally back out in the open. He climbed on stage with the others, got his guitar in his hands, let the pent-up energy flow through the tips of his fingers, playing riffs and melodies while the others were still trying to check their sound. The notes crackled and danced in his ears—crisp and layered and full of nuances he hadn't heard before, even when he was just hitting chords so their sound guy could adjust his monitor. It was like the truth of sound uncovered, and he could hear it in the others' playing too.

Watching the others, though, he could see they couldn't hear it. They just got the top layers, the usual stuff, not the new secrets underneath.

Their interviewer stood ten feet in front of the stage, watching with a grin. Turning her head every now and again to look around, like she was looking for someone to share the moment with.

"Was that a new song?" she asked when they jumped down a half hour later.

"One of the unreleased ones we were telling you about," Shawn said.

"Wow, what are you waiting for? Release it already!"

"Where you going?" Shawn said to Dean.

Heading for the door, Dean said, "Out of smokes," without turning his head. And he left. Left the girl, left the possibilities. Blood rushing in his ears—not his blood. He was dizzy, but this wasn't the place or time. The band needed the write-up on the unreleased album more than he needed another body to figure out how to get rid of.

He saw how easy it was, though—how easy it would be to lure someone off and do it. He rolled his shoulders, trying to shrug it off. Trying to stop feeling his teeth. They seemed to be promising him an even more satisfying experience than he'd had with the biker, if he'd just go ahead and use them.

Fresh blood, his teeth said. His throat. His fuzzed-out brain. *Fresh* blood.

The sun hit him like a cinder block to the face when he opened the venue's back door. His teeth slid back where they'd been earlier—either irritated by the light or disappearing now that he was out of range of blood. He closed his eyes. What he needed to do was case the area, figure out how he could get the body off the bus, find someplace to stow it where it wouldn't be found for a day or more. Give them time to put miles between themselves and it.

Slowly he cracked his eyes, using his hand as a visor again. The bus was easy to make out—big hulking dark shape haloed with light. Everything else…was anyone's guess. Some cars maybe, maybe their support act's van with a square blob of a trailer behind it. Telephone poles. Smaller blobs—a phone booth? A mailbox? He took it in a few seconds at a time, squeezing his eyes closed in between to try to clear them.

Every time he closed his eyes, he remembered the rush of that chick's blood. It tugged at his shoulders, wanting to lure him back inside.

He squinched open his eyes again, everything blocky and hard to make out.

He was going to be fucking useless in daylight.

He gauged the distance to the bus, put his head down, and strode toward it with his eyes shut. The temperature dropped a few degrees when he passed into the bus's shade. He put a hand out, finding its side. Walking the length of it, he finally reached the door.

Inside the bus, he put a hand in front of him, shuffling until his fingers bumped the bunkroom door. He slipped inside, pulled it shut, and pushed his sunglasses up with one hand, rubbing the afterimages away with his fingers.

At least at this point he could hide on the bus until show time—just him and dead Vampire McGee.

AFTER THE sun finally slipped past the horizon, he poked his head out. Now he could see well enough to read the plate numbers on their support band's trailer from thirty feet away. He stepped down from the bus, leaving the door open. Sauntered around the front—stretching his legs if anyone asked. His sneakers kicked up dust. The whole area behind the building was nothing but crumbling pavement and bone-dry dirt. Beyond that, a chain-link fence looked over a field of dried grass. High voltage power lines ran across it. He headed back the other way. An aisle of about fifteen feet ran between the venue's back wall and the length of the bus. A little farther up the building sat a welcome sight—he just wasn't sure how he was going to lug a hundred-and-seventy-pound corpse thirty feet without anyone coming out the back door and catching him at it.

First things first—he grasped the lid on the dumpster and hauled it up. No lock. That was a good start.

He peered over its lip.

Not quite half full—a mix of garbage bags and broken-down liquor boxes. He shot an eye toward the door before clambering inside.

Someone had taken garbage out since this morning; the sweet scent of doughnuts fought with the dregs of last night's alcohol.

Holding his breath, he worked his foot between the bags and started shifting them to the other side, piling them in one corner as he could. He didn't want to go all the way to the bottom—when the garbage truck came and dumped the trash into its mouth, the last thing he wanted was a body-sized torpedo crowdsurfing over the other garbage.

He pulled himself back out, sneakers thumping softly to the ground.

Back on the bus, he stopped halfway up the front lounge to peek out the window. No one coming yet. This was going to be risky as hell. But the alternative was, what—taking the dead biker on tour with them? *Get staked—see the country!*

He shoved his curtain back and reached in, dragging the head toward him, hauling the body off the bunk. He walked backward with it. The foot end thumped to the floor. The taped bags swished over the floor as he dragged it up the aisle. He hoped nothing tore. The smell wasn't too bad now—Hefty bag and lightly fermented meat—but he could imagine the stink rolling out if the wrapping opened up.

When he got to the steps, he lowered the package's shoulders to the floor and hopped down.

He glanced toward the venue door.

Coast still clear.

He rolled the biker onto his stomach and backed down the steps with it until he could lean forward and dig his shoulder under the biker's stomach. When he straightened, the biker's toes pulled off the top step, and all the weight was on him.

With an arm wrapped around the body and the other hand gripping the bus door, he backed away. His knees threatened to buckle.

He staggered a half circle, bumping the bus with the biker's heels before lurching, swaybacked, toward the dumpster—feeling like *any second now* that fucking door was going to open.

The weight grew heavier with every step.

The skin behind his ears pulled tight, listening for the slightest sound—though he had no idea what he'd do if he did hear the door swing open.

He staggered the last few paces and banged into the dumpster. With a shove, he managed to get the biker tilting away from him, its hips caught between him and the dumpster.

So close, so close.

Glancing toward the door, he scooped the biker from behind his knees and heaved him in.

Fuck yeah.

With another look toward the back door, he hauled himself over the lip. He stumbled over the bags—more tired now than the first time he'd been in there—and folded onto his knees. One of the bags—not the biker—squished under his hand as he pushed himself back up. He dragged the trash in the corner over the torpedo, half burying his own shins in the process.

Over the rustle of plastic and clink of bottles, he heard a door bang open and froze.

Crouched.

A bottle dug into his kneecap.

He'd left the bus door wide open. *Shit.*

His heart beat hard and steady. Slowly he settled onto his ass, his back against the wall of the dumpster. His heel next to the biker's head.

Voices carried, not loud enough for words, but he could guess what they were saying: nobody's on the bus, and the door is wide open.

Damn it.

He took a deep breath. Pressed his hands against his knees. If he didn't end the mystery, it'd turn into a full-out investigation, followed by a late-night lecture about bus security. He heaved himself up.

Shawn and Wayne stood just outside the bus, Wayne looking back toward the venue door. Shawn was scanning the road.

Dean crawled over the edge of the dumpster and dropped—not quietly—to the ground, stumbling back a few steps.

Wayne looked over. Shawn turned around.

Even in the dark, Dean could see Shawn's eyebrows furrow as he made out what he was seeing.

Dean stepped forward and swung the lid closed.

"Were you *in* the dumpster?" Shawn said.

"Lost my sunglasses. Thought they might have gotten thrown away." As he strolled toward his guys, he untucked his glasses from the collar of his shirt and slipped them on.

"You paid, what, three dollars for those at a gas station?" Wayne said.

"Yeah, but I like 'em."

"You're out of your head," Shawn said.

Dean smiled, close-mouthed, giving them a quick salute before heading for the building.

Let them go ahead and get on the bus. He had nothing to hide, aside from the two wooden sign posts he'd found in the aftermath, and those weren't going to get him in any hot water.

He wondered again who that guy'd been, where he'd come from. Was he some kind of vampire hunter?

Was that something he had to watch out for too now? Vampires, vampire hunters—*people* were the only things he wasn't worried about, now that he'd off-loaded his secret. To tell the truth, he wasn't all that worried about vampires and vampire hunters either. He felt too good to give a shit.

6.

CARL DROVE until his stomach growled. The horizon was orange. He might have time to scarf something down before night fell. He stopped at a Burger King, paper crowns piled along the half wall separating the dining area from the order counter. While he waited for his Whopper and fries, he walked back in his memory to Sophie, a cheap gold crown sliding over her eyes. She was laughing with a handful of ketchup-covered fries on their way to her mouth. She must have been seven or so then, and he'd probably rolled his eyes at whatever she'd been giggling at, the worldly nine-year-old and his silly little sister.

And maybe one day she would have had a seven-year-old of her own, crowned with her own ring of cheap gold cardboard. His heart clenched, thinking about how suddenly things could just…not exist anymore. People, possibilities, futures. All of it gone the minute you turned your head.

A teenager pushed a tray of cheap food across the counter toward him.

He didn't feel so much like eating now.

A family of six—five kids and a mom who was admirably on top of their needs—took up the middle of the dining room. He found a corner to himself, his back to them, and chewed woodenly while staring through the big windows, watching nothing. Thinking nothing. After days and days to himself, the last place he wanted to be anymore was his own head.

After an interminable five minutes, he wrapped the last bite in its wrapper and threw everything into the trash. He'd seen a pay phone outside on his way in, and after stopping by his car, he dropped change in and listened to the other end of the line ring.

It was five thirty where he was, four thirty in Los Campos. He still hadn't looked up what day it was. Tim would get home eventually. He hung up the receiver and collected his quarters from the coin return.

The gas station had cigarette advertisements plastered over its windows. While he waited for the Cougar's tank to fill, he stared back at the Burger King instead, the old habit crawling through him like an itch. Wanting that hit of nicotine. He fed it a candy bar instead, grabbed a bag of chips for later, a couple bottles of soda so he wouldn't have to stop after it got dark.

There was a problem, though, if he wanted to drive through the dark. The Cougar only held nineteen gallons. Even creeping along at forty-five, he'd run out of gas in the middle of Oklahoma, five hours shy of sunrise.

He tapped his fingers on the steering wheel as lodging, travel, and gas signs grew large and then fell away on the interstate, one after another.

When the sun kissed the horizon, he stopped angsting and followed one of the signs for lodging.

"Better safe," he said to no one.

The town he pulled into was as good as dead. But there was a motel. There was always a motel.

The late afternoon desk clerk had a blue cravat tucked into her button-up shirt. The desk phone rang as he got to the counter, and she said, "Single or double?" to him as she lifted the phone off the cradle. He told her a single, and she nodded as she told whoever was on the line that Joey could watch TV if his room was clean. She moved the receiver under her chin to tell Carl how much the room cost, put his key into his hand while talking to the babysitter or the older sister or whoever about just *what* Joey could watch—yes to *The Six Million Dollar Man*, no to *McCloud*, and definitely no to staying up for the Sunday night movie. Bedtime was nine, firm.

His room was halfway down the building. He dropped his bag on the bed and picked up the phone. Listened to the other end of the line ring—nine, ten, twelve. Gave up at sixteen—Tim was probably working—and turned on the TV. *Sixty Minutes* was just starting. His dad had watched that when Carl was a kid. He'd have been happy to see Harry Reasoner was back on.

Thoughts of his dad made him change the channel, settling on *The Hardy Boys Mysteries*.

He tried Tim three more times, including once around the time Tim usually got home from the bowling alley. After he set the receiver down, he got under the covers and listened to the motel noises—passing conversations, a radio in another room, someone's snores.

He tried to talk to Soph, but she felt gone, so he thought about his future instead, his head full of dreams.

After trying Tim at three a.m.—no answer still—he had a nightmare that he was letting himself into their apartment in the dark of night, the phone ringing and ringing in the kitchen. The light switch wouldn't work, and in the middle of their living room floor, he found a girl with her throat torn out, her eyes glassy and staring, one arm stretched out, pointing toward the other room.

OCTOBER 16, 1978

1.

LYING ON the bare mattress in his bunk, Dean knew the sun had come up. Maybe it was its warmth seeping through the bus's metal skin, maybe it was just the amount of time passing as he lay staring at the underside of the berth above him. Or maybe it was another new sense.

Whichever, he knew it was out there.

No one else was up, but after another couple hours the first restless rustlings of mattresses came. Feet padded quietly up the aisle. Dean turned his back to the curtain and covered his eyes as the bunkroom door slid open.

After another hour or so, no one was bothering to close the door behind them.

The bus's brakes hissed. Gravity pulled Dean's body. The engine went silent.

The whole thing swayed as passengers off-loaded.

He waited until he was alone with the driver before dropping on his back again. The others had left both the front and back lounge doors open. He felt along the edge of the mattress for his sunglasses. Found the biker's knife first. Held its grip in his hand while he put the sunglasses on.

By the time he was ready to put his feet on the floor, the bus was filling back up, chatter coming up the aisle. The venue must have a shower, everyone coming to get their bags so they could clean up.

He got to his feet, turned, and took one step toward the front lounge, carefully opening his eyes behind the glasses so he could see what was coming at him.

Brilliant white pain, so sharp it took his breath.

His knees gave. He wrapped his arms over his face, smashing the sunglasses against the bridge of his nose. His shoulder hit the bunk. He landed on one knee on the floor, hunched forward, squeezing his arms against his eyes.

His teeth clenched at the pain that throbbed at the front of his skull.

"Hey!" Shawn clasped his arm. "Hey, are you all right?" He dropped to Dean's level.

The sun was so hot in his eyeballs—even now that he'd blocked it—he couldn't even tear up. It felt like any moisture had been burned right off. He dug his fingers into his hair, crouching into himself even tighter.

"Dean. Talk to me." Shawn's voice bordered on panic. "What's going on?"

"Headache," he managed in a whisper between gritted teeth. "Migraine."

Shawn put a hand at the back of his head.

Dean's teeth were coming out, Shawn too fucking close.

Shawn was saying, "Okay. Okay," and when he spoke next, his voice was directed backward. "What do we have for painkillers?"

"Shut. The. Door." Dean's throat was as dried up as his eyes.

Shawn's jeans brushed his elbow as he rose and turned. The door slid shut. Dean crouched back, relieved at the distance between himself and Shawn. The *door* between himself and the rest of them. Shawn would open it again as soon as he found painkillers.

He couldn't stay on the floor.

He grabbed a fistful of curtain, nearly tearing it down as he hauled himself into the bunk, one arm still wrapped against his eyes. He untangled his legs from the curtain and dragged it shut, pushing its edges tight against the walls.

The backs of his eyeballs ached. He peeked around his bunk area. It was mostly black, floats sliding in front of his vision.

With a curse, he pressed his head against his arms as the door juddered open. His muscles braced, but it quickly shut again. The curtain flapped against his arm.

Then Shawn was there, crouched by the bunk. "Here." Knuckles touched his hand.

Grimacing, he rolled onto his side, away from Shawn. Away from the touch, which sent a jittery chill through his nerves.

He had his eyesight back, some of it—enough to make out the shadowy outlines of concern on Shawn's face.

Shawn held his palm flat. Dean couldn't see the pills well. His fingertips ghosted Shawn's warm palm as he felt for them, and the touch brought a tingle through his jaw. His body wanted to lurch forward. He broke contact, the pills pinched between his fingers.

He wondered what they were going to do to him, if he'd even be able to keep them down.

Shawn held out a cup of water, smelling both sweet and flat. Dean shook his head, pushing the pills into his mouth.

Dropping onto his back, he dry-swallowed them.

"I've never known you to get migraines," Shawn said.

"Haven't since I was a kid," he lied.

"Should we call a doctor?"

Details picked themselves out in the bunk. Dean held his hand over his face, could make out the grooves in his palm. He closed it. "I'll be all right." Come nightfall. "I just need a few hours. Can Teddy cover me for sound check?"

"He won't mind."

Dean rubbed his forehead.

"Are you sure a few hours are enough?" Shawn said. "We can pull out of the show. Better if we do it now than when people are lined up at the door."

"I'll be okay. It doesn't last long. By dinnertime I'll be good."

Shawn's heart beat, faster than usual. Closer to Nick's pace.

In the shadows of his bunk, Dean said, "Really. I'll be okay."

"All right," Shawn said finally, his brow still creased with concern. "We need to grab our stuff."

"Yeah."

"Maybe a shower'd do you good?"

"Maybe later." He massaged his eyes.

Shawn pulled the curtain shut, but not well enough. Dean pressed it snug against the wall, ducking his face into the crook of his arm, just as the door juddered open again.

Jesus, this was going to be a problem.

But what else could he do? Tell them to send him home, he couldn't do this anymore? Aside from the days of discussions and fights that would ensue—what would he do once he got back home? The band was all he'd ever done or wanted to do. The only thing he *knew* how to do?

And what would the band do, without their lead guitarist? He'd be leaving his best friends in the lurch.

2.

CARL HUNG up the phone. The echo of the ring tickled his eardrums as he zipped his bag and hauled the strap onto his shoulder. He checked the room—daylight spilling through curtains, rumpled bed, soggy towel. He got in his car, paid fifty-nine cents a gallon to fill the tank. Made a pit stop in the bathroom, then bought a fried egg sandwich from the counter inside. He ate it in the car, yolk oozing from its sides. He licked it off his fingers as he drove.

He was in northeast Oklahoma. Flat. Monotonous. He drove underneath a McDonald's built across a highway overpass. Well, that was something.

No more calling Tim. He'd be home around nightfall, speed and traffic willing. He'd just walk in the door—surprise!

It irritated him that Tim hadn't been home, hadn't been just a phone call away. He needed to *talk* to someone, just to get the fuck out of his own head. And Tim was all he had.

Approaching Oklahoma City, he got snagged in backed-up cars, his knee jiggling at the wait. Eventually he was past the accident that had held them up, two twisted Chevies, one a sedan, the other a station wagon. Ambulance lights flashed weakly against the hot sun in a pale sky.

He fought fatigue after Amarillo, every inch of highway looking like he'd already driven it ten times. He crossed into New Mexico at two thirty with his sun visor down, squinting in the brightness as he nursed another cup of caffeine. The car smelled like sweet creamy coffee. His mouth was thick with it.

He hit Roswell at rush hour, glancing at the dash clock nervously as traffic slowed to forty, but the slowdown only lasted a quarter mile. As soon as the city limits were behind him, he pressed the pedal down, hitting eighty-five, ninety, nothing but scrub as far as the eye could see, blurring on either side as he raced the shadows that collected behind him.

By Alamogordo, the shadows were catching up. In his rearview, streams of headlights trailed behind him, car windshields tinted orange and opaque. He turned on his headlights. When he checked the clock, he tightened his grip on the wheel.

He wasn't going to make sundown.

The guttural roar of exhaust pipes rose behind him. He looked in the mirror. Three bikes had appeared over the horizon, their headlights forming a triangle. He swallowed, checking the road ahead. *Thinking.* He was close enough to home to be somewhat familiar with the area, but the news wasn't good—no exit for another five miles or so. Nothing but highway, scrub, and, way off in the distance, brown hills.

The engines gunned.

His back tensed. He didn't even have the gun anymore, lost on the fucking bus. Would a gun even work, anyway?

Not that it mattered—he didn't fucking have it. Or the stakes. Not that they'd be much help either.

The bike lights swerved, shifting the shadows inside the car. The hair on his nape stiffened as the bikes pulled alongside. He wouldn't look.

He'd be just some guy on the highway, New Mexico plates, on his way home from work maybe.

He eased off the gas. The Cougar started to drop back.

The bikes roared again, shaking Carl's seat.

They surged ahead, and kept on going down the road.

The Cougar slowed—fifty, forty. Their taillights grew smaller. Cars pulled around him. A guy in a Cadillac laid on the horn. Carl let the Cougar ease to the shoulder, staring ahead, his heart pounding. His mouth dry.

He came to a stop, muscles like loose rubber bands.

When the road was clear—no one behind him, no one in front of him—he let out his breath.

Sweat slicked his brow. He swiped it with the edge of a shaking hand. He was losing his mind, seeing vampire bikers everywhere. A breath of a laugh eased out, brittle, wanting to be something close to relief but not quite making it.

He pulled back onto the road, keeping it to the speed limit, maybe a little under. Eyes darting toward the shadows at the edges of the road.

He rolled into Los Campos with a wave of relief. The familiarity of his own neighborhood washed against him like a tide. He'd been gone, what, six days? It felt like a year. He'd imagined things would be different back here, after everything he'd gone through, but not a thing had changed. The buildings—homes, apartments, stores—were beige like the landscape, like they'd grown right up out of the ground. He passed the car wash, its sign lit against the evening, and the vacant lot littered with shadows and trash. A blue bucket, cracked and tipped sideways in the dirt—it had been there for months now. He pulled up at the apartment building, two stories of beige fronted by wrought-iron railings. He nosed the car up to a curb. Shut off the engine.

The place was quiet, not a bike in sight—that was something. Not that it didn't mean they weren't hiding around the corner.

You're being paranoid.

He was. Why wouldn't he be, after what he'd seen? He let himself out of the car, ears pricking at the neighborhood sounds—a kid's shout from down the street, the tap of a horn. He grabbed his bag, climbed the dark stairwell. His footfalls echoed along the catwalk. The windows he passed were blank, their curtains pulled tight. He unlocked his door and let himself in. Clicked on the light. He didn't need to call out for Tim; the place just *felt* empty. He tossed his keys on the end table and headed for the bathroom, where he pissed, stripped, then scrubbed himself under a miserable trickle of water from the shower head.

By the time he was dried off, he felt both refreshed and heavy with the toll of a week spent in a car. He stepped over his trail of clothes and dropped on his bed face first, falling asleep with his arms spread, the warm apartment air skimming his bare legs. The ghost of the old Carl's scent, embedded in the sheets, mingled in his nostrils—the Carl who was over and done with now. New Carl was home, ready to move on with life. If he could find his fucking roommate.

3.

DEAN SLIPPED off his sunglasses at the bottom of the bus steps, the dark of evening upon them. Fans waiting outside the bus pushed albums toward him, scraps of paper for him to sign. They wanted photos taken with him. He dashed his name out a few times before apologizing for having to get inside.

Anything to avoid coming into contact with them.

The delicate pulses in the girls' throats whispered dirty things to him.

He was full of teeth.

He was nothing *but* teeth.

The door closed behind him, and he walked the cool, fluo-
rescent hallways to find his bandmates, show them he was okay,
that he'd be fine for the show. He'd need to figure out his food
situation at some point, but for tonight, his mission was to be
fine—because there was no other choice if he wanted to keep
doing this.

It wasn't just for himself. Shawn, Jessie, Nick—this band was
their life too. It was everything they'd worked for. The guys on
their crew; they needed to put food on the table. Teddy, Janx,
and Mike had families. The bus driver probably had a family.
The band was bigger than him.

It was also everything for him. Without it, he was no one.

One way or another, he was going to make it work.

The blood of the others pounded him as soon as he opened
the door at the end of the hall. He put a close-lipped smile on
his face and forced his fangs back up into his gums.

OCTOBER 17, 1978

1.

SUN peeked through the blinds when Carl pulled his eyes open.

The noise that had woken him came again, a banging at the door.

He pushed up, rubbing his tongue on the roof of his mouth, trying to get rid of the worst of the taste of sleep. He itched for a cigarette before remembering he'd quit. The banging came again. Tim wasn't answering it. Had Tim even been home? He fished a pair of shorts off the floor and buttoned them as he headed through the apartment. The banging stopped, but he had the sense that whoever was there was just waiting for him to get to the door.

He scrubbed a hand through his hair. Probably had sheet creases on his face. He'd have liked a cup of coffee before dealing with this—"this" being the landlord probably, looking for overdue rent.

He flipped the lock and was already saying, "Yeah, listen, I've gotta get to the—" as he swung open the door.

Two men in suits stood on the catwalk.

One held up a badge in a black wallet. "Carlos Delacroix?"

"Yeah, what—?"

"Detective Bays." Bays didn't bother with a comb-over, just let the bald top of his head shine the way God had intended. His wide blue tie rode the wave of his belly as he turned, lifting his hand. "This is my partner Detective Lewis. May we come in?"

"Um." He gripped the doorjamb. "What's this about?" How had they found him? Had he left something at the scene? Had he left some clue at one of the motels?

"We just need to ask a few questions. Do you mind?" Bays held out an arm.

Carl moved aside.

"Sorry to disturb you first thing." Bays came to a stop in the middle of the living room.

Lewis, a good ten years younger and four inches taller, fit his suit better than Bays did. He wandered the edge of the room, sweeping it with his gaze—Soph's photos on the walls, a loose stack of mail on a rickety bookshelf.

"Um. So, what can I help you with?" As Carl closed the door, the room darkened. He walked to the window and opened the blind.

"Can you tell us where you were the night of October eleventh?" Bays said.

The question shot through his groin. The dates were confused in his head; he needed time to work out just where he *had* been. He wasn't even sure what date *today* was.

Lewis lifted a ceramic piggy bank from the bookshelf and turned it over. Coins clunked against its insides. Soph's coins.

"Um. October eleventh?" He hadn't even seen the biker yet, had he? *Think. Think.* No—he hadn't. He'd left here that morning. "I was on a trip. I just got back last night. Why? What's going on?"

Lewis set the pig down, stopped in front of another Soph photo, the eight by ten that matched the smaller one Carl had hung in his car.

"Who's the girl?"

"My sister."

Bays said, "What kind of trip?"

Carl tried to keep his attention on Bays, but it kept getting pulled over to Lewis. "I was…I went out east to kind of follow around a band for a little bit. Man Made Murder, have you heard of them?"

"My nephew listens to that," Lewis said.

Bays said, "Were you with anyone?"

Carl pushed his hand into his back pocket, pulled it back out. No idea what to do with his fucking hand. This was so not good. Maybe he had his dates wrong. This was so not good. "No," he said. "No, I went alone. My roommate had to work."

"Got some ticket stubs? Something to show where you were?"

"Um, I didn't keep them, no."

"Do you have anything that can put you out of town?"

"Umm…" The whole time he'd been gone, he'd maybe talked to, what, a handful of people? He'd bought coffee, he'd bought breakfast. There was that guy in the bar, but he couldn't say anything about him. If Bays and Lewis were here about the biker, that put him right there in their territory. If they weren't but they talked to that guy to verify his story, it told the *bikers* where he was. He'd almost rather Bays put him in jail than have the bikers know where he was, in case they put two and two together.

"Where'd you stay?" Bays asked.

"A couple motels on the way back. I slept in the car on the way there."

Bays had a little black notebook in hand. He flipped the cover and a few pages. "Which ones?"

His mind was blank. He hadn't paid any attention. Zero fucking attention at all. His throat locked as he looked around the living room, gears spinning out.

"When'd you leave on this trip?" Bay said.

"The eleventh, about six in the morning? What's going on?"

"You were gone a week, you've got nothing to show for it?"

"I might have a couple receipts in the car." He hoped. "Let me get my shoes."

In the bedroom, sitting on the edge of his unmade bed, he pulled tennis shoes on, no socks, his hands shaking. He dragged a shirt over his head. Stuffed his wallet in his back pocket, just in case. Who the fuck knew where they were going with this.

"Can you tell me what this is about?" he asked as he grabbed his keys from the end table.

"Just part of an investigation. How long have you known Timothy Randolph?"

Lewis was pulling the door shut behind them, and Carl stopped, right in the middle of the catwalk. Turned around. "Tim?"

"Let's go see the receipts," Bays said.

Bays stood close while Carl unlocked the passenger side. Lewis wandered around the car, peering in the windows. Carl crouched in the open door to fish through the heap of fast food containers and empty cups on the floor, his heart beating like a bird trying to get out a window. The gun—thank God he'd lost the fucking gun. It was registered to his dad. He had no idea how legal that was, carrying around a dead person's gun.

Crumpled cigarette packs on the floor made him yearn for a smoke. His fingers trembled as he shifted dirty napkins aside. Morning shadows clung under the dashboard, trying to hold against the rising sun.

"Here." He spun on a heel, thrusting two slips of paper out. One was from the hardware store, for the goddamned stakes. Heat swept his face as he realized, but it was too late now. He could say he'd made signs for the show.

Bays studied them. "Twinsburg, Ohio."

He'd bought a carton of cigarettes at a grocery store on his way east. October twelfth. It put him a good seventeen hundred miles away from whatever had happened here that day. It put him a good bit of miles from New Hampshire too. Even from the body, if anyone had found that yet.

I didn't kill anyone. That was his story—that was the *truth*, and he was going to stick to it.

Bays tucked the receipts in his notebook.

"Can you tell me what's going on?"

"You don't read the news?" Lewis asked from the other side of the car.

"I haven't been home. What's this got to do with Tim?"

"Why don't we take a ride to the station," Bays said. "You can answer our questions, we'll see if we can answer some of yours." He tucked the notebook into his shirt pocket.

"Can I follow you?" Carl asked.

"Why don't you ride with us?"

"Am I under arrest? Am I a suspect?"

"Nope, and not at the moment. Car's right over there. We'll get this cleared up, you'll be back home in no time. Probably have a lot of unpacking to do, right?"

He got in the back seat, the metal belt buckle already so warm its heat bled through his shorts. He fidgeted as the detectives got in up front, Lewis behind the wheel.

Whatever this was, it didn't seem to be about the biker.

What'd Tim have to do with anything? Where the fuck *was* he?

And what if all this eventually led to the biker?

He crossed his arms, hugging himself. *Fuck 'em. Just fuck them.* He'd done the job they hadn't managed to do. He'd made sure that asshole was taken out. Whatever *this* was about, this was nothing. He'd done the job *they* couldn't fucking manage to do.

And he hadn't killed anyone.

He hadn't *done* anything except sit back and watch the other guy take care of it.

He pressed his palms to the warm seat and sat up straighter, looking from the back of one head to the other. Whatever this was about, it wasn't anything he couldn't get out of.

They rounded a corner, and there was the station. He pulled back. His last memory of the place was of yelling at a detective— not Bays. Wanting to know why the fuck they couldn't do anything. Why the fuck couldn't they find the asshole? He'd given them the description. The sketch artist had gotten the biker almost spot on. He'd had a fucking patch on his jacket, that had to mean something, trace back to some kind of motorcycle gang.

Why weren't they getting more press coverage for the sketch, the patch? Why wasn't it everywhere?

Why weren't they following up on leads, he'd wanted to know.

The detective had withstood it quietly, holding a hand up when another officer stepped into the doorway to see if he needed help. The detective had said, "We're not closing her case. We'll keep working on it. We just can't afford to keep every man on it." Then: "Can I get someone to drive you home?"

After that, Carl had just gotten phone calls, every other week, keeping him up to date. They'd dropped to once a month, then once a quarter. Last time he'd heard from the Los Campos police had been nine months ago, letting him know Soph was moved to the cold case pile, though not in so many words. But no leads, nothing to go on—what could they do?

He'd given them the fucking lead.

He leaned forward. "Did you guys find anything on my sister yet?"

"Who's your sister?" Bays said without looking back.

"Sophia Delacroix. She was killed two years ago."

That got him to turn around, take a second look at him. Carl couldn't read what was going on in his eyes.

"Fuck it," Carl said, pushing off the back of the seats, dropping back in his own. Looking out the passenger window.

"That was the girl in the dumpster, wasn't it?" Lewis said.

Carl's throat went tight with frustration.

They took him to an interview room. It was his first time in one, and it was just like the movies—table, couple of metal chairs, big two-way mirror in the wall. Bays asked him if he wanted coffee, maybe water—sent Lewis off to get that water. "Pull the files too."

He dragged out the chair on the other side of the table as the door closed behind Lewis. "Tell me about your sister."

"Why? You guys know everything I know about my sister. It's in the file."

"Yeah, but save me the time. I read slow." He sat back, his tie still surfing his belly.

Carl sped through it: the dance, the biker he'd seen, then she was gone. And they found her in a dumpster. The girl in the dumpster, that's who his sister was. That's how everyone would remember her forever, the pretty little girl in the flared-sleeve dress—in the fucking dumpster.

Lewis dropped off the water, two thick files. He stood back, hands on his hips.

"Tell me about Tim Randolph," Bays said. "How long have you been sharing a place?"

Carl looked from Lewis to Bays. "I don't know. A year, fourteen months."

"How long have you known him?"

"We went to the same school. It's a small town."

"Grew up around each other, decided to move in together?"

"We're friends, why not? Do you know where he is? He wasn't answering when I called from the road."

"So you knew him before your sister was killed. Did he know your sister?"

Carl gave him grudging credit for putting it that way, being straight about it. He hated when people fluffed around it with *died* or *passed*. Or *When it happened*. His aunt and uncle used *When we lost Sophia*. She wasn't fucking *lost*. She hadn't fucking *passed away*. Someone had slit her fucking throat. His eyes flooded with heat. He tried to push it back, tried to blink them dry.

"I didn't hang around with him before Soph was murdered," he said around a thick ache in his throat. "I don't think they knew each other, outside of everyone knowing who everyone else is."

Fuck—why did they keep asking about Tim?

"Any idea where Randolph might have been the night your sister was killed?"

The jolt dropped his jaw. He stared at Bays. His throat worked. Finally he pushed it out: "*What?*"

2.

BACKSTAGE, THE club was full of smells. Dean's fingertips vibrated against a pint bottle of gin. Thank God for runners willing to run out to the liquor store.

He couldn't put together two words of what anyone was saying. His head kept turning, following the beat of life around him. He tipped the gin to his mouth, thinking it probably wasn't the best idea, but he needed to roll the edges back. Needed to dampen the restlessness.

At least he hadn't had to worry about explaining his lack of sheets. His second "migraine" in as many days had put his bunk off limits when the driver had come around stripping bedding from mattresses. At one point, the guy had started talking to himself, saying, "What the?" Dean had clamped the pillow over his head. He didn't want to know shit about what the guy had found in his cleaning up.

Shawn whistled, drawing Dean's head his way. "Did you hear a word I said?"

"Sorry."

"He's turning the gun into the cops if nobody fesses up to it."

"What gun?"

"The one the driver found in his bunk. Is something up with you?"

"My stomach's a little messed up."

"A lot of you's a little messed up."

Dean dragged the corner of his mouth up.

"The liquor's probably not helping," Shawn said.

"Sure ain't hurting. What the fuck is this about a gun?"

Shawn sighed. "Phil found a gun when he was cleaning the bus today. It was in his bunk, the one he hasn't bothered to use all tour?" They were required to have bunk for the driver, but usually he headed off to a motel when they reached a venue and returned after a decent day's sleep around the time they were getting ready to leave. At their expense, but given it involved the safety of the band, it was a bill they were willing to foot.

"Nobody knows where it came from," Shawn said. "Do you know anything about it?"

"I don't know anything about a fucking gun." Had the biker brought it on? That kid who'd come on board with the stakes? He'd found the rest of the stakes when he was cleaning up, but he hadn't bothered to check inside the bunks.

Shit.

Though—maybe it had nothing to do with any of that at all. At any rate, it had nothing to do with *him*. For a fucking change.

3.

CARL WAS numb—the kind of numb you got when a Mack truck slammed into you: too much shit for your body to deal with.

Bays walked ahead of him, talking, telling him what was going to happen next.

None of the words got through.

He gawked at the rest of the station—typing and voices and phones ringing.

So much going on. It threatened to swallow him up.

People sat on wooden chairs, waiting their turn, one of them definitely a hooker. A desk cop spoke through vents in bullet-proof glass. Someone laughed, loud and cutting. Carl's scalp tightened, his teeth pressing together. All the activity made him dizzy. He needed another glass of water. He bumped a woman with a large purse who'd just gotten up from a chair at a desk, her attention still on the cop she was griping at. She turned it on Carl—"Well excuse you too!"—and Carl stumbled away, sucking in air.

"Carl!"

Tim's voice came from far away, barely reaching through.

He wanted to cry. He felt hollow inside, like a tin soldier. Anyone could step on him and crush him.

"Carl!"

Bays turned, his mouth pressing tight.

Carl started to look back.

Bay's gripped his shoulder, but Carl saw: Tim's face, on the far end of the room—stricken and hopeful at once. Like hey, Carl had come to get him out! His hands were cuffed behind him, his hair rucked up. What were probably yesterday's clothes hung from him. Or the day before yesterday's. How long had he not answered the phone?

"Just keep going," Bays said.

Of course they weren't going to let him talk to Tim. Weren't going to sit him in a room with him.

I spent two fucking years chasing the wrong guy.

And all fucking day in a police station, going over and over what little he knew. Hearing the fucking details of what he hadn't known.

Tim pulled against the hold a cop had on his arm, saying "Carl!" again.

Rage exploded over numbness.

Bays jerked him to a stop before he could get going, fingers digging into his shoulder.

All this fucking time. All this fucking goddamned fucking time. Acting like his best fucking friend and knowing, all along. All along.

All along.

Bays tugged on him.

His body pulled against it, wanting to charge in the direction they'd taken Tim, down that hall, maybe down to the end of it where he could fucking corner him and yell in his face: *TELL ME THE FUCKING TRUTH!*

His nostrils flared. The whole room narrowed to the corridor Tim had gone down.

Did you fucking do this?

Bays yanked him off his feet, holding him against his chest. A folder of papers pressed against his shirt, his statement among them, for what that was worth—what little information he'd been able to give about Tim and the night Soph disappeared, and the days afterward. He'd been able to provide even less information about Tim and the more recent killing.

If his fucking best friend had killed anyone, he knew all of fucking *nothing* about it.

His face screwed up tight, his throat aching. He couldn't see for the blur, tears welling, hot at the tops of his cheeks.

"We've got him, okay?" Bays' voice was gruff in his ear. "We've got him."

Did you? Did you get him?

What if the information he'd given had just screwed the only friend he had? Just because Tim had dropped off Jonesy for the game that night, just because he'd seen Soph standing on top of the steps.

A lot of people had seen Soph standing on those steps that night.

Did you fucking do it? Did you really fucking do it?

BAYS PULLED up in front of the apartment building in the same shit-beige unmarked car.

"Do you have somewhere to go tonight? I only ask because..."

Because why would Carl want to sit surrounded by the walls he'd lived in with the guy who might have killed not only his sister but some other seventeen-year-old-girl—slashed her throat, left her in a hole at a construction site. On October eleventh. The day he'd fucking left town.

Tim had gotten pulled over on his way home that night, speeding because he always went a good ten over, and the cop had noticed what looked like a blotch of blood on the collar of the tee shirt underneath his button-up shirt. He hadn't thought too hard on it at the time—guy could have cut himself shaving, right? Hadn't thought about it until Tim was pulled in for questioning two days later—not long after the last time Carl had talked to him. Pulled in based on one of the victim's friends saying the girl had complained about "that bowling alley guy" following her.

Routine questioning, probably nothing—Timothy Randolph
had no record aside from a couple speeding tickets. But while he
was in there the cop who'd pulled him over looked back at his
own records, checked the names and dates, pulled a detective
out of the interview room for a few minutes.

That night, they had a warrant and a collection of Polaroids
of the murdered girl from under Tim's mattress, photos taken
from a distance, from someone who was watching her. The next
day, they found the shirt in the apartments' garbage, in a bag
with a Columbia Record Club offer addressed to Tim.

While they had Carl in the interview room, the blood had
come back from the lab, a match for the victim.

*Did your sister ever mention him? Did they have any school
activities together? Did she have an after-school job she might have
met him through? Did you see him that night at the school? Did he
say what he was going to be doing while you were away?*

"I'll be okay," Carl said, pulling the door handle. He stepped
into the evening. Cars passed, tires swishing over asphalt. The
low noise of someone's too-loud television set seeped through
the walls of the building. Kids laughed, chasing each other in
the vacant lot.

The world felt almost *too* normal. He was locked out of it,
trapped on the wrong side of some fucked-up parallel world. He
could yell and bang on its surface, and no one would hear him.

He didn't even have *Tim* to hear him anymore.

"If you need anything," Bays said, leaning across the seat,
"or think of anything that might help the case, you've got my
number."

Yeah, the card was growing soft in his palm. He nodded
without looking back. The car door clunked shut. Bays pulled
away, leaving him there. Leaving him looking at the apartment
building he'd come home to for the past year plus. All of it
reeling out: him and Tim lugging cardboard boxes up the steps,
all the possibilities, all the freedom. Adults now. On their own.
Pizza for dinner that night, sitting on the carpet in the living

room, chattering away. Much better than a dorm, right? *Way* better than a dorm.

Going up the stairs was like dragging bags of sand, his muscles leaden. He clutched the railing, hauling himself up. At the top, a woman collided into him, laughing at something a man in a doorway had said. Carl's grip on the railing tightened. She apologized, still laughing, heading down the stairs, her steps clicking lightly.

The man in the door watched Carl with half-lidded eyes, a beer can in his hand. He stepped back and shut the door. Carl dragged himself past it, past two more, to the front of his own.

When he let himself in, the emptiness hit him in the middle of his chest. It was an off-kilter feeling, like his roommate would be home later, after work or after studying at the library, and this Tim guy the cops had, that was some other guy altogether.

Tim's baseball cap from the bowling alley hung on a hook by the door. A pair of his beat-up sneakers sat tumbled against the base of the bookshelf. An *X-Men* comic lay on a couch cushion beside an empty bag of chips, crumbs dotting the cushion.

He stood in the doorway to Tim's room, Tim all over it: his jeans, his skateboard, his *Texas Chainsaw Massacre* poster tacked to the wall. He pulled the door shut and leaned his forehead against it, wondering if it had been like *that* in Tim's head, if it had been like that movie. All those movies he loved so much.

He suddenly felt sick over the one he'd gone to, thinking of how while his own guts twisted over what was happening to the girl on screen, Tim might have been cheering the killer on. Relating to him. Going to those movies to commune with what was inside him.

Or not. It all depended on whether they were right about Tim.

He searched every closet and dresser, turning the drawers upside down to check their undersides, shoving Tim's mattress off the box spring to check that too. The cops had already been through—but what had they missed?

In the kitchen, he checked the freezer, all the way to the back. He rifled through the cabinets, flung open drawers. His fingers traced the knives in there. Secondhand, cheap-ass knives with wooden handles dulled from years of washing. He couldn't imagine Tim using one of these to cut someone's throat.

But he was unsettled by how easily he could imagine Tim slicing open someone's throat with a decent knife—the smile that might slip onto his face as he watched her bleed out. He was thinking of the other girl, not Soph.

No way could he think about that and *Soph.*

He checked the basin at the back of the toilet, underneath both the bathroom and kitchen sinks. He pulled the grille off the air conditioner and the fabric off the front of their hi-fi speakers.

There was plenty of evidence of his sister in the apartment, but that had all come in with him.

He sat on the couch with a glass of ice and soda, staring at a point in the middle of the carpet. All the pictures of Soph, some of her clothes, a teddy bear she'd had as a baby—all that stuff had come in with him. Tim had encouraged him to put the pictures up: *Don't put her in a box. She was your sister.* Soph smiled—squarely—from atop the TV set right now. Was dressed in a tutu for a dance recital on a bookshelf. Had her eighth-grade graduation cap and gown on at the wall by the front door. On the dresser in Carl's bedroom sat Soph the summer before she was murdered—early summer, before the tractor trailer overturned onto their parents' Cutlass. She was wearing white shorts and a blousy yellow shirt. She held an ice cream cone toward the camera, like she was offering it to their dad. Carl didn't have to get up and go look at it to know what flavor ice cream it was. He knew every fucking detail.

She'll be right there every morning when you wake up.

Was that what Tim got off on? Soph's face looking out at her killer every fucking day? Watching him watch TV? Watching him study—watching him go on with his life in a way that *she would never have the fucking chance to do?*

His fists clenched. *Somebody* had taken Soph away. He was one hundred percent with the cops on that.

What if they were wrong about Tim, though? Tim had been there for him. He'd been best friends with him for two fucking years, putting up with all his crazy biker/private investigator shit. His obsession.

Lots of people had the same blood type. There could be another explanation for his shirt. Yeah, they'd ruled out Tim's own blood, but there could be *another* explanation.

The fact that Tim was living with the brother of a girl who'd been killed in the same way—throat slashed, no sexual activity— that could be really fucking bad luck for Tim—really fucking shitty luck that made him look even more likely to the cops as their guy.

But either way—either way, if the guy who'd murdered Pauline Garcia, whoever the fuck he was, had also murdered Soph, then *Carl* had gone after the wrong guy. He'd wasted two years going after the wrong guy. And right now he thought he should be on top of that, on his feet and figuring out how to get the *right* guy. But he was wiped. Not tired; he'd gotten enough sleep, between the motels and his own bed last night. He was just emotionally, psychologically wiped.

He'd *done* his job.

He'd made sure someone had paid for his sister's death.

His spirit felt like it had paid its due, and he had nothing left in him to do all of it all over again.

He had nothing left, period. No mission in life, no family— no best friend and roommate, not unless this got straightened out. Just this shitty apartment, an academic suspension, and a dusty Cougar that probably needed an oil change and a tune-up.

He set his empty glass on the end table.

He *did* have one goal. One thing he had to do.

He had to convince himself that Tim hadn't done it. So he could sleep at night. So he could convince the cops. So he could get Tim out and get on with the big plans he'd dreamt up on his drive home: get a job, get back to school, move forward with life.

He added another one to the list: move. Leave this shithole behind. Maybe he could prove Tim didn't do it, and they could move to another town altogether. Someplace less beige. Tim could transfer his credits. They'd start fresh, where no one knew Tim as the guy the cops had pulled in for Pauline Garcia's murder, and no one knew Carl as the guy whose sister had been found in a dumpster.

Armed with a knife from the kitchen, he went to Tim's bedroom and flipped the mattress over. He'd looked into everything he could open or turn upside down, and he hadn't found anything that said to him that Tim was anything other than who he thought he'd been all along. If he could walk out of this place in the morning satisfied that nothing showed to him that his roommate had done anything worse than speed on the wrong street at the wrong time, he'd be ready to fight for him, the same way he'd fought for Soph these past two years.

He slashed the mattress open to its stuffing.

Shoving it aside, he flipped the box spring. Sliced right through the flimsy fabric tacked to the underside. Nothing but wooden slats and metal coils.

See? he thought. *See?* A handful of Polaroids of some girl at a bowling alley didn't prove anything. It *didn't.*

Gripping the knife, he headed back to the living room. The cushions on the couch and chair unzipped. Square foam inside. He tipped the chair over. A piece of the upholstery fabric hung loose from the bottom of its seat. He ripped it off completely, exposing the wooden frame underneath. *Nothing. Absolutely fucking nothing.*

Heart thudding, he dragged the couch away from the wall and turned it over. Tim's parents had donated it to their cause when they'd moved in. It had come from their basement, from the corner down there where Tim had hung out during high school, reading comics, listening to music, trying to draw some comics of his own, pages he'd burned on the charcoal grill behind the apartments, saying they were stupid. Carl hadn't even gotten a chance to look at most of them. He wished he had now. Maybe they were stupid superhero stuff. More likely they were slasher comics, like the movies he watched—but what would that prove, unless the victims were young girls, right?

Some of the staples holding the fabric to the frame were of the black upholstery type, some were thin steel, like you'd use for paper. Carl sliced the thin cloth down the middle and began yanking it free.

More wooden frame, and then more, and then, at the far corner, where all the staples were thin and steel colored—a battered and creased envelope slid into his hand.

OCTOBER 18, 1978

1.

THE BUS pulled into a hotel parking lot at five in the morning.

Nick stumbled as he pulled himself up from the couch in the front lounge. Throwing his hand out to catch himself, he caught Janx in the face with his knuckles. Janx said, "Hey!" and Nick fell anyway, sprawling back on the couch, saying, "Fuck," in a kind of half daze.

They'd brought a lot of booze onto the bus after the last show.

Dean was barely feeling it, sitting there at the table, sliding the bottle cap between his fingers. He waited for the others to get by, get their stuff from the bunkroom. Tromp back up the aisle toward the door.

He was keeping himself in check mostly by imagining himself in a small cage, his restlessness pacing inside of him while his nostrils flared and hearts beat just by his ears.

"Coming?" Shawn said.

That's what he'd been working on figuring out, pushing the bottle cap back and forth. A bed sounded good. Getting the fuck off the bus sounded really fucking good. But he'd be trapped in the hotel room from sunup to sundown.

Not that he'd be any less trapped on the bus.

Shawn smelled strong—the shower at the venue the other day had worn off, but it was just dried perspiration.

Dean felt like he was drowning in that other rich smell, Shawn leaning with a hand on the table. Waiting for his answer.

He shot the bottle cap off the edge and stood, holding himself in check. Holding himself in that imaginary cage. "Yeah."

Shawn's eyes met his—brown, inquisitive, but not alarmed or wary.

Jesus, he should be.

Dean needed to take care of himself tonight. Needed it because his teeth were sliding down behind his lips, and his eyes were dragging his attention to the pulse at Shawn's neck.

In the lobby, Mike handed him a key. He trudged up the stairs, behind Shawn and Wayne. Kept going past them, heading for room 208.

He took the time to hang the Do Not Disturb sign from the doorknob before dropping his shit on the room's single bed.

A toilet on the other side of the wall flushed.

Another door in the hall fell shut.

He could breathe, though. He was alone, walls between him and everyone else.

(But the smell of Shawn lingered, dark and tempting.)

He stripped and showered, then padded with wet feet out of the bathroom to tug the room's drapes shut. The sky was taking on a purple hue near the horizon, his nemesis readying its climb into the sky.

He peeked along the edges of the drapes. Still able to see the parking lot's lights, he adjusted the curtains again.

Dropped his hand.

Could still see the fucking lights. This wasn't going to work.

He stripped the bed and dragged the bedding into the bathroom. The tub was wet, so he threw the bath mat over its side and made himself a bed on the floor, his feet pushed between the toilet and the tub.

After a few minutes, he got up and locked the door, then settled back down.

He crossed his arms over his chest, leaning his forehead against the bathtub's cool side. He tried to get some sleep, even as the roots of his teeth pulsed. His stomach felt like it was gnawing on itself, and the sun—he could tell even lying there in the cool bathroom—started to glimmer at the edge of the horizon.

2.

"Are you sure?" Bays said. It was eight in the morning, and Carl's eyes stung. His nerves were raw from lack of sleep. He nodded, clutching the back of the chair parked in front of Bays' desk.

Bays set down the envelope. That was going to have to go into evidence. Cops were on their way to the apartment right now to do another search. Lewis was on his way to the D.A., looking to get a warrant to search Tim's parents' house, because who knew how far back it went. Who knew what might be in boxes in their basement, or the back of the closet in Tim's old room.

The girl in this envelope, Carl had no idea who she was, but she was very, very not alive anymore. It had been taken outside, and it didn't look like it had been taken around here—too lush, fat drops of rain on green leaves, pale fingers resting against moist soil. The Polaroids were a little faded, overexposed at one edge. They predated Soph, probably.

The darkness at the girl's throat, at first he'd thought she'd tied a thin scarf around her neck. He'd seen girls with that look. But the blood bled red in the fabric of her white blouse, and he'd had to take another look at her throat—and then look away, his guts clenching like a fist.

"Have a seat," Bays said.

"Are you going to get him?"

"I'm going to go have a chat with the captain. Sit tight." He left Carl staring at the envelope, his fingers gripping his knees. Nerves jangling. Heart thudding. The photos might be from

Oregon. Tim had spent a summer with his cousins there when he was seventeen.

Fuck. Fuck. Fuck.

His cheeks washed cold and hot all over again. He squeezed his eyes shut and dug his fingers into his knees.

When Bays finally got him, almost two hours later, and brought him back down the hall they'd been down the day before, Carl didn't know what to do with his hands—pockets, hair, crossed and stuffed under his armpits. He let Bays sweep the door open, then he walked in.

Tim, his wrists cuffed in front of him, looked up. His lips twitched. His eyes went from Carl to Bays to Carl.

Carl wondered what he was thinking.

"Five minutes," Bays said, but Carl had a feeling he'd let it go on as long as he needed to. Knew Bays would be standing on the other side of the two-way mirror, and he wouldn't be alone.

Bays closed the door.

Carl approached the table.

"Crazy, huh?" Tim said. "I don't know what the fuck's going on. They're saying I killed some girl."

Carl dragged the other chair out, unable to meet his eyes.

Tim leaned across the table. "You've gotta believe me. I couldn't kill anyone."

Carl couldn't stop his gaze from flicking toward the mirror. His chest was tight. He had no idea where to start.

This was his *only friend.*

"When'd you get back?" Tim asked.

"Night before last."

"Anything exciting to tell?"

Carl shook his head.

"But you found him, right?"

His shoulders tightened. He very pointedly did not look toward the mirror. He couldn't let Tim talk him into trouble. "I met one of the guys in the band," he said. "Briefly." The crack of the stake snapping. The palpable memory came at him: the guy's shoulder bumping him out of the way, the rich scent of blood, like being in a butcher's cooler.

"What happened?" he asked Tim, shifting in the hard chair. Gripping its seat.

"I don't fucking know. They gave me a lawyer, and he's not worth shit. I think he graduated from law school like two days ago. *Contract* law, I bet. He just keeps telling me this bullshit—"

"Did you do it?"

"Jesus! How can you even ask me that? You fucking know me!" He spread his fingers against the table. "You fucking know me!"

Carl stared at one of Tim's fingernails, grime wedged underneath it. "They said they found blood on your shirt."

"I told them—one of the kids at the alley had a bloody nose. I told them to ask around, but they're telling me not one fucking person remembers the kid with the bloody nose."

"They found Polaroids of the girl under your mattress."

"From a couple months ago! I met her at the bowling alley. We went on a date, *one date.*"

"I don't remember you going on any dates." Not in all the time he'd known him. And he hadn't bothered to think about how *that* was strange, because it wasn't like he'd been seeing any girls himself. It had been a relief, actually—no pressure to join him on double dates, no laughing and making out in the other room while Carl pored over his folder.

"You don't remember shit about shit. All you care about is that guy that killed your sister. Your head's so far up your ass on that—"

"Did you?"

"Did I what?"

He felt like he was on a steamroller with no brakes. He gripped the seat harder, fingernails digging against metal. "Did you kill my sister?"

White showed around Tim's eyes. He drew back, his cuffs clinking as he dropped his hands in his lap. His mouth gaped open. "I can't even believe you just said that to me."

The chair under Carl shot backward. He was halfway across the table, holding on to its far edge for his life, right up in Tim's face. "Did you fucking kill my sister?"

He expected the door to fly open, the cops to spill in.

Instead there was silence. The in-and-out heaving of his chest. His spittle on Tim's lip.

A vein in his temple throbbed.

His knuckles ached from gripping the table.

The two of them were frozen in that tableau until Tim pushed his chair farther back and rose, hands dangling in front of him. "I don't think I want to talk to you right now."

Carl lowered his head, his eyes squeezing shut.

His arms trembled.

A hot tear pushed against his lashes.

"I'm ready to go!" Tim called, turning his face to the door. And while they waited for someone to open it, Tim, antsy, said, "I think you need to think about our friendship. You'll see I didn't do it if you think about it. Why the hell would I hang out with you if I'd done that to your sister? To little Soph? Really? I mean, Jesus Christ, who the fuck do you think I am?"

Without lifting his head, Carl said, "What about the other girl?"

Now the door flew open. Uniformed cops pushed in, Bays standing at the door, a folder clutched in his hand. Watching Carl as they hauled Tim out by the elbow.

Tim turned his head and said, "Whatever happened with that guy you were chasing across the country? Huh? What'd you do to *him*?"

3.

KNOCKING WOKE Dean. It had to be hours later—he could feel the sun out there, its fingers digging into every crack.

The light was out in the bathroom, the dark close and comforting. He tugged the blanket higher and curled up again.

Eventually the knocking stopped.

Time ticked.

He woke again, stiff, and rolled to sitting, patting the floor for his cigarettes.

The sun was still out there. Handy to know—it'd suck to accidentally walk into something like that.

He had a feeling the next time he tried facing the sun, it was going to more than hurt.

He smoked and paced and sat. Stood and splashed his face. Looked at himself in the mirror, with that eerie visual clarity despite the dark. The man in the mirror wasn't the person he'd been looking at for twenty-five years. He peeled his lips back. Touched the tip of his tongue to a tooth.

He snarled at the reflection, impressed for a second with how that looked. Smiled a little even.

The pantomime stirred up a need in him to *do something* with these teeth. He turned and paced the tiny space. Sat on the toilet, tapping the rhythm to "Boiler Room" on the edge of the tub. Fucking *waiting*.

He felt like a lion, shut up in a cage, but in a few hours, the cage door would swing open.

4.

WHEN CARL got to his apartment, the cops were just leaving. He closed the front door as their cars pulled out of the parking lot. The neighbors had to be enjoying the excitement. The guy a few doors down had been standing on the catwalk with his can of beer when Carl had come up. His lip had curled as Carl passed by him.

He pressed his forehead against the door. The weight of the apartment leaned on him. The place was a mess, just a different mess than when he'd trawled through it.

Bile soured his throat. He clenched his teeth, sweat beading on his forehead.

He strode to the bathroom, landing on his knees in front the toilet just as everything came up—the morning's coffee, the half of a dry Pop Tart he'd forced down with it, the bite of sandwich Bays had prodded him into eating.

He dropped back and collapsed against the wall, an arm on his knee. A hand over his face. Contents from the vanity drawer lay scattered across the floor. The towels had been ripped out from under the sink. He'd probably done that. The cops might have been neater about it if it had been them.

He felt like things were about to fall apart. Bays hadn't asked him about the guy Tim had mentioned in the interview room, but Tim had enough information to get their curiosity up if they wanted to be curious.

He should be worried about that. He should be down at his car right now, cleaning out the evidence that connected him with the biker, but all he could think about was pizza. All the fucking pizzas he'd shared with the guy who'd killed his sister, talking the whole time about a guy who'd had nothing to do with it.

He'd gone after the wrong fucking guy, for two fucking years.

He'd been a party to *killing* the wrong guy.

You saved a guy's life, showing up when you did on that bus.

Small consolation.

Things happen for a reason.

Soph hadn't happened for a reason. There had been *no* fucking reason for that to happen to Soph. She hadn't fucking died just so he could show up at the right time to save some musician from a vampire.

Why would he do it? Why?

Bays had had a piss-poor answer: *Son, some people are just wrong in the head.*

Not good enough. Not good enough by a long shot.

His hands shook as he stuffed clothes into a bag. Clean clothes, dirty clothes—he paid no attention. Tim had come right up to him that day he'd sat on the gym steps, blaming himself for not hanging around after dropping off Jonesy. *She would have had two sets of eyes on her, man.*

Fuck you and your fucking eyes.

He wished he'd seen that falling apart piece of shit car after Jonesy'd gone in. Wished he'd seen Tim with his fucking eyes on her.

And he got mad at himself all over again: if he'd glanced up and seen Tim Randall chatting with Soph, he'd have just gone back to reading his fucking book.

But at least then—at least then he could have said, "I saw her talking to a biker, and Tim Randolph."

The bag was overstuffed. The zipper wouldn't close. He yelled at it with everything he had, until his head felt hollow and light, his blood pulsing hard in his temples.

HE PARKED in front of a convenience store, its front windows lit against the evening. A woman came out clutching a brown bag, cheap white bread poking out the top. A couple of teenagers went in, arguing with each other. He had nowhere to go. He had two dollars in his pocket, and the banks were closed. No parents' house to run to. His aunt and uncle—he hadn't been able to face them since Soph. Every exchange with them afterward had been awkward, impossible. They didn't blame him; they told him they didn't blame him. But *he* blamed himself, and he couldn't deal with their not admitting they blamed him too.

And, God, now look at him. His chest caved. He'd not only let her get killed, he'd moved in with her fucking killer. How he wasn't in jail himself right now—he could only credit some keen sense on Bays' part. Because if Carl were a cop, he'd have put his ass in jail right alongside Tim's.

Who moves in with the guy who killed his sister and doesn't know it?

Anyone would think he'd been in on it. His aunt and uncle—
the minute they heard, they'd have to think he'd been in on it.

He yanked his key from the ignition and went into the store.
Bought two packs of Camels and asked for matches. Lit up as
he walked out the door, and man *that* felt good. That was the
first thing that had felt good in days.

He climbed into the back seat, right in the convenience store
parking lot, shoving the beach ball of a duffle bag he'd packed
against the back of the passenger seat. He curled up, knees pulled
up, jacket draped over his shoulder. He had no idea where else
to go. The thought of the apartment made his stomach buck, his
throat clench. The wreck of the place—all their things strewn
on the floor, ripped apart, gone through.

A shadow appeared in the car's windows, peering in.

Carl tugged the jacket higher, covering his eyes. He listened
to the soles of shoes walk away, crunching grit in the parking lot.

Twenty minutes later, a car pulled alongside his. A flashlight
shined in the window. The cop knocked, and Carl folded himself
out of the backseat, rumpled and unsteady. The cop listened to
his brief, halting story, no expression on his face. Checked in
with the station on the radio in his car. Came back telling him
he needed to find someplace to go; he couldn't sleep in the
convenience store parking lot.

He dragged himself behind the wheel and moved to a diner
a few blocks away, someplace lit up inside with people coming
and going. He parked closer to the street this time, less obvious,
and climbed into the back seat again to wait for morning with
the school photo of Soph in his hand. He was going back to
talk to Bays. Tim Randolph was going away for killing his sister,
he was going to make sure of it. He didn't know what he could
offer, but there had to be something.

5.

SHOES ON his feet, room and bus keys in his pocket. Dean took the stairs down to the ground floor, turning toward the hotel's side exit instead of the lobby. He didn't need the desk clerk remembering him leaving.

He'd lost track of what town they were in. He remembered the early tours, the first ones they'd done by bus. The excitement of going to the next town and the next. Chicago! St. Louis! Hell, I even can't wait to see what Boise's like! Teddy'd pipe up, saying he'd been to Boise, and he'd have some story about it—a van broken down, a club manager that shorted the payout, a crowd so wild three people came out of the show with stitches.

He had no fucking idea where he was.

Bland hotel, McDonald's on the corner, a gas station across the road, interstate beyond that, headlights flickering through the overpass guardrails.

He hiked to the convenience store, his shoulders bristling at the heavy, greasy smell of burgers and fries at the McDonalds. The store was bright, making him squint—he had to stop himself from shielding his eyes with his hand as he moved past the candy bars and motor oil, antacids and cases of cold drinks. The clerk, a skinny guy in his fifties with a faded anchor tattoo on his forearm, sported nicotine stains on his fingers. An unfiltered cigarette burned in a beansack ashtray by the register.

"Coupla Winston softpacks." Dean pulled folded-up bills from his pocket. "Matches too."

The clerk rang him up, gave him change back from his two dollars.

Out in the parking lot, he peeled a pack open and stuck a cigarette between his teeth. He turned his head to follow a woman hurrying from the pumps to the store, her coat held closed, her hair flapping in the wind.

Apparently it was chilly out. He didn't feel it, in his thin shirt and jeans. As he stuffed the two packs of smokes in his jeans pockets, though, he still missed his jacket. He had to move the buck knife to a front pocket to make room for the smokes in the back.

It took some walking to get to a place where it didn't look too strange, some guy out on foot. Places these days had too many roads set up for cars, too few accommodations for pedestrians. But he'd made it to a neighborhood off the main road, one with houses that didn't all look the same, a place with sidewalks and gnarled trees, their branches casting dark shadows over the concrete.

He'd thought a lot today about what would be ideal. Ideal would be a private place to do it, someplace indoors. Someone home alone, a house not an apartment in case there was noise. He smoked another cigarette, casing buildings as he passed—big houses, not a lot of yard between them but not too crowded together. Some had tall wooden fences between, which would be a bonus, but probably not necessary.

His only plan was to cover ground and keep an eye out for opportunity—or make an opportunity if he had to. If things got desperate.

He needed to do this tonight. His fangs weren't staying retracted. His thoughts were hard to get hold of, squirming away like greased pigs when he tried to catch one.

And the blood. He wasn't even near any, and the thought of it consumed him.

Several blocks later, as he was considering breaking into one of the houses, maybe one of the dark ones so he could stand in the foyer and wait for its owner to come home, he turned a corner and found a woman unloading groceries from her trunk. The driveway was so short, she was practically standing in the road.

Before his brain could put together a plan, a sack in her arm spilled a can onto the road. It rolled in his direction, almost like the biker had bowled it toward him: *Here.*

Start here.

He bent and picked it up.

"Thanks," she said, giving him half a glance as she struggled to adjust the bags in her arms.

"Here, let me grab that." He slipped the can into the bag it had fallen from as he took it from her arm.

"You don't have to—"

"Not a problem." He grabbed two more sacks and still managed to close the trunk while she backed up with the other bag in her arm.

"I should have just made two trips." She turned, her hair swinging across the back of her coat. "I always hate to have to make two trips, though." Looking over her shoulder, she said, "My husband's gotten used to broken eggs."

He wondered if the mention of the husband was a tactic or the truth. She was in her mid to late twenties, he thought. Her modest pumps clacked up the asphalt as she drew her keys out of her coat pocket. She gave him another quick glance, her face tight.

He took in the house's front windows—dark, both upstairs and down—as she climbed the porch steps.

He was halfway up when she turned at the door, hugging the bag with both arms. "Well, thank you for your help." Blocking the way.

"I'll just leave these here." He set them against the wall. He didn't want her on high alert. Let her think she'd run across a real Samaritan. "You have a good night," he said, turning down the steps.

"You too. Thank you."

He whistled as he walked away, fingers pushed in his front pockets.

When he got back to the sidewalk, he glanced back. She had her keys in hand, watching him go. Making sure he did. He didn't blame her. There were dangerous people out here.

When he circled back, coming up behind the house through a neighboring yard, the windows glowed with warm light. He imagined her in the kitchen, pulling items out of paper sacks, putting them where they belonged. Maybe while a kettle of water heated on the stove, tea to take the chill out.

Their trash cans sat by the back porch, two metal bins with a large cardboard box, broken down flat, leaning between them. He had a use for that. Later. First came the woman, whose warm flesh he could already imagine in his grip.

Keeping to the shadows, he skulked to the front, slipping between the house and a neatly trimmed hedge of hawthorn. He crouched below a window, listening for sounds inside.

Cars passed, tires whisking over asphalt. He didn't hear anyone walking around, inside or out. The nearest neighbor's home was dark.

Five or so minutes passed, time pressing against him.

He came back around the side of the house, to the back porch, climbing it quietly. Figuring it would be better to surprise her— and better for the neighbors to not see him pushing his way in.

Holding his breath, he unlatched the storm door and eased it open. He'd expected to feel at least a little uneasy about this; instead he felt a rush, his fingers thrumming, his breaths coming fast. He peeked in the spaces around the curtain in the window. It looked onto a hallway. Up the way was an opening to the kitchen.

He tried the doorknob. Locked. He'd expected that, but it didn't hurt to try.

He looked for a doorbell. None on the back door. So he knocked before taking half a step back, holding the storm door open. Excitement buzzing through him. He cut a glance to the side. Neighbor's house still dark.

It took a moment before her shadow started to grow against the white curtain.

The cloth shifted as she peeked out. He smiled a little bashfully and lifted his hand, a little wave. Her eyebrows drew down. He nodded a little, in the direction of the doorknob.

The curtain fell back. The door opened a crack, her eyebrow raised as she peered through. Lower down she had her shoes dangling from two fingers, like she'd been taking them off when he'd knocked.

"Sorry," he said, moving closer, putting his hand against the door. "I was wondering—" He shoved with this side of his arm, his other hand coming through the widening gap to propel her back.

"What are you—"

"Shh." He touched his finger to his lips as he closed the door behind him. "I won't be here long, darlin'. Let's go in the other room."

Her shoes clattering where she dropped them. Her stockings slipped on the smooth floor as she ran through the doorway.

The Eagles' "One of These Nights" played softly from the direction she ran. When he rounded the corner, she had her back against the kitchen sink, both hands gripping the handle of a cast-iron skillet.

The music came from a portable radio on the counter.

A lock of hair had fallen loose from where she'd had it tucked behind her ear. She drew closer to the sink.

"Relax. You're not gonna need that frying pan." He had his palms up, like she had this all wrong.

Calm, even though his pulse raced.

Hers was running a mile a minute too, hot and fast and sweet, playing a song he could feel all the way up into that new sense, high in his nose.

"Just take what you want and go," she said. "I won't tell the police what you look like."

"I actually don't have a lot of time, so if we could just make this quick."

Her breast heaved. "Then take what you want and get the hell out of here!" White rimmed her eyes. "I'm not stopping you!"

"How about we put that down, okay?" He moved closer, hands still up.

She slid over, lifting the skillet over her shoulder, her arms shaking with its weight, her fear. The fear gave a sharp scent to her perspiration. He found he didn't mind it a bit.

His mouth was full of teeth.

"Listen, I have a knife in my pocket," he said. "I don't want to pull it out. Just set that down on the counter—" Sweeping in, he twisted the skillet from her hands, easy as anything. The skillet, big and heavy, was easy to catch hold of, even as she tried to slip away.

With her hands empty, she yanked a drawer open, throwing utensils out of it—ladles and spatulas, looking, he supposed, for a knife.

He wasn't afraid of a knife. Those shish kebob skewers she was throwing to the floor were more problematic than any knife.

He dropped the skillet in the sink, put his arms around her waist from behind, and pulled her backward, away from the counter.

She dragged the drawer right out of its guides, kicking as he hauled her off her feet. The drawer's contents rattled to the floor.

His head rushed, at the warmth of her, the smell of her, the *pulse* of her as she fought to bring the drawer over her shoulder and hit him with it.

He dodged. It glanced off his neck.

"It's nothing personal, darlin'," he said as his teeth grew two sizes, right into the side of her throat. Right where that delicate pulse was beating its signal out to him. Blood burst into his mouth, going right for his throat. Right down it as he took a big swallow, breathing in, feeling his feet go unsteady for a second.

He cut off her scream with his hand over her mouth. She jerked against him, like she was orgasming, and the hot blood rushed down his throat. He clamped her tighter, his own pulse racing, her blood singing a sweet song in his ears as he drank it.

Her weight brought him to one knee, her body going limp—a twitch here, a twitch there. Blood kept coming, as fast as he could swallow it. He felt like he couldn't breathe, and he felt like he couldn't stop, not until the spurt petered to a dribble.

He slipped his hand off her mouth.

She didn't gasp in air.

Light and warmth and jangles filled him. He drew back, panting. The woman's body lay like a ragdoll on the kitchen tiles. She had a hand curled against her chest, like she was keeping something secret, but her fingers were empty.

Even the high-noted sting from her fingernails raking across his face had a sweetness to it. A reverence. He touched the side of her throat that hadn't been mangled. It felt like silence.

The Eagles had given over to Linda Ronstadt, telling him he was no good.

He probably was.

A set of metal measuring spoons reflected light from the ceiling. He was mesmerized for a moment, his hand resting on her chest. His body full of her warmth.

A floorboard creaked.

His ears pricked.

He was on his feet in a flash, his insides still jangles and light. He shoved a kitchen chair out of his way and launched into the living room.

He caught the guy by the neck as he was grappling with the doorknob, trying to get back out of the house after what he'd seen. The fabric of his wool coat was cool. His hair smelled like outside.

He smelled like blood.

The guy yelled, "No!" as Dean's weight slammed him into the door.

"No, please," he whispered. "Please." His voice cracked into a sob.

"You want me to let you go?" Dean whispered. It sounded like the biker's voice. He felt the biker grinning right along with him. Light came off the biker. Off him. Light and heat.

"Oh please, God, what did you do? What did you do to Pam?"

Dean backed up a few steps, hugging the guy's back against him. The guy whispered prayers, clutching Dean's arm. His chest caved with a sob.

Dean murmured in his ear, whatever the biker came up with to say as he brought his arm across the guy's face. Brought his teeth close to the guy's neck, his skull pulsing with excitement. He licked the side of his throat, tasting sweat, aftershave, stubble.

Feeling the beat of his pulse, fast under his tongue.

He didn't have any room, though. His eyes slipped closed as he breathed and tasted, as the guy sobbed in his arms. He had no trouble holding him, this guy who had a couple inches and forty soft pounds on him. Sobbing in his arms.

Coming up along the guy's jaw, he tasted salt.

The guy's chest heaved as he gasped in air, still pulling at Dean's arm.

You got it, the biker said. *You got this.*

Holding the guy's body against him, he cracked the guy's head to one side, sharp and hard. He felt the neck snap in the backs of his teeth.

There, the biker said. *Just like I'd have done it.*

Fuck you.

The guy's body dropped.

Dean stepped back, letting it thump to the floor.

Linda Ronstadt hadn't even finished her song.

Let's get this cleaned up, the biker said.

"What do I do?" He glanced at the walls, the staircase. Pulled the toe of his sneaker from under the body. Back in the kitchen, the wife hadn't moved. The radio played a commercial for a used car dealership. He stepped over her and knelt. He wasn't sure feeding on her till her heart had stopped beating was enough to finish her off. She had no pulse. She wasn't moving. But he sure as hell didn't want to take the chance of her ending up like him.

He snapped her neck before getting up to find the door to the basement.

Pam wasn't too difficult to drag down the stairs. Her husband had a good hundred pounds on her. The backs of his dress shoes thumped down each step. By the time he reached the bottom,

Dean was panting—but he was energized too. Warmth and jangles and light, right to the tips of his fingers.

He left the bodies side-by-side near the boiler, sightless eyes pointed at the wooden joists in the ceiling.

In the kitchen, he righted the chair, picked up the drawer and fitted it back on its tracks. He collected the scattered utensils and dropped them inside. Pushed it closed. He left the skillet in the sink, and turned out the light.

He glanced toward the stairs again, on his way to turn out the foyer light. On a whim, he made a detour up them. He pawed through their bedroom closet until, in the back, he found a jean jacket, not even all that worn. He shrugged into it. It worked for him.

There ya go, the biker said.

He gave him the finger as he headed out of the room.

The cardboard box was still there, by the porch. He clamped it under one arm. Enough for what he needed.

On the street, he pushed his fists into the jacket pockets, hunched his shoulders, and strode with his head down, back in the direction of the hotel, still all jangles and light on the inside, the edgy restlessness eased for the time being. He was breathing easy. This hadn't gone badly. It wasn't how he'd ideally be spending his nights off—but it showed he could do this.

He'd probably bought himself a few nights of peace. At least, he hoped he had.

OCTOBER 19, 1978

1.

THE SUN crept across the parking lot, pinking the sky like a blood orange. Carl twisted on the back seat of the Cougar, his tee shirt sticking to him. He moved his jacket over his eyes. Traffic picked up, car doors slamming, shoes shuffling over pavement. His stomach rumbled, and he gave up and crawled out.

By eight, he was at the police station, waiting for a turn at the desk so he could ask to see Bays, when he spotted the man's balding head moving through the bullpen. He backed up and ducked around.

Bays was bringing a jelly doughnut to his mouth when Carl caught up.

"What can I do?" Carl said.

"What can you do about what?" Bays set a cup of coffee on his desk. With sugar-dusted fingers, he smoothed his tie, and his chair squeaked as he settled his weight in it.

Carl took a seat beside the desk. "To help. Is there anything you need from me to nail him for this?"

"Did he mention the Garcia girl before you left on your trip?"

"No."

"Did he mention anything about any girl? Act strangely? Was there anything different about him before you took off?"

"No—but what about Soph?"

"What about her?" He slid a legal pad toward him and set the doughnut on it. Another detective stopped to say something to him—he nodded and waved two fingers: *In a minute.*

"Is there anything I can do help you nail him for Soph?" Carl said.

"Son…" Bays sighed, wiping his hands. "Come on." The chair squeaked again. "Let's take a walk."

They swerved through the desks in the bullpen, and Bays stopped and turned halfway up a dim, gray hallway. "The D.A.'s not charging him with Soph's murder," Bays said, and as Carl popped open his mouth to protest, Bays put a hand on his shoulder. "They're going to use Soph and the girl from the Polaroids to see if they can pressure him into confessing, giving up some info on that girl so we can identify her and notify her family, but if he doesn't crack, they're just going to push the Garcia killing."

"But—what the hell?" His cheeks felt cold. His pulse raced, reedy and distant.

"We have a…let's just say he's a very conservative D.A. He wants wins. He thinks he's got a good chance with the Garcia girl—fresh in people's minds, blood on his shirt, testimony of a witness who says the victim was unnerved by him."

"But with Soph—"

"With Soph the D.A.'s thinking two things. First he's thinking about what the defense is going to present. They're going to look at the case, subpoena you—maybe as a hostile witness if they have to—and they're going to have you admit that while you saw Timothy Randolph drop his brother off at the game, no one saw him anywhere near your sister. Then they're going to force you to say that there *was* this other guy, a rough-looking character, you saw speaking to your sister right before she disappeared. And when they're done with you, they're going to call Detective Medina to the stand. You remember Medina?"

"Yeah."

"Not a bad guy, but they're going to ask him who the suspects were in this case, and he's going to tell him about this rough-looking character you saw. Then they're going to ask him what eliminated that character from their list of suspects, and you know what Medina's gonna say?"

"They didn't believe me?"

"No, he's gonna say they never eliminated him—they just couldn't find him."

"Okay..." Carl's head felt tight. His temples throbbed. He was trying to grasp at the problem, but...so what if they didn't find this other guy? He didn't *do* it.

"So the first thing the D.A.'s worried about is the defense's next question to Medina—and the judge may overrule it, but it doesn't matter, because the jury's still going to hear it: Did you ever think you couldn't find him because he didn't exist?"

"He existed—"Carl's face beat hot. "I *saw* him. He fucking—"

"You may well have," Bays said, reaching into his jacket. "But that brings up the D.A.'s problem number two." He unfolded a sheet of paper and turned it around for Carl to see—a half-legible fax on slick thermal paper, but legible enough to make out one important detail: they'd found Grip Gershon.

"He had the patch you described in your statement on his jacket. Same height and build, seems to match the sketch you said was a good likeness of what you saw. And he had an empty knife sheath strapped to his thigh, just like you said."

"But he didn't do it," Carl said, the paper turning sticky against damp fingertips. "Tim— I mean, he killed the other girls the same way, and—"

"And this guy's prints bring him up as a suspect in a killing in a military hospital. He's been off the grid for years. Roaming the country, I guess. Involved in an outlaw biker gang."

"But he didn't—" He wouldn't have sliced her throat and dumped her. He'd have killed her to feed.

Bays took his arm and pulled him to the end of the hall, where it teed off and led to the restrooms, a utility closet. Sunlight came through windows on the opposite wall. "It doesn't matter if he did it or not. It's how the defense can present it. They can say, 'It's possible Timothy Randolph committed this

murder, yes, but isn't it *just as* possible that this rough character"—he waved the fax—"this obvious criminal, could actually
have killed this girl like her brother said he did two years ago?'
And if they can convince the jury that yes, that *is* possible, the
D.A. doesn't get his win."

"This is bullshit," Carl said.

"Listen, maybe Randolph will talk. Maybe something else
pointing at him will pop up. But don't hold your breath. If I
were you, I'd consider him caught for *something*. He'll go away
a long time for the Garcia girl alone."

"But that's not—"

"The same? I know, kid, I know. I'll keep tabs on if they find
out anything about Gershon guy. Maybe something'll turn up
that says he was on the other side of the country when your
sister was killed."

"Are they investigating that?" Of course they were fucking
investigating that. A dry heat itched across his eyeballs. Of
course they were fucking investigating that—and now with
Bays asking questions related to this case, there was going to
be a connection, however tenuous, between him and the biker.
Who was dead.

"I don't know that they're going to knock themselves out over
it, but the way they found him's got them a little curious."

Carl swallowed. He figured he knew the answer to this, but
Bays would expect the question: "How'd they find him?"

"He had no heart. I've seen a lot of things, but I haven't seen
anyone's heart sawed out of their body yet."

"What happens now?" Carl asked, shifting his weight to his
other foot. Itching to get out of there. Out of Los Campos
entirely. He just wanted to be in the middle of nothing so he
could scream.

Bays took a breath, stretching his back. "Like I said, they'll
lean on him and see if they can get a confession. There's a long
road to go yet, but they'll get him indicted, try him, hopefully
get the Garcia charges to stick, and he'll go to prison for a very
long time."

Carl dug his fingernails into his palms. He felt like he was being peeled apart on the inside.

"You should talk to someone," Bays said, clasping Carl's shoulder again. "I know this is a lot on you. I can get someone to get a few names to recommend you. And hey—everything I said just now? It's between us. I thought you deserved to know, but you can't go talking about what the D.A.'s going to do. Not if you want to see him go down for at least some of the shit he did."

Carl gave a curt not. There wasn't enough air in the police station. The sun streaming through the windows mocked him with its brightness. It heated his cheek and burned the eye that was still half turned toward it.

He said, "Got it," as he pulled out Bays's grip.

"Do you have someplace to go?" Bays asked.

"I'll figure it out." All he had was emptiness. No friends, no family, no enrollment in college. Not even his sister was here anymore, just an empty space he used to talk to, photos with eyes that looked out but didn't see. He was a husk without a seed. "Thanks for your help. I'll figure it out."

"If you need those names…"

A young woman hauling a box of files in front of her stepped aside as he strode up the hallway. The bullpen was a burst of noise that immediately seemed to muffle. He felt like everyone was looking at him. The shells of his ears itched hot.

Back in the car, he clutched his keys.

He needed to get the fuck out of Los Campos. There was nothing keeping him here—no family, friends, no job, no classes. Just a shitty apartment he never wanted to see again. And if he got connected with what had happened to Gershon, he didn't want to be here for it.

He hit the bank, fidgeting in line until he could close out his account and stuff the cash in his pocket. Back in the bright sunshine, he climbed into the Cougar and drove to the middle of nowhere—a dusty road, brown ledges of mountain the distance, nothing but scrub in between.

No idea where to go.

He hit his steering wheel with his fist. "Fuck!"

He could stay. He could get a hotel room, find a job, enroll in school, move into a studio apartment on the other side of town. Visit his aunt and uncle. Try to piece together a normal life. Attend Tim's trial—a bitter victory when he got convicted. Maybe the biker would never trace back to him. Ten years from now, he'd just be a regular schmo, maybe with a girlfriend, or even a family. Like none of this ever happened.

"FUUUUCK!"

The yell left the back of his throat raw, made the veins in temples throb.

He slammed out of the car to piss on the side of the road, a hot breeze drying the sweat on the back of his neck. He was thirsty as hell—and he had *nothing*. Nothing but a duffle bag of clothes, and a stupid manila folder he should have destroyed before he booked out of town that last night he spent around the band.

He popped the trunk now and dug it out. Back in the passenger seat, with the door open and one foot on the ground, he flipped through the reports. A semi rumbled past. He slipped the photo of the soldiers out and held it against the wheel. Sergeant David "Grip" Gershon, smirking at the camera. Sergeant David "Grip" Gershon who probably hadn't killed his sister—but he'd killed someone. Probably a lot of someones.

And the other bikers, they were probably just like him.

And one of theirs had been killed.

Did Dean know about these other guys? The rest of the biker club? They knew who Gershon'd been after before he bought it. If they were the vengeful type—and why wouldn't they be— they'd at least be looking to see if the guy Gershon'd been after had had anything to do with why he's not around anymore.

Tucked in the back of the folder was a stack of papers he'd taken from Dean's house. On top was page two of the tour itinerary. The date at the top—New Orleans—was two nights away.

He looked up as a station wagon hurtled past, heading toward Los Campos.

He'd be in Louisiana in plenty of time if he left right now.

2.

DEAN WAS on the bus when they pulled up to the venue because he'd gone back to his room after his kill for just long enough to collect his things. He'd climbed on board while the night was still dark, and he'd taken advantage of the darkness—sitting in the front lounge, stretching his legs. By the time the sun had risen, though, he was cocooned in his bunk.

The curtain scraped lightly against the cardboard he'd taped over the bunk's opening.

"What's this?" Shawn said, tapping it from the other side.

"Keeping the light out."

"Still getting migraines?"

"Not as long as I keep the light out."

"How long's this gonna go on?"

"I don't know. It lasted three weeks one time," he lied.

"All right," Shawn said with a sigh. "We'll see you inside when you get there." He started to walk away—then his sneakers scuffed back to the bunk. "People are going to talk, you know. You're going to be the enigmatic, eccentric guitarist who doesn't give interviews and no one ever sees until after dark."

"That's me." He ran a thumb along the gaffer tape at one edge, smoothing it as Shawn left for good this time. He had no urge to light a cigarette; most of the smoke from the last one was still trapped in the air with him. He settled back on the pillow, hands over his stomach, and played the night before over in his head, one minute chastising himself—he should have worn gloves—the next letting his eyes roll closed at the memory of the woman's blood hitting his system.

The jacket he had on smelled vaguely like the guy, with a trace of the wife's perfume in its threads.

What did you do with all the hours? he asked the biker, but the biker had no interest in talking back if Dean wasn't on the hunt.

The bus swayed, the last of his guys getting off it.

He played with the knife, propping the pommel on his leg. He was going to need to explain to someone, sooner or later.

Pull someone in to help keep his secret. Who, though, was the question. It had to be someone *in* the band—they'd be the only people with as much at stake in keeping him going.

Jessie'd freak out. He wouldn't be able to deal with the truth of it. Dean could already see him shaking his head, his eyes wild—trying to get Dean to admit it was a joke. Backing away as he became convinced it wasn't.

Nick and Shawn were tougher to calculate. He wanted to lean toward Nick, not because he trusted him more—there wasn't anyone he trusted more than Shawn—but because he wouldn't see the implications as clearly, over the awe of it—wouldn't really digest the fact of what he had to do to survive.

The fact that he was going to be leaving a trail of dead people in their wake.

A fact he had a hard time being bothered by himself. An old part of him, standing a ways away from the new him, tried to work itself up over it, but it was a small voice, overwhelmed by the way his brain worked now. All the changes this thing had made in his body—the healing, the teeth, the blinding headaches—it hadn't left his mind alone either.

"Rotting from the inside," he murmured, tapping the blade against his chin. Rotting to the point that it hardly bothered him that he'd killed two people the night before.

Killing a dog would have hurt more than what he'd done.

Shit.

With hours to go, he had nothing to do but light another cigarette, close his eyes, and relive the rush of blood.

3.

TEXAS UNSPOOLED under the Cougar's tires. Some middle-of-no-where radio station was playing Cherry's one hit, the jangly "Three Deuces," reminding Carl of the summer he was twelve—and Soph, singing the chorus loud and wrong, giggling every time he tried to set her straight. She was doing it on purpose, and the corner of his mouth crooked up, remembering.

"We're going somewhere else, Soph," he said. "I don't know where yet, but we're going someplace new."

He didn't know what he should expect, bringing this news to Dean, if the guy would just say, "Yeah, I know," and walk away, or if he'd want to see his folders—if he'd tell him it was bullshit, or if he'd take him backstage to talk about what had happened. He adjusted the rearview, the setting sun flashing into his eyes.

A sign whipped by, gone in a flash. He glanced at the speedometer, took his foot off the gas until the needle dropped near eighty-five.

He thought about how Tim had handled his search for the guy who'd killed Soph, how he'd seized on the story about the biker early on. He'd provided Carl with his first motorcycle magazine, his introduction to the lurid crudeness of biker gangs. He'd filled his head with the terrible sorts of things guys like that did. Encouraging him to focus on the biker.

The New Hampshire trip—the morning Carl was leaving, Tim had gotten up too, early enough to grab a coffee with him before he headed out the door. In a good mood. He'd said, You're an idiot for thinking this is going to turn out to be anything, but he'd also asked if he'd had a map, if he had enough cash in case the car broke down. When are you going to be back?

Well, like, minimum, how long do you think you'll be gone?

Bays had wanted to know if Tim had acted any different, and Carl didn't know how strong the evidence was for that. He was afraid he'd slip up, anyway, if he tried to tell Bays about the morning he'd left without giving away what he was leaving for.

Well, like, minimum, how long do you think you'll be gone?

Because he'd already decided on another target. Another little girl, barely seventeen. Cute. Dark-haired. She had a brother, but he was just fifteen. He wondered if Tim had tried to insert himself in the kid's life. *I remember your sister from the bowling alley. She'd come in sometimes. She always seemed really happy. In fact, I saw her that night. I can't believe I saw her that same night. Who would do such a thing?*

Fuck him.

Just fuck him.

"What do you think, Soph? Time to put that behind us?" The medal hanging from the mirror swayed. His tires bumped over broken asphalt as he pulled up by a gas pump.

HE ROLLED into New Orleans in the dark, the city pressing close, thick with sweat, humidity, and something dark and earthy, despite all the streets and sidewalks.

Lack of sleep tugged at his eyes. He'd caught a half hour here and there in the back seat of the car last night, then driven through the hot sun, the never-ending interstate hypnotizing him. But this city—it was like driving into another world. If magic existed, he thought as he craned his neck to gawk at a graceful porticoed mansion, it existed right here.

For the first time since he'd come home, he felt like he'd found something. Like he'd come to the right place.

4.

PREY.

The young girl in the venue shirt working her way around people to empty ashtrays. The tour-manager-slash-roadie for Thieves, with his beige leather jacket, wide collar, and gold chain peeking through the V of his shirt as he swept a carrot stick through a plastic tub of dill dip. The two music journalists talking to Shawn, one of them sweeping a curl of blond hair behind her delicate ear, smiling at him; the other—a guy with a paunch and Who tee shirt—crowding her out of the way, probably oblivious to the fact he was even doing it.

They all made Dean feel like a mouthful of teeth.

A short *pop* turned his head, the rise of a cheer.

"Can't Win" had hit number one for the week.

Another *pop* went off, Janx opening the second bottle of champagne as Mike poured the first into plastic cups, passing them around. Sparkling effervescence spilled over people's hands. Nick slurped champagne from the crook of his thumb with a smile. Mike moved onto pouring the second bottle, Wayne still handing cups around.

Jessie brought him one, grinning, raising his own and saying, "Prost!"

Dean lifted the cup, vibrating in his fingers—from the bubbles, from the noise in the room, from the impulses inside of him—and said, "Prost," before lowering the drink to his waist. He could tell by the smell; champagne wasn't going to sit well with him.

When Shawn came by, it was to whisper, "This sucks," in his ear, but he was smiling.

They had four more bottles of champagne on ice, a gift from High Class. A reminder of who they were yoked to.

But Dean was thinking, right now, that that was probably for the best. If he had to leave, they'd still have a label, still be a band. Someone would replace him. He even had a couple vague ideas on that.

And he was thinking this because even Shawn, standing beside him with his drink, watching the crowd hoot and holler—even Shawn was prey.

A dimple creased Shawn's cheek as he smiled at Nick riding Wayne and Janx's shoulders under the spray of a shaken bottle of bubbly. A featherlight pulse at the side of Shawn's throat broadcast his smell.

He was a walking bag of blood, and Dean, wondering how he tasted, dropped his eyes.

OCTOBER 20, 1978

1.

CARL woke in a hotel room that smelled like mildew and cleaning agents. It took a moment to orient himself. He was twisted in the clothes he'd had on last night, and the colored lights of Bourbon Street were still flashing in his head. He'd gotten some spicy chicken, ate it while he watched the crowds. Thinking about how Tim had talked about the French Quarter once, about Mardi Gras, how you could buy liquor there at eighteen—and kill someone in the middle of that parade going on, and nobody would ever figure out who did it.

He'd bought liquor last night, and his head ached with it. He dragged himself out of bed, unsure whether he was looking to pee or puke. The cool of the bathroom tiles helped his stomach settle some. A shower put him in half-decent shape.

He checked the clock—fuck. Yanked wrinkled clothes from his duffle bag.

In the lobby, he got directions to the venue from the desk clerk. Too far to walk. The Cougar's air conditioning blasted as he crept down Poydras. City buildings towered over him through the commercial district. He caught a glimpse of Port of New Orleans before turning off, and then he started looking for signs.

He spotted the bus instead, its cargo doors gaping open. He wound around the block, looking for a place to leave his car.

Anxious to get out there. He walked three blocks back, a bounce in his step. He was here, and they were here, and if nothing else he was going to see a show tonight.

Men in tee shirts and boots lugged equipment into the venue. The upper part of the bus was silent—door shut, blinds down.

He leaned against the corner of the venue and hooked his thumbs in his belt loops. Far enough away that he wasn't in the way, close enough to watch what was going on. He did his best to look nonchalant. He still had no idea how this was going to go, but it might be best if he wasn't too memorable.

The door in the bus came open with a creaking complaint. One of the musicians stepped off, his hair a bush that had grown wild. He stretched his arms over his head, interlocking his fingers, arching his back as he squinted toward the sky. One of the roadies slapped him on the shoulder, and the musician treated him to an *I'm-not-quite-awake-yet* smile.

Another came out, sticking his head through the bus door before deciding to step into the humidity. He looked elfish to Carl, his dark hair splitting to either side of his ears, like rivers parting around a rock. He was all elbows and knees as he bent in front of one of the open bays to haul a bag out. Dropping it on the sidewalk, he unzipped it and started rummaging through.

The third walked down the steps backwards—blond, All-American good looks—talking to an older man coming down after him. His hands flew as he spoke. He had an easy smile and a solid, lean build that was exactly the frame his faded jeans and tight tee shirt had been made for. The older man nodded, his eyes flicking toward the building. He carried a coffee in one hand, a roll of papers in the other. He pointed toward the open door as roadies shut the bus bays, and the blond spun on his heel and walked along with him, into the venue, his hands shoved into his front pockets, a smile on his face as he talked.

The other two followed, the elf stopping to light a cigarette. He dropped the match on the sidewalk. The wild-haired guy held the door for him.

Carl watched the bus door, hanging open and silent.

Dean hadn't come out.

The bus jostled as a roadie hopped up its steps, agile for his size.

A cab pulled up behind the bus. Short toot of the horn. Engine idling.

A few seconds later, the driver came down with his bag over his shoulder, wearing the same faded work trousers he'd had on that day in the alley.

The cab drove away.

The roadie closed the bus door on his way back out. At the venue, he nudged a brick out of the way and pulled the door shut behind him.

The sidewalk was empty—oddly quiet against the street noises around them.

He could have missed Dean getting off earlier. The guy could be in the building.

He pushed off the wall and walked the length of it, away from the bus, his steps slow. Around the corner, the ticket window—literally a hole cut into the brick façade and framed out with red-painted wood—was shuttered. He pushed his fingers in his pockets and watched oncoming traffic, the bus visible in his peripheral vision.

The breeze from the morning was gone. Sweat stuck his hair to the back of his neck.

He sat at the corner, propped against the building. He dropped his pack of cigarettes between his tennis shoes and lit one up, letting it dangle between his fingers as he blew smoke and watched the bus.

For the next few hours, people came and went, but never Dean.

He told himself the musician was inside, tuning a guitar, whatever it was they did before a show.

But, as his attention returned again and again to the back of the bus, with its blinds drawn, he felt like Dean was still on *there*. Hiding from the sunlight.

What happened afterward, Dean? What are you now? What'd you do with Gershon's heart? Because that was kind of crazy, wasn't it? Bays didn't say the heart had been stabbed up by something blunt. He'd said it was *gone.*

The venue door swung open, the guy with the wild hair coming out, an unopened can of soda in the crook of his arm, his other hand bringing a half-eaten banana to his mouth. Carl watched him jostle the soda so he could get the bus door open. Someone—a fan, heading for the entrance to stand in line—called out his name and he smiled and called back a "Hey," before climbing inside, stopping to pull the door shut again.

He leaned against the wall and watched the bus.

2.

"ARE YOU going to wear the fake teeth again?" Shawn asked from the other side of the cardboard barrier. A soda can top popped with a hiss.

Dean winced. During last night's encore, he'd gotten too into—charging the front of the stage with a snarl. A shiver had gone through one of the girls who'd been reaching for him.

"Yeah, probably." The bunk was close and stuffy, the mattress hard, his hips tired of being on it. He'd done a lot of thinking while the sun warmed the wall by his shoulder. A lot of thinking about what he'd almost said last night—and how he did need to say it. *How* to say it. Dread was growing in him again, just like before the biker had shown up. It was distant, but the tips of its fingers reached deep.

He didn't know what was coming, only that it couldn't be good.

And he needed to tell Shawn at least some of this. At least *something*—in case he had to leave. In case Shawn could think of a way to keep him from having to leave, which was really what he wanted—someone to say, *We can figure this out.* They'd always figured things out.

His breath gathered in his throat.

And Shawn, out there clueless, said, "I called Evie."

Dean realized that was why he was here in the first place, to confess to someone he'd called his pregnant ex. To talk that out.

"What'd you do that for?" Dean asked—half relieved to be off the hook for a few minutes longer. Maybe his situation wouldn't seem quite as bad to Shawn, compared to a pregnant ex. He pulled his pillow under his chest, lying on his front.

"I had some crazy idea in my head that maybe, with us hitting number one, she'd change her mind."

"And?"

A silence stretched out.

Dean bent his head, stretching his neck.

"I was never that great of a boyfriend, you know. Always on the road, in the studio, writing, practicing, rehearsing. She used to accuse me of spending more time with you guys than her, and I'd say, 'That's my job. What do you think pays the bills?'"

Dean picked at the seam of the pillowcase.

"I'd tell her, 'You knew what I did when we met.' And I was just…an unmovable brick wall about it, you know? All 'This is what you signed on to.'"

"She knew what you did," Dean said.

"Yeah but…I don't know. I just thought…if this is the tip of something, if we can get High Class to release *Mercy* and really get a handle on this thing, I could afford to bring her out for some of the tours. I could…I don't know, find a way to make a better balance."

"And the kid?"

"That'd be just more reason to make it work, right?"

Dean leaned his forehead on his pillow, his insides fighting against this disruption. This *change.* And it was old Dean's insides pulling tight at the idea of it, old Dean who would have wanted to keep the band just the fucking way it was. Girlfriends came and went—or hell, maybe even a wife, as long as she stayed home, stayed out of the studio, stayed out of rehearsal. "What if it's not your kid?"

Shawn let out a breath of a laugh. It sounded like it was turned in on itself. "I was thinking if we got back together, I'd tell her to not even try to find out. We'd just call it mine."

"And?" Dean had his face turned, cheek to pillow, scanning the manufacturer's name printed on the bottom of the cardboard he'd taped against the hole in his bunk.

"She was glad I called so she could give me her new phone number. She moved in with the guy over the weekend."

"You want to hit something?"

"Really bad."

"I'm sorry," Dean said. And meant it. He may not have wanted Evie tagging along, but he could feel Shawn's hurt like it was his own. Or, like it was old Dean's own at least. He could still reach out and touch old Dean, if he stretched far enough.

And old Dean needed to talk to Shawn about new Dean. He put his fingers against the cardboard. "Are the doors closed?"

"The— Oh." A half second passed, during which Dean felt Shawn looking toward each end of the bunkroom's hallway. "Yeah."

"Okay, I'm—"

"Shawn! You in there?" Wayne's voice, coming from farther up the bus.

Gonna come out of here because I need to talk to you.

"Yeah!" Shawn called.

"They're ready."

"'Kay!" To Dean, he said, "Sound check. Up for it?"

His chest tightened, his moment to explain slipping away. "No, I'd better not. Can you come back right after?"

"If Mike doesn't have shit lined up for us."

"Try to come back. I need to talk to you."

"Okay."

The door to the bunkroom closed.

Dean stayed where he was, hugging the pillow.

An hour passed. Two.

The sun sank away until it was nothing but traces tugging at his mind.

He hugged the pillow tighter, against the dread in his chest, until he couldn't take lying there. With the edge of his thumbnail, he pried up the tape. Folded the cardboard out like a door. Slipped through the opening into the dark hallway and let himself into the back, just to check. He put a knee on the couch and tweezed two slats in the blinds open with his fingers.

Still enough sun out there to bother his eyes some, but it wouldn't last much longer.

He scanned the crowd, all those kids come to see them. The traces of sun weren't so bad where the building blocked it.

His gaze fell on a face he recognized.

He put his hand against his chest, against the swamp of dread there.

The biker hadn't been the only thing to show up the last time he'd felt this. And the biker hadn't been the only thing that'd been gone when the dread had disappeared.

The kid who'd brought the stakes, his head dropped back into the crowd. He must have risen up on his toes. Another dark head was next to him, light shining around it. The sun playing tricks on his over-sensitive eyes.

He let the slats snap back into place.

Guy comes on the bus with a handful of stakes, he knows what he's after.

And now he was back.

Dean sank to the couch, wondering what he should do. What he *could* do.

He nixed the idea of telling Shawn, at least right now. Better to keep everyone out of it until he figured this latest development out. Maybe by not knowing, they wouldn't wind up caught in the middle of it.

3.

THE CROWD wound around the corner.

The wild-haired guy had come off the bus with one of the roadies fifteen minutes ago; now music rumbled from the building, so distorted by the brick it was hardly music at all. It kept up for a good forty minutes. Another forty minutes later, the first band on the bill was playing in fits and starts, their sound higher than Man Made Murder's but still just a distorted mess.

Carl stood among the other fans, his shoulder against the wall. He faced the back of the line. Every minute or so, he lifted up on his toes to check the bus.

He had to have missed Dean somehow.

The band's fans were there in groups—pairs at a minimum, but four or five or ten at a time who all seemed to know each other. He tuned them out and lifted onto his toes again. Shadows hugged the edges of the building beyond where the security lights reached.

Cars came up the street, headlights leading the way. Concert-goers held them up as they crossed to the venue. One flipped a driver off, laughing with his friends.

Carl came up on his toes.

The bus door shifted.

His heart did a quick beat. He stepped away from the wall, his fingertips ghosting it. He peered around the shoulders of the people behind him.

A few at the end had caught the movement too. They nudged each other, nodding toward the bus.

The door opened to a black hole. Then Dean Thibodeaux clodded down the steps, looking like he'd just woken up. He stopped halfway between the bus and the venue, ducking his head to light a cigarette.

He looked up as he shook the match out. His eyes went straight to Carl's.

Carl held his breath, his fingers pushing against the wall. Trying to decide if now was the right time to try to have that talk.

Wariness crossed Dean's face. He shoved the matchbook in his pocket as he started walking again, *not* looking at Carl. The door at the band's entrance, and a second later it fell shut. Dean Thibodeaux had entered the building.

Chatter broke out, excitement about the sighting.

Carl leaned his forehead on his arm, his hand braced on the wall. He stared at the bricks.

Lit by the jaundiced security light, Dean's cheeks had been sculpted out, his lips pale. Dark smudges crouched below his eyes.

He looked like a drawing Carl had seen once of a wendigo.

Someone jostled him, the line moving. He pushed away from the wall, stepping out of the crowd, letting people behind him spill into his empty space.

Dean hadn't set foot outside until after dark.

Carl's head twitched, unconscious little jerks.

A hand touched his back, someone slipping past to get to the line.

He took another step back, coming off the sidewalk completely. Staring straight ahead, his breaths drying his mouth.

The shadow that had crossed Dean's eyes. The pallor of skin.

He'd just seen a vampire.

The pavement vibrated under his feet. A noise rattled him. It took a few seconds for it to connect. He dragged his head around. His mouth opened, throat dry.

The rumble echoed off cobblestones and brick. The line kept moving forward, mostly oblivious, people disappearing into the mouth of the door. A few fans craned their necks to catch a look at what was coming, jumping forward to keep their spots.

And there they came, five outlaws in leather and denim, straddling steel beasts, their gloved hands gripping throttles, their hair rippling like flags behind them.

Carl turned as they roared around the corner, the noise beating his ears.

They pulled up behind the bus. Kickstands came down, engines cut off. A tension stretched the air. Carl backed another step into the road, distantly seeing the front corner of a car slamming on its brakes just shy of his thigh. He touched the hood of that car, still watching the bikers, felt it slip from under his fingers, the driver going around him.

The bikers split up, three striding to either side of the bus. On the side Carl could see, two canvassed the windows, the edge of the roof, the dark space underneath. The one in front—the broad-shouldered blond Carl remembered from the bar—strode toward the door, looking neither right nor left. Chin high.

The venue's back door swung open. A roadie stepped out, not realizing what he was walking into. When he saw the blond reaching for the door handle, he stiffened. "Hey, show's inside."

Carl wished it had been the bigger of the two who'd come out, the one built like an ape.

"Ticket booth's around the corner," the roadie said.

The blond looked the bus door up and down.

"Come on, guys," the roadie said, striding toward the bus.

The blond jiggled the handle. Stepped back, craning his neck.

Carl caught movement at the end of the bus's roof and darted his gaze over as boots landed. He'd missed how that one had gotten up there—climbed? Jumped? A red-headed kid—probably not even as old as him—with an unpleasant sneer clomped his way across the roof to one of the ventilation hatches.

"Hey!" the roadie called. "Come off there before I have to call the police."

The blond's arm came out from his side. Black-gloved fingers clamped around the roadie's throat. The blond hadn't even looked over to see what he was grabbing for.

The roadie clutched the biker's hand, saying, "Hey," his voice strained. Saying, "I'm not looking for trouble. You guys just—" The roadie's eyes widened. He tore at the biker's hand, his breath rasping as he tried to get air.

The redhead on the roof levered a hatch up, pushed it over. Dropped to his ass, his legs dangling through the hole.

The blond watched him slip through before turning to the roadie, walking him backward with long, sure strides until the roadie's shoulders slammed into the wall, followed by his skull.

He stared at the roadie while the roadie's mouth gaped like a fish's.

"Oh my God," whispered a girl beside Carl. Her elbow bumped him as she brought her fingers to her throat.

He swung his gaze back. Another biker dropped through the roof. The bus swayed on its tires as the men moved around inside.

The other three stood guard, arms crossed, watching the crowd, the street, the back door to the venue. They were all solid, one with a gut pushing at the tee shirt he wore under his Black Sun Riders jacket.

The line to get inside had stopped moving, people bunching up. The guy taking tickets had his hand up, holding back the crowd while he yelled to someone inside.

The blond watched the bus, ignoring the roadie at the end of his arm. The toes of the roadie's sneakers scraped at the pavement.

The bus door squeaked open. Boots clunked down the steps. The two bikers emerged, the older one giving a curt nod before tossing something the blond's way. The redhead was already heading for his bike.

The blond looked at what he had in his hand. Looked back up at the bus.

He let the roadie drop back to his feet, and the roadie clutched his own throat, gasping for air, staggering against the club's wall.

The crowd bowed back as the blond strode to his bike. He shoved whatever he'd gotten from the bus into an inner pocket in his jacket.

He threw his leg over his bike.

The engines revved. Their riders walked them out of the mouth of the alley, pointing them toward the street, then they took off, the riders lifting their feet to the pegs, their bikes swerving through cars. They rounded a corner, hair flagging in the wind.

It seemed to take an eternity, but finally the sound of their engines died off.

The crowd breathed a sigh of relief.

Carl's chest felt like a weight had sat down on it.

The chatter started around him. "Did you see? What the hell was that?"

Four guys spilled from the back of the club, bats and sticks in their hands.

Too late, motherfuckers.

One bee-lined to the roadie, taking him by the arm, looking into his eyes. The roadie rubbed his throat, his eyes wet, his face dark even under the security lights. He nodded at whatever the other guy asked.

Thirty minutes later, sirens finally came up Tchoupitoulas. The cops paced the bus, walked through it with the band's manager. Talked to the roadie who'd been choked, some of the crowd. Carl faded back, not eager for questioning.

The bushy-haired musician came out. His manager caught him by the elbow, trying to pinwheel him back into the club, but the musician clearly didn't want to go—didn't even look at the manager or the club. He jerked his arm free, asking one of the cops questions, even as one of the other roadies dragged him back in.

Music vibrated the walls, spilling through the open doors. The support act had come on.

Two of the cop cars left, leaving one behind, its two officers standing by the back of the bus.

The guy at the door started letting people in again—tearing tickets quickly, moving the line along with his hand. His eyes darted toward the road, the sky, as if he was expecting a storm to be rolling in.

Carl crossed the street. He sat against the wall of a building, hugging his chest. Watching the scene. He should get out of there, but he couldn't bring himself to.

Where else did he have to go?

What do you think, Soph?

She'd have wanted him to stay and warn Dean. Maybe he already knew, just from the fact that there had been bikers here. But what if he didn't?

So Carl waited, hugging himself. Hoping the bikers didn't come back.

4.

A COLLEGE jock backpedaled into Dean, his focus on a set of bright green beads flying through the air—or the cleavage on the barely dressed young lady who'd tossed them off the balcony over the strip club. He grinned at his friends, who clapped him on the back.

"That's a sign. Let's go in," one of them said.

"I'm outta cash."

"Fuck—already?"

After getting off the bus, Dean had gone in one door of the venue and right out another, fans calling after him out front. He'd tossed a wave over his shoulder as he headed toward the Quarter.

The jock said, "I left some in the room so I wouldn't spend it all."

"Well go fucking get it!" one of his buddies said. "I'd say it's worth spending. Look at her."

"Don't go in without me!" The jock still had the beads clutched in his fist. He tossed another look toward the balcony, and the girl up there gave him a wink.

Dean's veins thrummed with the earlier feed—the night seemed to bring him back to light and jangle. He'd needed space after the bus. Needed to be out in the open, moving around, not cramped into another club, hemmed in by another four walls. And he'd needed to get away from the dread. Tendrils still slid through him, but the focus had been a lot stronger at the club. Around that guy.

He hadn't left intending to go on another hunt, but as the jock pushed into the crowd, he gave him a twenty-foot lead before wending through the bodies, keeping his blond head in sight.

When the jock let himself into a hotel four blocks later, Dean dropped his cigarette and jogged to catch the door. He stayed far enough behind that he didn't look like he was following, but he caught the elevator door before it closed.

"What floor?" The jock stumbled a little over his own foot, happy. He'd hung the beads around his neck. They flashed Christmas-bulb green in the overhead lights.

Dean gave the number that was already lit.

"That makes it easy then," the jock said, grinning. "Having a good time?"

"Oh yeah." Dean leaned against the elevator wall, smiling with his lips closed. The guy smelled like alcohol, fresh sweat, expensive cologne. The pulse at his neck throbbed like a hard-on.

When the door swept open, he let the jock go first, pushing off the wall to follow—hoping the guy wasn't in the last room in the hall. That would get awkward.

Halfway down, the guy fumbled his key from his pocket. Dean gave him a nod, started to walk on past.

Stopped and backed up.

"You wouldn't have a light, would you?"

The guy was busy unlocking his door.

"Uh, yeah. Sure." He shouldered the door open, held it with his foot as he reached back into his pocket.

Dean strolled past him, pushing the door wider, walking right into the room like he wanted to have a look around.

"Here," the guy said, his brow creasing. He came inside holding out the lighter, a yellow Bic, his other foot still trying to keep the door open, but he had to let it go before Dean would raise his hand for the lighter.

The door clicked shut. "Thanks." He slipped it in his pocket.

"Uh—I, uh, don't know what you're— Uh."

"*Shh*," the biker said with Dean's mouth, raising a finger to his lips. "They'll hear you."

"Uh…" The guy looked around. "Who?"

A bed in the next room over banged the wall.

"Them." Dean crossed the space between them. The guy backed up, still confused.

He shoved the jock against the wall. Still he was confused, his brow drawn down, his mouth soft as he tried to work it out.

"Stay still," Dean said.

"What?"

Dean whipped forward, his teeth going right into the jock's throat. Hot blood spurted from that pulsing vein.

The guy punched him in the head, trying to pull away.

Dean tangled his foot behind the guy's knee, and down they went with a thud. The jock yelled. Dean shoved his hand against the guy's mouth, wide open, his finger catching a nostril.

The guy tried to bite, but Dean's hand wasn't positioned in a way he could catch it.

Dean cupped his hand over his mouth and pinched the guy's nostrils shut.

He bucked. His sneakers banged the floor. He punched Dean in the head again, but there was no way his teeth were letting go, not with all that light and heat sluicing down his throat. He twisted the guy's fingers back. Heard a crack. A yell as the guy worked his mouth free.

Dean dug his face in harder, sucking, swallowing.

He drained the jock until he was kicking weakly, then took a breath, and bit back into his throat to finish it off.

He left him with a twisted neck, glassy eyes staring toward the suitcases that had been spilled onto the floor, the cheap Bourbon Street liquor cups that dotted the nightstand.

He stopped long enough to splash his face. His shirt collar was wet, but the shirt was black: the blood wouldn't matter, not at night, walking through the streets. Not in the few minutes it would take for him to get a clean one once he got to the venue.

Back in the elevator, Dean glanced at his watch.

Cutting it close.

Thieves had probably come off stage by now, and he still had a ways to walk.

Toward the dread, feeling it press against his chest with each step.

That fucking guy. He should have torn *his* throat out instead. On the one hand, the guy from the bus had saved his life—Dean had been ready to let the biker finish him until he'd heard that door unlatch. But had he only left Dean alive because he hadn't known what he'd become?

Was that why the guy was back now?

The stakes didn't worry him—the one the guy had tried to jam into the biker's chest snapped like a toothpick. The stupid stakes didn't worry him, but the press of dread on his shoulders did.

Like maybe the guy had some kind of power. Bad power.

Bad for Dean, because the kind of feeling he had in him, it couldn't signal anything good.

As he neared the club, the feeling was like a half ton of concrete settling on his sternum. He took deep breaths, trying to ease it. Trying to breathe through it. And part of him was still jangles and light, his head all rushy-feeling.

Most of the crowd had gone in. He didn't bother going around the corner, just swung through the front entrance like he belonged there. No one stopped him.

The place was packed—hot already with bodies.

Like he'd thought, Thieves were done. Their own gear was set up, ready to go. His guys were probably pacing in the back, cursing him for holding them up. He pushed along the outer perimeter, dodging people who only at the last minute realized who was walking by, turning big eyes and gaping mouths toward him.

He didn't mind them. He was sated. He felt like he could fuck a girl and it wouldn't bother him. On another night, it might be fun.

The door to the back swung open as he approached it, Wayne wild-eyed. "Where the hell were you?"

"Getting some air."

"Jesus, we've been looking all over. Even the cops are looking for you."

His back stiffened. Cops looking for him couldn't be a good thing. Had they tied him to the couple in the basement? Or the fucking biker in the dumpster. That had been a dumb fucking move, leaving the body behind a club. "That's a little overboard, isn't it?"

"Nothing's a little overboard tonight," Wayne was saying as he rubbed his throat like there was something wrong with it. He was about to say more when Mike seized Dean by the arm.

"It's about fucking time. Are you ready to go on?"

"What's the rush?" But Mike was turning him toward the stage doors, where the other three waited, their faces anxious and relieved at once.

This couldn't be good—but no time to ask about it. They stepped onto the stage to the cheers of the audience—raucous, pent-up. Spilling over. The mass of sweat made Dean's nose twitch; the smell underneath made his fingertips jitter. It smoothed out as they headed into their first song, music taking over everything. His whole being becoming jangles and light.

Every now and then he glanced up, scanning over the crowd. Looking for cops.

Looking for his vampire hunter.

OCTOBER 21, 1978

1.

"LET'S GET this out quickly," Mike said, stepping around a piece of equipment Wayne and Teddy had left in the hallway.

"You don't have to tell me twice." Wayne rubbed his throat again as he moved a flight case along with his other hand. Once his point was made—Dean wasn't sure what that point was, still—he dropped his other hand to the case and hustled it out the door.

"Stay here." Mike put a hand against Dean's chest before he could head out.

"What the fuck's going on?"

"We're making the fastest break out of town ever."

"I'll feel a lot fucking better when we get on the road," Shawn said, rubbing his arms.

"What—"

"D'you hear that?" Jessie pushed between them to look out the venue's back entrance. Everyone leaned toward it, listening.

All Dean heard was the traffic going by and the sped-up beating of people's hearts.

He caught the sleeve of Shawn's jacket. "What the fuck's going on?"

Shawn told him about the guys on bikes, about them getting on their bus, choking the shit out of Wayne for trying to stop them.

"They just took off?" Dean said.

"Yeah. We thought they'd gotten you or something when we couldn't find you.'"

"I was just getting some air."

"Nice of you to tell someone."

"Thought I had. Maybe not." He watched the bus, its belly doors open like mouths. Teddy shoved gear in while Wayne and Janx jogged back in to get more, pushing through the guys crowded at the door. Fans hovered at the edges, hoping to catch sight of the band, a few of them pointing at the doorway.

The situation wasn't helping his dread one bit. He rubbed his chest, backing out of sight, into the shadows of the corridor.

The bikers could have only come for one reason—looking for one of their own who'd disappeared.

Not finding him on the bus, had they just taken off?

He rubbed his chest. It sounded like too much to hope for.

2.

THE AUDIENCE came out first, a few to start, then a stream of them, spilling through the doors, widening into the street, flowing up the sidewalk.

Roadies jogged out the back, handing equipment off so it could be shoved inside.

The cops moved the straying fans along, telling them the show was over.

The roadies slammed the bay doors shut, throwing worried looks at the street as they headed back to the club.

The place went quiet.

Carl was ignored—he'd been hunched against the building across the street for so long the cops had stopped seeing him. He wrapped his arms around his shins, propped his chin on a knee.

After another fifteen minutes, the band came out, flanked by the roadies. The one who'd had the run-in with the bikers craned his head, like he was expecting the bikers to be back, waiting in the shadows.

The bus shook as they piled in, Dean's head appearing for a moment before it went through the door.

The one Carl thought was their manager took one last look outside before hauling the door closed.

Carl jumped up. He'd figured they weren't going to hang around here after what happened. His ass hurt from the cobblestones in the sidewalk as he strode along the same side of the street, heading the three blocks to his car. Heart racing—hoping he made it back in time. On one hand, it didn't matter: he knew where they were headed.

On the other, who knew what might happen between here and there.

He dug his keys from his front pocket, jammed one in the door lock. Hit himself in the shoulder as he yanked open the door. Anything could happen between here and there. He pulled away from the curb and circled back to the venue in time to see the bus's taillights turning onto Tchoupitoulas.

He got stuck in traffic, tapping the wheel, watching for an opening. When he swung onto the road, the rumble of engines roared in his ear. He slammed the brakes. The car bounced, jerking him into the seat.

Chrome flashed by his window.

Hair rippled in the wind.

"Shit."

The sharp blast of horn came from behind. Heart pounding, he finished entering the intersection. A van had gotten ahead of him, blocking his view of the bikes but he could see the roof of the bus ahead, trundling along. He jiggled the gas pedal, restless, wanting the van the fuck out of his way. It finally turned off, just before the bikes did. Carl followed the bikes, pretty sure the bus wasn't too far ahead.

THE CITY's lights faded in his rearview mirror. His stuff was still at the hotel—his overpacked duffle, his toiletries, a plastic cup he'd brought back from the Quarter, sticky with the pink dregs of a hurricane. All he had with him was the manila folder, riding on the passenger seat, sliding as he sped up to move around a slower car.

Did they know, in the bus? They had to, though the bikes were riding in two columns, their front ends even—the pairs of headlamps could be mistaken for a line of cars in a quick glance.

Skeletons on the backs of their jackets grinned in Carl's headlights. Bony hands gripped black throttles. A full moon loomed over their backs.

Massaging the steering wheel, Carl dropped back more, giving the Cougar a little gas whenever someone looked like they were angling to pull into the space he'd left.

The city scattered into outskirts. The land was flat, the guardrails short. Beyond the reach of lights, trees of a sort he couldn't identify made strange shapes in the shadows.

They drove for two hours, traffic thinning as night crawled onward. Somewhere at their backs, the sun was rising, too many time zones away to lighten the sky.

They swung the over top of Baton Rouge and crossed the Mississippi, its dark waters sucking light from above. Long stretches passed without sight of a building, without another set of headlights lighting the road.

Bats swooped. Eyes flashed green from clumps of trees along the road. An animal darted from a ditch and pulled back, turning tail and jumping through the scrub.

He left two football fields between himself and the bikers, slowing occasionally to let them get farther ahead before giving the Cougar enough gas to bring their taillights back in sight.

He had no idea what the fuck he was doing. There were *five* of them. And what'd he have? A manila fucking folder? A gas can in the trunk? Whoop-dee-do.

He gripped the wheel and gritted his teeth. He needed, at least, to see what happened. He'd look, get the *fuck* out of there, and then he'd take himself someplace safe, set up a new life, and maybe buy a typewriter. *The Vampire and the Rock Star*. He had nothing else to do with himself. "Why not that, Soph?" He glanced toward the passenger seat, like she was actually along for the ride.

A little past four, two bikes split off from the pack, arcing wide and torpedoing back his way. In his lane.

Their headlamps grew brighter. He squinted, started to lift his arm to ward it off—and realized the bikers had no intention of stopping.

He cranked his wheel hard, stomping on the brakes. The Cougar's wheels skidded sideways, its rear end sliding toward the bikes.

They kept coming, slow now—rumbling and deliberate.

Grinning at him.

He stepped on the gas, yanking a look at their lights as the car careened. He straightened out and floored it, racing back down the strip of road he'd come.

The bikes' lights pierced through his back window, illuminating the inside of the car. It made Carl feel hunted. His shoulders tightened. A sharp lump stuck in his throat.

His heart pounded. He flexed one hand, then the other, fingertips tingling. He had to pee. He whispered *shit shit shit* as a crawling heat made its way up his face.

The Cougar hit seventy, eighty. Started to shake as he pushed toward a hundred, afraid to take his eyes from the road.

The cabin filled with light.

The bikes' engines shook his windows.

Everything outside the car was black. The road in front of him ate his lights as fast as the car could shine them.

A sign flew past, too fast to read.

His shoulders ached. Breaths huffed from his nostrils.

He gritted his teeth and drove, hard as he could, knowing this was going to end with his car upside down, vampires feasting on whatever was left of him. He saw himself glassy-eyed—dead—hanging half out his window.

His teeth chattered as the car shook under the power of its engine.

A curve came up fast. He remembered going through it from the other direction, when it hadn't seemed like much of anything. A choke jumped from his throat as he turned the wheel.

The bikes roared forward, jumping toward him like horses that had been held back.

He pushed the pedal to the floor, trying to hold to the car as he eased the wheel toward the curve's apex.

His rear tires slipped like they were on ice. He lifted his foot off the pedal, jerked the wheel. Overcorrected, and the world spun in the windshield. He yelled, his voice pushing against the interior of the car, trapped in with him.

His tires hit dirt, and the whole thing kept spinning.

His front corner slammed a signpost, jarring him to his bones. His shoulder knocked against his door. A cloud of dirt sifted into the air.

His heart pounded.

With a shaking hand, he reached for the keys. Turned them. The engine was already running. His brain was short-circuited.

He couldn't see a thing through his own dust.

But he could hear—

Nothing. Silence. The emptiness beyond his own engine.

He waited with his hand on the keys, his toe ready to make the move from brake to gas. Waited for the dust to finish falling in the air and let him see for sure the dead-empty road.

He was afraid to get out of the car. He was pretty sure they were gone. If they were still around, they'd have smashed his window open and dragged him out.

He was pretty sure they were gone—but he was still afraid to get out.

His heart banged so hard it thudded against his back. A muscle in his leg twitched. He had his foot jammed against the front of the floorboards like he was still trying to stop the car—his whole leg stiff.

He was shaking all over, he realized. Trembling.

He needed to piss like he'd never needed to piss in his life. He was surprised he wasn't sitting in a puddle already. Or a pile of shit.

The car's cigarette lighter had disappeared during the spin. So had his pack of smokes. He found the pack on the passenger floor, stuck a bent cigarette in his mouth. Felt around under his seat until he got hold of the lighter. It took three tries to push it into the hole. He sucked on the dead cigarette, his eyes on the empty road. Waiting for the lighter to pop out.

He leaned back as he breathed the cigarette to life. He *needed* that. It was his last fucking one, and it was the best cigarette he'd ever had in his life.

He smoked it slow, enjoying it to the last drag.

He pulled on the door handle. Shouldered it open. Put a foot on the dirt and rose from the car, wincing as he pulled his other leg from under the dash. He set his other foot down, gingerly, his ankle sore. Limped along the hood of his car, holding onto it with one hand.

Crunched-in metal along the side, but nothing that would keep the car from driving.

He dragged a hand through his hair, fingers shaking. His headlights picked out the shape of a disfigured bush crouching along the opposite side of the road, leaves whipping with the wind. The sleeves of his tee shirt flapped. Goose pimples prickled on his arms.

Jesus. He needed to figure out which direction was which.

3.

DEAN SAT stiff-backed on the side of his bunk, hands on knees, staring at a point low on the bunks across from his.

Chatter came quick and fast through the open door, Wayne the center of it, him and his sore throat. All of them speculating what the fuck the bikers had wanted on their bus. Nothing was missing. Nothing was even out of place, as far as they all knew. The bikers had just shown up...and left.

Except something was missing, all right.

Dean's cheeks were cold with the implication of it. His skin crawled.

He'd checked three times. He'd torn the blanket and pillow off the bunk mattress.

A corner of his blanket lapped the toe of his sneaker.

He ran the heel of his hand up his forehead, nerves prickling. The dread wasn't going away, and it should have if they'd left the vampire hunter behind.

Assuming they'd left him behind.

"There's some crazy shit on the tour, isn't there?" Jessie was saying. "Crazy fucking shit."

"I don't get what they wanted." Shawn's voice was closer. The seals on the mini fridge in the galley gave as he finished speaking.

They wanted the knife. At the very least, they'd wanted the biker's fucking knife.

He bent forward dragging through his bedding one more time. *Tell me the knife is still fucking here.*

Because if they had the knife, they knew the biker'd been on this bus. If they knew he'd been on the bus...

"You all right?" Shawn said from the doorway, a beer can in his hand.

"Just a little freaked out," Dean said. He moved off the bunk to stuff the bedding back inside. Then he leaned over it one more time to shove his hand behind the mattress.

FUCK.

He swayed as the bus picked up speed. He pulled his head out from the bunk, and Shawn was still standing in the doorway, but his head was cranked the other way.

"I wonder what that's about," Shawn said.

Gravity pulled them the other way, the bus's speed dropping off. Shawn held onto the doorframe.

Dean caught the edge of his bunk as their speed picked up again.

"What the hell?" Shawn pushed away from the door, beer spilling down his hand. He strode up the aisle. The others were looking around, some of them getting to their feet.

"You guys might want to sit down and hold on," the driver called back.

Shawn caught hold of the back of the driver's seat. "What's going on?" The others crowded behind him.

"Holy shit—seriously?" Nick said. Over his shoulder, Dean saw headlights, then taillights zip in front of the bus. The bus leaned forward again, the driver pressing the brakes. The taillights zipped back out, leaving the road dark.

But they could hear the engines buzzing, pulling forward and back, pestering the bus like mosquitos.

"Should we pull over?" Teddy asked.

Wayne said, "No!" as Mike was saying, "How far until we hit a town?" He had a hold of the pole at the front, watching out the windshield.

Dean stepped back from the crowd. The engines outside grew louder. Through the hole in the blinds Nick had opened, he saw a headlight surge and drop away.

Jessie's head ducked in, his hand gripping the back of the couch. "They're trying to pull over a bus with bikes? This is *crazy!*" The engine racket surged again. Jessie said, "It's a fucking *bus* for Christ's sake. How many are out there? Three?"

"That's what I count," Teddy said.

"They have a lot more to fucking lose than us," Jessie said. "I mean—fucking bikes! I'm gonna have a look in the back."

Dean stayed where he was.

Wayne rubbed his hands on his jeans, pacing. "Do you think they can do anything?"

"I don't know," Nick said.

Teddy crowded in with him, mashing the blinds against the window. He widened the space between another set of slats.

Nick said, "More headlights."

"What?" Janx fought with the blinds on the next window, trying to get them pulled up.

Dean took another two steps back.

"Shit," Jessie said. "That's five."

"That's how many were at the club," Wayne said. "*Fuck!*"

Dean walked up the aisle, his hand against his head. All his fault. All his fucking fault. That he hadn't thought someone would come looking...

Someone banged into his shoulder on the way to the back of the bus.

The bus swerved.

Drinks on the table and counter toppled, cans rolling to the floor.

"They can't force us over, can they?" Wayne's voice edged toward panic.

"Do *not* pull over," Shawn was saying to the bus driver.

"I got no plan of that!"

Mike came back up the aisle, his arms swinging out. "Everyone sit down. Grab hold of something. We've got another show tonight. We don't need anyone injured."

The bus jerked and swerved again.

"Jesus they've got some balls," Teddy said, watching through the window.

"Sit *down*."

Dean dug his fingers into his hair. He should have them stop, let him walk off the bus. Give the bikers what they were after, and the rest of them could take off.

Fucking Christ—*would* they?

He dropped his hands, started striding toward the front—Shawn's eyes on him.

Maybe they could just slow down. He could jump out the door. The tumble might hurt, and what would come after was almost definitely going to, but the bikers would have what they wanted—and maybe it'd keep them distracted long enough for his guys to get away.

Shawn's eyes were on him, his mouth opening. Dean shoved past him.

As he put his hand out to grab the pole seat, the bus braked hard. He stumbled toward the driver, reaching for the back of his seat.

The driver cranked the wheel.

The back end of the bus slid.

The whole thing jerked as the driver tried to right it, tapping the gas. It was like being inside a fish on a hook.

Tires hit shoulder. The bus bounced. Shouts rose.

Dean was knocked into the front lounge couch.

The bus started to tip.

4.

HE CRUSHED out his last cigarette, kissed the St. Michael medal dangling from his rearview mirror, and pulled slowly back onto the black road.

No cars passed from the other direction, no headlights rose up from behind. His dash clock ticked to four thirty. His speedometer stayed around forty. Every now and then, he forced his toes down to move it back up to forty.

He dreaded catching up—they weren't fucking around. He knew at this rate, he wasn't about to.

That was okay too.

He was only going this direction because he couldn't talk himself into going back. And he was having a hard time talking his foot into going in this direction with any hurry.

The needle slipped under forty again.

He wished he had another cigarette.

And a drink. Not one of those sweet frozen ones he'd had in the Quarter either.

If he did go back, the bars would still be open, maybe.

His stuff would still be there. He could get a newspaper, find a job. Just stay in fucking New Orleans and forget all this shit.

Throw the folder into the dirt and put miles and miles between himself and the motorcycle riders.

He could, but at the same time…he couldn't. Because he hadn't been able to save Soph—and he hadn't even had the chance to try. This time, he at least had the chance. However much it made him want to piss his pants.

5.

WAYNE AND Teddy screamed—two completely different sounds, Wayne's the apex of his fear; Teddy's a high howl of pain.

Dean struggled to get himself up from the side of the bus that had become the floor. The couch, now on its back with Dean sprawled over it, was in his way. The driver, on the other side of the seat, was groaning. Dean tried to untangle his legs from the pile of jackets that had landed with him.

Shawn clambered over him, going to see to Teddy, who was on the floor—or what passed for the floor now—wailing.

"Mike?" someone yelled.

"Is everyone okay?" called someone else.

A thud hit the bus, over their heads.

Teddy cried, "My fucking leg!" and Shawn said, "Is it broken? Can you walk on it?"—shoving a guitar aside so he could crouch next to him.

Dean got his feet under him, using what used to be the ceiling of the bus to keep his balance while he rose.

More thuds from above.

The sound of metal.

A wrenching noise.

Nick rammed his shoulder against a bus hatch, halfway up the lounge, his teeth gritted. Blood trickled down the side of his face from a gash at his hairline.

Wayne stumbled through the bunkroom doorway, landing with a clatter of limbs among the bunks.

Nick caught Janx's shirt as Janx stumbled into him. "Help me get this open."

The bus door made another creaking, wrenched sound.

"We've gotta get him out," Shawn said, clutching the leg of Dean's jeans as he came near.

Teddy had hold of his leg, his knee bent, his face shining with sweat. His lips were pulled back from clenched teeth as he rolled with the pain.

A window smashed. Glass cascaded over them. Dean ducked, bringing his arm over his head reflexively. He looked over the edge of it.

Black boots vaulted into the mess.

Teddy yelled as one landed on his ribs.

Shawn back-pedaled away, hunkering down. His sneaker hit a rolling beer can, and his arms flew out before he landed on his ass.

The hatch Nick and Janx were working on popped. Fresh air raced in.

Janx hauled himself through, Nick crowding him, ready to go, whites showing all around his dark eyes.

Dean didn't see Jessie or Mike.

He saw Wayne, his throat caught in a biker's grip as another biker leapt down through the broken window. Saliva shone on Wayne's lips. He was croaking, "Please. Please."

Another dropped in, hauling Shawn up from where he was trying to lift Teddy by the armpit.

Janx was out. Nick was squirming through.

The biker who'd lifted Shawn threw him into what used to be the bus's floor, Shawn's head thunking against the leg of a chair.

Dean watched him slide to a heap and reach out, trying to pull himself forward.

Dean stepped toward him.

An arm came across his chest, sending him tripping over Teddy.

Teddy screamed, and even through that scream, he heard Shawn's neck snap in the biker's hands.

The toes of Nick's sneakers were scrabbling against the bus ceiling. Dean grabbed his hips and shoved them forward.

"One loose!" came a yell from above, and they could only mean Janx.

Fucking run your ass off.

He pushed Nick's feet through the hatch and followed with his head and shoulders, finding there wasn't a lot to grab onto on the other side, nothing to help you pull yourself through.

Nick ran straight into the darkness, heels kicking up dirt and clumps of weeds in a field. Dean didn't see Janx.

A *thump* came from the road ahead of the bus, followed by a whoop. Reaching for the ground with one hand, Dean tried to see what had happened.

From inside the bus came yells, thuds, a rushed pleading that was cut off mid-word.

His heart broke. His throat locked up at the sound of Teddy's voice silenced mid-scream.

A hard grip closed around his ankle.

He dug his fingers into the dirt, kicking back with his other foot, connecting with a body. That ankle got caught up too.

He kicked the first free, staring toward the field.

Nick stumbled in the tall grass. Got back up. Started going again, favoring a leg.

Keep going keep going keep going. At least one of them might get the fuck out of there.

He kicked back again, leaning all his weight on his hands as whoever had him tried to drag him back in. The lip of the hatch scraped his hips.

Another yell inside started and cut off—another voice silenced. It fueled Dean: he kicked hard, using the biker's body to launch himself forward. He tumbled from the bus hatch onto the ground. Rolling to his feet and took off, following Nick into the field.

6.

CARL CRANKED the window halfway, letting a rush of air whip the side of his face. Cooling the sweat on his skin.

He drove another mile, telling himself that at the next crossroad, the next turn-in, he was calling it quits. He had no business chasing bikers. No business chasing girl-killers. No business being a fucking brother.

He wasn't cut out for anything.

But he didn't have anything left, either. He was, he thought as his tires whisked over the road, the most expendable person in the world. So why not him?

Yeah? And what are you going to use against them when you find them? Your good looks?

He heard them, the engines. Distant.

His foot jumped off the gas.

A crowd of revs cut across the night, high and far off, but near enough to make his bowels cramp.

Then the sound was gone. Just wind against metal, tires over blacktop. The race of rushing air at his ear.

The speedometer hovered at twenty before he got it climbing again. It didn't have to climb for long. Red lights started as distant insects and grew into bus taillights as he came down the road. He made out the shape of it in the dark, the bus on its side, its nose canted into a ditch, just its rear corner touching the road's shoulder.

He slowed to a stop, his turn signal ticking.

Nothing moved.

He popped his glove box and found the little flashlight Soph
had given him when he'd bought the car. He turned it on, its
bulb dim even after he shook it. He stared through the window,
uncertain whether he should get out. Waiting to see if anything
moved at all out there, if anyone came crawling out, waving their
arms, relieved that someone had arrived.

His engine ticked.

His heart beat his ribs.

He caught his breath, swallowed, and caught it again.

He grasped the door handle, his skin prickling.

The door weighed a ton, and he swung it on its hinges, cring-
ing at the creak against the quiet night. He scanned the ragged
field alongside the bus, the tops of weeds swaying with the wind
that was threatening to bring rain.

He checked the road—dark both ways. Put his foot on the
pavement. Hauled himself to standing, one hand on the Cougar's roof.

The skin behind his ears drew tight. He turned his head,
picking out noises: a soft rustle in a tree branch, an owl's hoot
that sent shivers along his neck.

His sneakers sank in the moist dirt by the side of the road as
he approached the bus, walking with a hitch to favor his ankle.

Light spilled through an open hatch in the roof. He kept his
shoulder against the bus as he picked his way toward it, sweeping
his meager flashlight beam along the edge of the field. It was
scraggled, and it narrowed a bit, encroached by trees, before
widening out for a good bit in the distance. Hard to tell what
was on the ground—clumps of weeds, maybe rocks. A bush
here and there. Nothing moving but the wind.

He peeked around the edge of the hatch, found himself surprised by the sight of the inside of a bus turned over. Like he
hadn't been expecting *that*. A table bolted to the floor jutted
from what was now the side of the bus, like it was levitating.
Bodies lay heaped on the windows below him. The big roadie
faced upward, his body bent toward the couch, a broken metal
rod standing up from one eye. It looked like the broken leg of

a chair, snapped off right at the weld. Gore oozed around the base of the leg, and Carl had to look away, swallowing back acid.

The one with the wild hair looked all right from here, except he wasn't moving.

A leg—still attached to a body he was pretty sure—hung over the edge of the door to the back of the bus. Carl didn't think it was Dean.

He took a deep breath of night air before putting a foot through, his flashlight pointing toward the sky as he held onto the bus's roof. He put his other foot on the edge of the hatch and lowered himself until he was ready to slide that foot out, shimmy himself inside.

Something gave under one of his heels. He shifted it over, working his toes underneath. Knowing—*knowing*—it was the roadie's arm, and not wanting to look and verify in case he caught sight of that eye again.

He wriggled his upper body through and stumbled as he stood up, reaching for the floating table to brace himself.

The wild-haired guy hadn't moved. Carl crouched, touched his neck. Felt nothing. He pulled himself back up.

The pantry had spilled out, as if the salt and pepper and plastic cups and bags of chips had jumped out of the cabinets in surprise. The bathroom door dangled open from above. Carl grabbed hold of it as he made his way through the galley.

He ducked to climb through the sideways bunk door, trying to avoid the roadie hanging from it, nudging a leg lightly aside when he had to.

The roadie's upper body rested in a bunk, the curtain leaning against his back, hiding the look on his face. Carl was okay with that.

He crawled along the braces between the bunks. The back lounge's door was caved in. Two people lay intertwined against the windows at the bottom of the bus. The blinds from above hung down crooked. He flashed his light on the window over his head. They'd gotten it half open before they'd been killed.

Carl remembered the easy smile one had had as he'd walked backward off the bus just earlier that day—his hands flying through the air as he'd talked. Now he lay underneath the body of their manager, a trickle of blood from his ear, and Carl did his best not to step on either of them.

No Dean, though. Had they come to snatch Dean instead of kill him?

He grasped the edges of the window above and dug his tennis shoes against the couch to lift himself up to fresh air. It was hard to breathe in the bus, like he might catch what the others had if he pulled in too much of the air down there. With his face pressed to the opening, he gulped the night like it was water. Then he dropped down.

Moving back the other way, he made himself go all the way to the driver's seat.

The driver's skull was crushed, the window under his head cracked.

No Dean.

This would be it then—the end of the story. The vampires came and killed everyone, and Dean Thibodeaux had disappeared with them.

And the elf guy. He didn't see him either. He flashed the light over the wreckage one more time, wincing at what it crossed. He dropped his head, eyes closed, and moved his lips in a silent prayer.

Then he crawled back onto the dirt, the night air fresh and welcome against his skin—even the dark was welcome after what he'd seen inside.

He stayed on his knees, crawling until he'd put a good ten feet between him and it. Then he dropped on his ass.

Man—a cigarette. He really fucking needed a cigarette.

Thinking he'd flag someone down if they passed, he looked up the road—a clear view from where he sat. That's how he saw the body humped on the ground in the bus's headlights.

He pushed up and limped over. Another roadie, face down on the pavement. The bus's headlights lit up the dark blood seeping into the asphalt.

Carl walked back, his eyes on the ground. On the flattened weeds. On the dirt he'd torn up, he guessed, on his way out of the hatch.

The torn-up divots reached out farther than his just toeing his way out.

He stopped and backed up, toward the bus.

Grooves had been scratched into the ground.

Crouching, he put his fingers in them.

Looking toward the field, he made out mashed down weeds, a jagged path breaking through taller scrub.

He shined his weak flashlight toward them, getting to his feet. Walking slowly.

Following the broken shrubs, losing the trail, finding it again. The flashlight was almost worse than no light at all, giving him just enough illumination to make every shadow look like it was about to jump at him.

At first he thought he was coming up on a rag, a bunched up piece of cloth.

His toe bumped something solid. He swept the light downward, and realized the rag he thought he'd seen was a denim jacket, rucked halfway up a back.

Face down, neck at an angle that made a shudder run through Carl's shoulders, one of the two missing bodies lay unmoving in the weeds.

He recognized the way a pale ear stuck out in a fork in what he'd at first thought was some kind of strange grass.

He crouched, touching a slice of white skin showing beneath the hair, just above the jacket collar. Still warm. Still malleable. With the angle of the neck, he didn't expect much, and when he pushed his fingers around the side of it, feeling for a sign of life, he wasn't surprised when he found nothing.

He swept the beam away, covering all directions, circling outward from it.

Maybe this was the last of them. Maybe they'd gotten Dean. He stared across the swaying reeds, all the way to the dark tangle of trees a hundred yards off. If Dean had gotten to those trees, he could be anywhere. Running his ass off. Getting the fuck out.

Carl didn't blame him one bit.

He swiped an arm across his brow. Clicked the light off. Squeezed his eyes shut behind his arm.

This was better, wasn't it? Not finding Dean, instead of finding him dead.

The edge of a sob spilled out of him, mostly air. Half a laugh—at himself. He'd been betrayed by one killer, so what had he done? Come looking for another. Come looking for a different killer to fill the fucking hole inside of him with.

He sniffled, dropping his arm, lifting his face to the breeze. Rain was definitely on the way.

He walked away from the body, his ankle still pinging, weeds pulling at the legs of his jeans. He wasn't heading straight back to the bus. He didn't know where he was heading—in circles probably.

Fuck.

He swiped his brow again.

Fuck.

A spray of pale mushrooms peeked from under a clump of grass. He turned the flashlight beam on and dropped toward them.

He stopped.

Took a step closer and crouched.

Moved the grass away with the side of his hand.

Pale fingers, not mushrooms. The palm of a hand. A slim wrist disappearing into a denim cuff.

Breathing quickly, he dropped to a knee, crawling forward, sweeping the rest of the clump of long grass out of his way.

What he saw made his breath suck in.

He jerked his head up to check the field, the road. The roar of the bikes was long gone. No other cars were coming. It was just him, him and the bodies.

He played the light over Dean's face. He could only stand it for a few seconds, his chest feeling like it was breaking. He stared inside at the shoulder of Dean's shirt. If he hadn't eliminated everyone else on the bus already, he'd never have fucking known this was Dean.

He crept his gaze back up the side of Dean's cheek, to those staring eyes, the night reflected in their shine. Eyes bigger than any he'd ever seen, and he gagged a little as he realized what was so fucked up about them.

No eyelids.

Shadows flickered over the body—reeds of grass fluttering in the wind.

Flesh had been chewed from his face, his neck, his stomach. They'd ripped right through his jeans and taken chunks out of his legs. The only thing they hadn't touched was his chest.

Carl put a hand on it.

It didn't rise or fall under his touch.

Half his neck was gone. Half his cheek. His tee shirt was dark and wet where blood had soaked through.

And those eyes, staring upward, never blinking.

This hadn't been about killing him quickly.

This was revenge.

They'd left him here to watch the fucking sun come up.

He played the light along one splayed arm, bone showing through ripped flesh, the skin on his untouched wrist a milky blue in the moonlight. He stopped at the fingers that could have been mushrooms.

He was about to move the light away when one twitched, so slightly it could have almost been a breeze shifting it.

He leaned over Dean, looking into those startled eyes. His stomach churned, slick and hot and slow.

"Are you in there?" he whispered.

A flicker crossed the shine of Dean's eye—it could have been a cloud moving past the moon, it could have been a pulse-beat in Carl's eye.

He leaned closer, his skin prickling. "Dean?"

God, he reeked of blood, the stench earthy, sharp, and strong. He had to bite back his bile.

Another flicker. Weak.

Cool night air curled under the collar of Carl's jacket, buffeting his hot neck.

A coyote howled in the distance.

And Dean. The slightest movement in his hand. So slight, again, he could have imagined it, but he hoped he hadn't. He wanted to believe in it, the shift of a muscle, there and gone. But *there.*

They'd left him for the fucking sun to finish him off.

He looked back to his car. A hundred feet.

They'd counted on rescue crews coming, eventually. They'd counted on no one knowing they had to get Dean the fuck out before the sun crested the horizon.

They'd counted on the rescue crews being too fucking busy with the bus to go looking for strays until it was too late.

"All right." His voice was quiet as the night. "Let's do this." He gripped underneath Dean's arms, Dean's head lolling between his sneakers. He had to squeeze his eyes shut, hard, for a moment, get his belly back under control.

He lifted and dragged.

Under his jacket, his armpits started to slick with sweat. His shirt clung to his back. He focused on the tree line, far off and getting farther with every step. He couldn't fucking look at Dean, the white of his shinbone showing through the gore.

He stopped halfway to catch his breath, straighten his back.

From there, even in the dark, he could see the twisted hump of the other body they'd passed.

Lift and drag. The heels of Dean's boots flattened scrub, digging twin trails in the dirt. Lift and drag.

When he got to the car, he laid Dean down in the dirt at the shoulder and dropped against the Cougar's flank, wiping his forehead. Thirsting for water. Wanting a cigarette.

Really wanting a cigarette.

Just a little ways more.

The trunk lid popped with a tired *clunk*. He levered it up, holding it open as he peered in its shadows. A physics textbook, its pages bent. An oil funnel. The gas can he'd bought last week. He dropped it all on the ground. Pulling a scratchy blanket out last, he let it fall beside the heap.

Bending his knees with Dean's body between them, he grunted and lifted with his legs. Dean's arm swung lifelessly, the denim jacket sleeve dark with blood. The smell of blood pushed into Carl's nostrils. He felt like he was never going to smell anything else again.

He heaved Dean back-first into the trunk. Got under his hips to lift them. Folded his legs in.

Straightened and listened for cars. He didn't want to have to explain why he was putting a body in his trunk. He lowered the lid, not hard enough to latch it, just letting it rest there, closed.

He walked the long way back to the other body in the field.

When he lifted it under the armpits, the neck lolling in a way that was *all wrong*, a pack of cigarettes dropped from the musician's jacket.

Carl laid him back down, got a cigarette out, and lit it. He stuffed the rest of the pack in his pocket and grabbed hold of the body again. Dragging, inhaling, dragging, exhaling. Stopping to enjoy the final puff before crushing it underfoot and grabbing the body by the armpits again.

When the heel of his shoe bumped his back tire, he let the body drop. He opened his trunk with two fingers. With a grunt, he hauled the other body over the lip, letting it roll onto the mess of Dean's body.

Dean hadn't moved.

There was every possibility Dean was really dead.

He had no explanation for why he was trying to rescue a vampire, like it was some stray dog that'd been hit by a car. He tossed the blanket in with the two of them, bundling it near a taillight, and lowered the lid again, lightly, before walking around the side of the car.

He popped the glove compartment and yanked out his car registration, the car's manual and maintenance schedule, a couple of folded road maps, tossing them onto the passenger seat. Underneath all that, he found a screwdriver.

Back at the trunk, he raised the lid. Dragged and shoved the top body until it was positioned how he wanted it—where it, and gravity, would be the most use.

He ducked his head, wiping his brow on the inside of his arm. *Are you really doing this?*

Who's it going to hurt? He's already dead.

Yeah, but—Christ, are you really doing this?

He put a hand on the musician's skull, which, unlike Dean's, still had a trace of warmth in it.

Placing the end of the screwdriver against the guy's neck, he closed his eyes. Bit his lip. Dug the end of the screwdriver against skin. It dented. The metal tip slid. He gritted his teeth, grabbed the skull harder, and dug in again.

He made the hole, and at first nothing came out of it.

He turned his head, wiping his face on his sleeve again, then put his mind elsewhere while he ground the tip of the screwdriver into the hole, jamming hard on it.

It took a couple tries before he got any worthwhile bleeding going.

As the thin stream trickled down the dead guy's collarbone, he shoved the body until the wound was over Dean's mouth. Crouching, holding the body, he looked between them.

Dean's lip glistened but didn't so much as twitch.

He shoved the lid shut and hoped for the best.

The worst case scenario was he'd be finding a place to dump two bodies later.

He took one last look at his stuff piled on the side of the road.

He didn't need any of it. Every gas station had gas cans and oil funnels, and if he never sat through a fucking physics class again—his name was written in it. Wind buffeted him as he grabbed it from the side of the road.

He realized he was never going to sit through a physics class again. Whatever way this all went, he was a shadow. No home, no family. No interest in living life above ground with the rest of the world. Not now. Not after all he'd been through.

How could he ever possibly fucking connect with another human being?

He limped through the dirt. Opened his door. Dropped behind the wheel.

He fished the cigarette pack out of his pocket and pulled one out.

As he raised the car's cigarette lighter to it, the car jostled.

He inhaled a lungful of smoke, leaning his head back.

The back end bounced a little.

A *thump* came, like someone shifting in a confined space.

His gut squirmed. His cheeks felt cold. Maybe trapping a vampire in your trunk wasn't the smartest move. He rubbed his temple, elbow leaning against the window.

Another light *thump* came from the back of the car.

It wasn't the sound of someone trying to get out.

He could only imagine what actually was going on back there—and he dragged long and hard on the cigarette, sucking the thought from his mind.

He started the Cougar's engine.

As he pulled onto the road, the cigarette pack slid across the dash. The St. Michael medal swayed. A fat drop of rain hit the windshield.

The bus's roof played at the edge of his vision, and then it was gone. He pushed the pedal down.

7.

THE SUN glared orange in Carl's eyes as the door to a small-town hardware store swung closed behind him. The Cougar sat parked at the curb. The trunk had been silent for hours. He didn't know if that was good or bad news. He unlocked his door and slid his purchase between the seats. It dropped with a *thunk* on the rear floorboards.

He got in and drove, still a good hour from twilight.

He stuck to the back roads, not entirely sure what he was looking for but hoping he'd know when he found it.

He took a pull off a warm can of Pepsi he'd bought when he'd stopped for gas.

The sun dipped lower behind him. Shadows stretched across the county highway. The woods on either side were lush still, only a few leaves changing color yet. The road wound upward for a while before dipping back down.

He took a chance on a turn-off that looked like it headed back into the mountains, and as he climbed, the road brightened, the angle of what was left of the sun hitting when he was on the right side of the switchbacks.

Another lane came off that one, a dirt road climbing at a steeper grade. Two weather-beaten posts guarded the end of it like someone had once meant to put a gate across. He geared down and took the Cougar up slow and steady. It might have been a forest service road or a logging road. Whatever it was, it curved and kept climbing, wide enough for a car, with the side to his left dropping off sharp and quick, the tops of trees bumping past his window.

He was thinking—had been thinking most of the day—that this was like when he'd bought the Cougar. His aunt and uncle had tried to talk sense into him at the time: thirty good reasons why he should get something used, something dependable and well cared for but not too expensive. He had college to think about. His future. He'd regret spending all that money when all he had to show for it a couple years down the road was a used car.

He'd been dead set on the Cougar, though. Dead set on pissing money away on something he could shove into the hole inside of him, however poorly it fit. If he couldn't have parents, he'd have this fucking car.

Now he was nothing but hole.

The *only* thing he had was this fucking car…and a vampire in his trunk.

Another road teed off the one he was on, this one in worse shape but not climbing as steeply. He took it about three hundred feet, circling around near the end of it, and found himself parked in a bare clearing, the Cougar's nose pointing at the last vestiges of sunset.

When he stepped out, it was to the light rustle of leaves, the rat-a-tatting of a woodpecker, the soft drop of acorns to the ground.

He stepped to the edge of the slope and put his hands in his pockets as he looked over the shadowed valley. A white church steeple caught the last of the orange light.

Before it got too dark to see, he walked around, testing the ground.

Walked into the woods to find himself a stick.

Then he went back to the car and reached between the driver and passenger seats.

Hefting his purchase and stick in one arm, he continued around, fingering the car key from his ring.

It should be dark enough now.

He leaned down, putting an ear to the dusty metal.

Something shifted, like a sneaker against carpet. His heart quickened.

The anticipation was like a spring, and he felt it not just in himself but trapped in the trunk too. Waiting.

A spring so tight it might burst the lid open.

He turned the key.

The latched popped, and he back-pedaled out of immediate reach as the trunk flew open.

8.

Nick's shoulder dug into his chest. Dean's arm gripped his waist, over the blanket he'd covered him up with. All his tears had been rattled and bumped out over the endless hours of road.

His jaw ached from gritting his teeth.

Trapped with the smells of exhaust, spare tire, and Nick, he'd had no escape from his brain replaying what had gone down. The worst was the urge to change the outcome. *If I'd just done this. If I hadn't done that. If I'd headed out of the French Quarter in the other direction and never looked back.* Would that even have saved them? *If I'd told them to go back inside and gotten on the bus alone.* Would they have listened? They'd have thought he was out of his head.

The car rocked to a stop. He had no idea who had him or why. If they'd wanted him dead, though, they wouldn't have put Nick in with him. Unless they just didn't know better.

The sun was still out—not by much, but he could feel its sizzle through the metal trunk lid. He listened to footsteps on soft earth, the rustle of grasses and weeds.

As the sizzle crept away, the footsteps came near.

A key scraped. The latch let go. The lid lifted, just an inch or so, and night air tumbled in.

He grasped the edge of the trunk and scrambled out, eager to get out of there. Get away from Nick and the pain of all of it. He stumbled backward, staring at the lump of blanket lying in there. Panting, he took another step back, his arms stretched to his sides. He didn't know what to do.

The last glimpse he'd had of Shawn, the sound of Shawn's neck snapping. The whoop when Janx was killed. The way they'd dove on Nick.

He had no fucking idea what to do.

A twig snapped behind him, and he spun, breathing hard.

The vampire hunter was there, a shovel in one hand, a stick laid across it, making some kind of cross. His posture was wary, his eyes showing a little too much white. He stepped one foot back abruptly, lifting the makeshift cross higher.

Dean glanced at his arm—his jacket torn, the skin underneath looking fine. Or, at least, fine enough for government work. The scars would fade, the gouges would fill in.

He had no fucking idea what to do.

By the guy's shoulder stood a girl, a wisp of a thing with dark hair parted down the middle, a haze of light shifting at her edges. She watched him with dark eyes.

The guy with the shovel, his chest rose and fell fast. They stared each other down.

The blanketed bump in the trunk was calling to Dean though, beckoning like a ghost. He turned his head back toward it.

He'd spent the day with the emptiness that had been his band, his friends, his entire life, feeling his wounds heal—feeling the ones inside that never would.

He'd feasted on his dead friend, and when the blood he could get through his neck had run out, he'd split him open to get at more.

Behind him, the tip of the shovel thumped.

Dean looked over his shoulder.

The other guy had given up on the cross, letting the stick fall to the ground. He lifted the shovel, holding it out. "I thought you could bury him over there."

Dean followed the pointing finger to a spot near the edge of the slope.

"It's got a view," the guy said.

"Where are we?" His throat was dry, his voice like torn paper.

"Kentucky."

Jesus.

He lifted the shovel again. The girl beside him looked over her shoulder toward the plot of earth.

"Got a smoke?" Dean said.

The guy drew a pack of cigarettes from his pocket and tossed it over. Matches were shoved under the cellophane.

He tugged a cigarette out as he walked toward the spot that had been pointed out—he took the shovel as he passed, exchanging it for the pack. He put the cigarette between his teeth, leaned the shovel against his hip, and cracked a match to life.

When he had the smoke going, he started digging, the girl standing at the edge, watching while the other guy walked away to stare over the dark valley.

Moving dirt—working his muscles—was better than lying in a box with his thoughts. He was raw inside. Empty. The mound of dirt grew, and the guy offered him another cigarette. Dean smoked it as he dug, dirt sifting onto his jeans, streaking his hands.

Eventually the guy said, "Help me with this," from over by the car.

He leaned the shovel against the dirt and went to help pull Nick's body from the trunk, the other guy tugging the blanket to keep Nick covered, saving Dean from having to see it again. The girl drifted alongside them, her hand resting on Nick as they carried him. She stepped back as they lowered him into the ground.

The guy picked up the shovel while Dean still stood in the grave, his sneakers on either side of the blanket. He waited with a load of dirt for Dean to climb out.

And Dean walked away, raking his hair back. Leaving the girl watching the dirt get filled in.

He wondered what the fuck came next. What the *fuck* came after this.

He was unmoored.

For the first time, he had no one.

In the emptiness between his ears, he heard Teddy's voice cry out and cut to silence.

The other guy tamped the dirt with the shovel. Dean watched from the side of the car, fingers pushed into his back pockets. Thinking the pair of them strange, the guy never looking at the girl, never acknowledging her.

"Do you want to say anything?" the guy said.

Dean shook his head. He'd already said enough to Nick in the car. Already said he was sorry a hundred times over.

"Do you have any money?" the guy asked.

Dean shook his head again.

The guy leaned on the shovel. "Can you take over driving while I catch some sleep?"

"Where are we going?"

His body seemed to sag, the shovel taking his weight. "I don't know." Lifting the shovel to his shoulder, he said, "I don't suggest going back there, and I don't suggest going home. I don't suggest getting pulled over by the cops either. Just drive. Stick to the speed limit. Maybe stick to the back roads."

"I thought you were some kind of vampire killer," Dean said.

The guy laughed, the sound soft and sour. He tossed the shovel to Dean. "Keys are in the ignition." He started toward the passenger door.

Dean looked at the girl, and she looked back at him. The haze of light was so soft, he was pretty sure it was his eyes playing tricks, the new way he saw things.

He put the shovel in the trunk. When he let himself in the driver's side, the other guy was curled on the backseat, using his arm for a pillow. The girl sat in the passenger seat, her eyes tracking him as he settled behind the wheel.

He started the engine. "Mind if I turn on the radio?"

"I wouldn't."

"They've been talking about it?"

"Every half hour, it feels like." The springs creaked in the backseat as he shifted.

Dean thought about how Travers would be all over this tonight. Almost wished he could listen in, but WHAK didn't make it as far as Kentucky.

It would probably hurt a whole lot more hearing Travers turn their deaths into gossip. He asked the guy instead what they were saying.

"That there was a wreck. That they can't find two of you. That they're not sure what happened but they hope that when Jessie wakes up, he can shed some light on it."

"Jessie's alive?" Dean's fingers felt cold.

With another shift in the backseat, the guy said, "Don't go back there. They'll expect you to go back there."

Dean sat, breathing heavy, his chest tight with energy he didn't know what to do with. Nick hadn't been enough blood to bring him to light and jangles, but it had brought him back to life. The energy was from helplessness. From being all the way out here, and not being able to go back there.

The guy in the back seat said, "Don't go back there."

Dean moved the gearshift. He threw an arm across the seats so he could look out the rear window as he backed up. He said, "Nope."

"Lights," the guy said.

Dean had forgotten he'd need them—if he were a normal person, driving at night. He pulled the knob.

As they bumped back down the mountain road, the guy in the back seat said, "Wake me up before it gets light."

Dean glanced in the rearview, nothing but moon behind them. "Yeah."

The girl settled back, closing her eyes, her small lips parting. In the dark of the car's interior, a white line showed across her throat. She turned her face away, the haze of light shifting with her.

When he hit the main road and saw the sign, he turned in the direction that would keep them heading away from the sun. And with the soft, shallow breaths of the guy who'd saved his ass not once but twice hitting against the back of his seat—he drove.

† † †

The Story Continues...

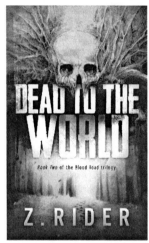 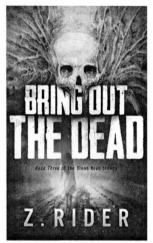

February 23, 2016   June 21, 2016

Join the mailing list to be notified when the next book in *The Blood Road Trilogy* is available.

Sign up here: http://eepurl.com/ZbGGP

Also from Z. Rider

SUCKERS—Out Now   INSYLUM—Out Now

Acknowledgements

Huge, huge thanks to Nick, who believed in this book even on the days when I didn't and who had total faith that I would manage to get it written. Also thank you, once again, to the invaluable Mr. Rider for his multiple readings of the manuscript and help along the way, as well as to my wonderful (enormous) family who have been incredibly supportive. I love you all.